MARBECK AND THE GUNPOWDER PLOT

MARBECK AND THE GUNPOWDER PLOT

John Pilkington

This first world edition published 2015
in Great Britain and the USA by
SEVERN HOUSE PUBLISHERS LTD of
19 Cedar Road, Sutton, Surrey, England, SM2 5DA.
Trade paperback edition first published
in Great Britain and the USA 2015 by
SEVERN HOUSE PUBLISHERS LTD.

British Library Cataloguing in Publication Data

Pilkington, John, 1948 June 11- author.
  Marbeck and the Gunpowder Plot.
  1. Marbeck, Martin (Fictitious character)–Fiction.
  2. Fawkes, Guy, 1570-1606–Fiction. 3. Gunpowder Plot,
  1605–Fiction. 4. Great Britain–History–James I,
  1603-1625–Fiction. 5. Spy stories.
  I. Title
  823.9'2-dc23

ISBN-13: 978-0-7278-8514-2 (cased)
ISBN-13: 978-1-84751-616-9 (trade paper)
ISBN-13: 978-1-78010-667-0 (e-book)

All Severn House titles are printed on acid-free paper.

Severn House Publishers support the Forest Stewardship Council™ [FSC™],
the leading international forest certification organisation. All our titles that
are printed on FSC certified paper carry the FSC logo.

Typeset by Palimpsest Book Production Ltd.,
Falkirk, Stirlingshire, Scotland.
Printed and bound in Great Britain by
TJ International, Padstow, Cornwall.

PROLOGUE

The sun was shrinking.

It was the twelfth day of October, and the outbreak of plague that had blighted London over this uneasy summer was receding into memory. The city basked in autumn sunshine, the clatter of hooves and the shouts of market sellers filling the air. Noon was approaching, the streets teemed with people, and at first few realized that the cries of birds had ceased; even the red kites were no longer wheeling about London Bridge. Then, as the sky began to darken, eyes turned upwards: the sun had changed, from a sphere to a narrowing crescent. A dark shape was sliding across it from east to west, and soon an eerie silence fell.

The phenomenon lasted for two hours. When the shadow finally passed and the sun assumed its proper shape, a sense of relief pervaded the city – indeed, pervaded all of southern England. But one word was on the lips of many: *omen*. It was a little over three weeks since the moon's eclipse. Two such occurrences within a month . . . surely this was a portent?

At least one individual, however, remained in ignorance of the entire event. This man knelt in a tiny, windowless space fashioned by a mason's skill within a thick limestone wall. Though the wall was but one of many in this grand country house, his only bodily comforts were a candle, a bottle of watered wine and a pail in which to relieve himself. From time to time he heard the searchers knocking on ceilings and panels, stamping on floors with their heavy boots, calling to one another. Yet Father Cornford of the Society of Jesus had no concerns for himself; if he were discovered, so be it. Capture and imprisonment, even execution, were the least of his fears. With eyes closed he intoned a desperate litany, all the while lashing himself over the shoulder with a whip of knotted cords: thirty or more of them, interwoven with scraps of twisted wire. Blood ran down his bare back, yet still he plied the scourge.

'*Peccator infirmus sum . . . indignus sum . . . domine, ignosce me . . .*'

Yet, as fervently as he prayed through the pain, lips moving in a whisper, the truth sat starkly in his mind, as immovable as a rock. It was a secret known to very few: a burden that weighed so heavily upon him, he could hardly bear it. Mayhem was set in motion: a murderous scheme that would tear England apart. But because the priest had learned of it under the sacred seal of the confessional, he was forbidden to speak of it.

Men would die, he feared, and likely in large numbers: some quickly, others slowly and in agony, yet Father Cornford could warn no one. A fortunate few might survive, but by then the city of London – and soon the entire nation – would be in turmoil. Tears ran down his cheeks; he was prey to the sin of despair. His response was to increase his efforts, to force the bloodstained thongs to bite deeper into his already lacerated flesh.

Outside a shadow had passed, the sun shone and birds flew again. But in the priest's hiding-hole the candle flickered and went out, and all was dark.

ONE

Marbeck sensed the big man's presence before he heard him. By the time he felt a tug at his sleeve, his hand was on his dagger-hilt – whereupon a voice sounded close to his ear.

'Ye've no need for that fancy toy.'

He turned and let out a breath. 'MacNeish.'

'Aye. It's been a while, has it not?'

The man's clothing had that familiar scent of coarse Scottish wool and old leather, while his breath smelled of strong drink. Marbeck looked him over before turning back to the lantern-lit platform, visible through the throng of shouting men. The roar of the cockpit, the amphitheatre of hope, was all about them.

'D'ye have money on Spiky Jack?' Colum MacNeish pushed himself forward, his rough coat brushing Marbeck's good doublet. 'I hear they put brandy in his water – raises his temper, but slows him down in the end. He'll tire before the black does.'

'What is it you want?' Marbeck asked. In fact, he had wagered five crowns on the red cock known as Spiky Jack, but he wasn't about to admit it to MacNeish. The man had been known to lack discretion on occasions, and in an informer that was a serious flaw.

'I thought we might do business,' came the reply. 'I have tidings . . . the kind that are worth more than the shillings you palmed on me the last time we spoke.' The Scotsman had raised his voice above the din, which made him cough. Turning aside he spat heavily, his spittle narrowly missing a gallant who glared at him, before quickly deciding that the huge, russet-bearded fellow was likely to prove more than he could match.

'Another time, perhaps,' Marbeck said absently; the squawking of the gamecocks was reaching fever pitch. He glimpsed a flurry of dust and feathers through the press of bodies. The shouting grew louder as gamblers urged both birds on to the kill.

'What'd I tell ye? Yon black cock's a dancing speedwell.' MacNeish craned his neck, peering above the throng. 'His spurs are better fashioned, too . . . Your bird looks a sorry sight.'

'My bird?' Marbeck frowned. 'How do you know which one I favour?'

The other gave a wry grin. ''Tis written on your brow, John Sands.' He used the old cover name; he could not know that just now Marbeck was Lawrence Tucker, country gentleman and self-confessed spendthrift. Meanwhile, men surged about them, bawling and gesticulating. Spiky Jack was cursed and berated, but to no avail. Finally, a cry of dismay sounded from someone at the front, followed by a chorus of jeers and laughter.

The cock-master's voice rose above the din. 'The red has lost the field – Black Plume wins!'

A cheer went up, followed by scattered applause. Marbeck sighed and was about to turn away, then suddenly remembered why he was here; his gamester's instinct had almost got the better of him. Raising his head, he caught sight of the man he'd been following for the past few days: Ferdinand Gower, Papist and ex-soldier, seemingly flushed with victory. Friends clapped him on the shoulder, while the fellow's smile was confirmation enough.

'Who's that smirking cove?'

For a moment, Marbeck had almost forgotten MacNeish too. 'Some lucky devil who bet on the black,' he answered tartly. 'How should I know?'

Seeing he was about to move off, the Scotsman put a hand on his arm. 'Wait, I pray ye . . .' His grin had faded. 'I said there are tidings, and ye know I have a good ear for intelligence, Sands. I've been speaking with one of the Palace servants—'

'Whitehall gossip?' Marbeck shrugged. 'I can hear that any time I please, from a dozen throats.'

'Not this, you can't.' The other eyed him keenly: despite the drink he'd taken – or perhaps because of it – he was in earnest. 'But I can't talk here, you understand.' He waited expectantly.

'You spoke of shillings,' Marbeck said dryly, reaching for his purse. 'Take one for charity's sake, and go quench your thirst somewhere.'

'I thought ye knew me better than that, sirrah,' MacNeish retorted, with a dismissive gesture. 'There are stirrings . . . cloudy matters that touch on the King's own children! Is that not worth a little of your precious time?' He jerked his head to indicate the fighting table. Men were milling about, clamouring to place wagers on the next bout. Marbeck's quarry, it seemed, was among them. Encouraged by his win perhaps, Gower moved closer to the table. Likely he would be here for at least another hour.

In spite of himself, Marbeck relented. 'Perhaps I'll take some air . . . it's stifling in here.'

He turned and threaded his way through the gamblers: men of all stations, from noblemen in cloaks and crowned hats to noisy apprentice boys in plain fustian. MacNeish followed, bonnet in hand, stepping through the dirty straw. At the doors he waited for Marbeck to pass through before making his own way out. There in Shoe Lane, the main route between Fleet Street and Holborn, they stood in a biting wind.

'Well?' Marbeck raised an eyebrow.

MacNeish lifted his face to the sky, drawing deeply of the cool air. The evening was drawing in, and the city gates would soon be closing. A few people were in the lane, moving towards Holborn and the church of St Andrew. Lights showed at windows, while from the cockpit behind noise rose again; the next avian battle was about to commence.

'I've not one, but two tales to relate,' the Scotsman said finally. 'One came from the fellow at the court, a servant to Lady Carey. The wife of Sir Robert Carey, that is—'

'I know who she is,' Marbeck broke in. 'What is it you're so keen to tell me?'

'Very well . . .' MacNeish sniffed. 'I've a notion to save my heaviest news for last. That way you'll listen, while I tell my first – which is of grave import too, I might say. It stems from among my own folk . . . Aye, I mind your impatience,

Sands. I mean Little Scotland – that's what you'd call it, is it not?'

Marbeck said nothing. The district so named was but a short way from where they stood: the crowded tenements about Portpoole, where the poorer countrymen of King James clustered. They were the ones who had followed their sovereign south over the past two years in hopes of preferment which, for most, had proved groundless.

'Aye, they're grave tidings,' MacNeish was saying gloomily. When Marbeck still waited, he moistened his lips and in a sombre tone announced: 'There's a stratagem in train to obliterate us.'

Marbeck looked blank; then he wanted to laugh. MacNeish's heightened sense of the dramatic had always amused him. The man's face was so dour, he could be preaching of Judgement Day. 'When you say *us*,' he said, 'do you mean—'

'I mean the Scots, of course!' The highlander's beard twitched. 'There's a scheme to decimate us and to force those that are left back to our own country . . . to the mountains and glens, if you will. It's no secret that we're hated here – has King Jimmy not outlawed the swaggerers who assail us in the streets? Yet the attacks persist, along wi' the barracking and the slander. Many have given up and gone, while others grow bitter and carry arms—'

'While a few have grown rich and loaf about the Palace, or ride to hunt with the King,' Marbeck put in mildly.

But the other was not to be gainsaid. 'Likely that's a part of it too!' he snapped. 'Jealousy, I mean . . . Either way, Sands, you should hear me out. Have I once lied to you, or spun you a—'

'Enough.' Marbeck raised a hand briefly, then glanced about to see that no one was within earshot. 'I need more than fears and rumour. Do you have names, something to point me at?'

'In the matter of what I've just related, I do not,' MacNeish admitted. 'Though I swear it's beyond mere chaff; there's a stirring, a danger ye can almost smell. Besides, what of the late portents of sun and moon? We've had plague already, and the year isn't over. Or do ye scoff at such notions, as others do?'

Marbeck gave a shake of his head, which might mean assent or otherwise, whereupon MacNeish let out a sigh. 'Well now, I've spoken of that threat – which is as real as I stand here – and I'll leave you to turn it about,' he said. 'Which ye will in time, John Sands – mayhap I know you better than you think.'

They eyed each other; for all this man's faults, Marbeck had never been able to dislike him. He knew it was time he went back into the cockpit to continue his surveillance. But seeing MacNeish's eagerness, he said: 'What is it you meant, about matters concerning the royal children?'

The other lowered his head. 'I believe it's a matter of a kidnap,' he said.

Eyes narrowing, Marbeck peered into his face. 'Kidnap by whom – or should I say *of* whom?' he asked. 'Prince Henry, the Princess Elizabeth or the young Duke Charles . . . or do you mean the infant Mary?'

'Now I have your ear, at last.' MacNeish drew himself up with renewed dignity. 'To tell truly, I know not which of them it is. I doubt it's the bairn, since she's but six months old. As for the princes—'

'Wait – are you serious?' Marbeck stared at him; the information was only just sinking in. 'Where did you hear this?' he demanded. 'I need testimony – all you've got. Or I swear, MacNeish, I'll have you in front of the—'

'Then will ye let me finish?' The highlander glowered at him. 'I told ye already – I got it from a servant to the Careys. Lady Elizabeth has charge of Duke Charles . . . she dotes on the lad, clumsy and sickly as he is. She has a servant named Prestall, who has a Scots mother. That one knows my wife, and so—'

Impatiently, Marbeck brushed the details aside. 'The substance. What did this Prestall tell you? You or your wife, I care not which.'

'He told me little,' MacNeish admitted. 'And he was drinking at the time . . . but I saw how the matter weighed upon him. There's a man . . . a royal official and a steward of powerful family. He travels a lot, collecting rents in the North Country for his lord. When he's here, he keeps an uncommon eye on

the young princes – both of them. Prince Henry in his household at St James's, but especially the young Duke in his
chambers at Whitehall. For all I know, he watches the princess
too. She lives at some great house in the Midlands . . .'

'Coombe Abbey,' Marbeck broke in, his frown deepening.
'But this means little. Many keep an eye on the royal heirs,
for their safety. The King encourages it—'

'Aye, that he does.' MacNeish nodded gravely. 'He was
kidnapped himself as a boy and will never forget it. But this
man I speak of . . . He's different.' Pausing dramatically, he
delivered his revelation. 'He's a Papist.'

'Is he indeed?' Marbeck sighed. 'Then how did he get to
be a royal official? He'd have had to prove his allegiance –
swear the Oath of Supremacy.'

MacNeish put on a grim smile. 'Because his lord and
kinsman got him the appointment and arranged it so he didnae
have to take the oath – d'ye see now?'

At that, a suspicion arose in Marbeck's mind. 'This lord,'
he ventured. 'Who might he be?'

MacNeish's face fell. 'If ye ken it already, then speak his
name,' he muttered. 'Or I might suspect ye merely want to
skimp on my payment.'

Marbeck found his purse and tugged it open. 'Well then,
will an angel serve?'

Somewhat swiftly, MacNeish took the proffered coin. With
a look almost of shame he stowed it away, then said: 'The
lord is Henry Percy, Earl of Northumberland – captain of the
King's Gentlemen Pensioners.'

'Yes . . . that I can believe,' Marbeck said, almost to himself.
The notorious 'Wizard Earl', one of the richest men in England,
was rarely free of suspicion of one kind or another, especially
with regard to his Catholic sympathies. 'So this rent collector,
the one who snoops about the Court—'

'Is his cousin, Thomas Percy,' MacNeish broke in. 'A sly
devil, hated by the Scots – but that's not why I name him.
'Tis he you should be following – not the dandy within, who
won on the black fowl.'

He jerked his head towards the cockpit doors, prompting a
wry look from Marbeck. 'You've still a good eye, when all's

said and done, MacNeish,' he muttered. Then as a thought struck him: 'How did you know I was here?'

'I didnae, John Sands. I'm here most days, if truth be told. 'Twas pure fortune . . . but when I saw you, I knew what I should do.' The highlander rubbed his thick beard, then looked away. 'You're the only one I know who might act on Prestall's words, spoken in drink but so ill-laden. And I may be no admirer of our wily King Jimmy, but I'm loyal – same as you are.' He turned to face Marbeck, adding: 'Where might I find you, if I need to? That old wreck of a place in St Martin's?'

After a moment Marbeck nodded, whereupon the big man bade him goodnight, threw his thick cloak over his shoulder, crammed his bonnet on his head and stalked off in the gathering gloom. He was making for Holborn, and no doubt thence to the tavern known as the Iron Kist, to carouse among exiles like himself: strangers in a country where, despite being ruled by their own king, they found themselves unloved and unwanted. Marbeck watched him turn the corner by St Andrews, then went back inside the cockpit.

He entered to a murmur of approval from the cluster of men about the fighting table. Two new cockerels, their feathers ruffled out in defiance, were being shown by their handlers. Easing himself through the throng, he looked about for the bright mauve-pink of Ferdinand Gower's satin-lined cloak, but couldn't see it. Moving faster, he made a circuit of the building, scanning the entire crowd, jostled by eager gamblers, before ending up at the spot where he had stood earlier. He cursed silently: the man was gone.

Abruptly, he went to the door, made his way out and stood once again in Shoe Lane. But the street was darkening, and there was no sign. Then he stiffened and looked round sharply. He saw nothing amiss, yet the feeling persisted: that someone had an eye on him. He glanced at the cockpit door, saw that no one had followed him out.

Finally, he dismissed the notion and resigned himself to the plain fact that he would have to explain to his masters how he had lost his quarry.

TWO

In the dusk Marbeck crossed the Fleet Bridge and entered the city at Ludgate. Fortunately, the doors were only now closing, and he was one of the last to be admitted. From there he walked by Paternoster Row to the conduit, and thence to his room above a disused bowling-house in St Martins. It was the most unsavoury lodging he had occupied in years, and he planned to vacate it soon. On entering he was greeted by the sight of his landlord, a beetle-browed rogue named Skinner, seated at a table opposite a frowzy woman in a low-cut gown. The downstairs was dimly lit, strewn with stale rushes and smelling of fish, the remains of a turbot that lay on the table. The faces of both Skinner and his companion were flushed with drink.

'Here's Master Tucker – you are right welcome, *sir*!' His voice thick with wine and sarcasm, the landlord leered at Marbeck. 'Will you join us in a cup of muscadine, or have you supped?'

'I have,' Marbeck said, moving to the staircase. 'I'll give you goodnight.'

'He gives us goodnight!' Skinner echoed, prompting a chuckle from his guest. 'Never one to waste his time on conversation, is our friend from the shires. What county is it you hail from, master? I never did discover it.'

'Perhaps because I never vouchsafed it,' Marbeck replied over his shoulder. Having reached the stair he put a hand to the balustrade, but at the landlord's next words he checked himself.

''Tis pity . . . but since you're in such a hurry, I almost fear to speak of the message that was left for you.'

Slowly, Marbeck turned. 'A message . . . was it verbal, or otherwise?'

'*Verbal?*' Skinner was enjoying himself: impressing his guest, it seemed, and giving vent to his dislike of the tenant who never troubled to pass the time of day with him. 'Well, 'twas brought by a servant with a limp, as I recall . . . or was that the fishmonger's boy? I forget . . . but no matter. The message was not *verbal*, sirrah, but *otherwise*: in short, a letter without a seal.' He paused for effect, then added: 'But I forbore to read it. I'm a man of discretion, who respects another's privacy.'

'Where is it?' Marbeck asked, his voice flat.

'Yes . . . now where did I place it?' Putting on a puzzled look, Skinner made a show of scratching his head. 'This afternoon it came . . . I was at my prayers.' He grinned at his companion, who laughed aloud.

Marbeck waited, keeping his temper with an effort.

Finally, aware that the jest had worn thin, Tucker slapped a hand to his head. 'Of course – I put it under your door, Master Tucker! How could I forget . . . I was distracted, thinking of my sweet guest and the joy she brings me.' His smile broadening, Skinner lifted his cup and saluted the woman, who smirked before taking up her own drink. The two of them soon forgot Marbeck, barely registering his footsteps ascending the stairs.

In his chamber he found the paper on the threshold, lit a candle and sat down on the bed. Unfolding the letter, he leaned close to the flickering flame, and his heart stirred; it was from Meriel, whom he had not seen in months. He knew the hand before he read.

He paused briefly to wonder how she knew where he lodged. They had parted in the summer, when he went to France . . . a hasty farewell, with hurt on her side and impatience on his. She was still living at her sister's then, but had spoken of returning home in obedience to her father. He looked at the writing and saw but a single sentence:

> *Come this night to my father's house in Crutched Friars,*
> *and wait by the gate where I may see you.*

It was signed with an M, its tail extended into a pattern of descending loops.

Lowering the letter he stared into the candle's flame, seeing her face when they had last been together. It was important; she would never write otherwise. Questions rose in his mind, but were unanswered. He'd intended to get a night's sleep, then go to Levinus Monk first thing in the morning. His spymaster would be angry at his having lost Gower, but there was now the matter of MacNeish's testimony . . .

In agitation he stood up. Though poorly furnished, the room was large, spanning the bowling alley beneath. The beams under his feet creaked alarmingly; the building was unsafe, though it was more on account of the uneven floor – something hotly denied by Skinner – that it had long been shunned by gamesters. Marbeck paced to the window and back, knowing he must go at once to Crutched Friars – how could he not? It meant a walk the length of the entire city, almost to the Tower, and he would have to explain his presence to the watch. But he would bluff, as always; the urgency in Meriel's words was plain.

Stowing the letter inside his doublet, he took his cloak from a peg and went out. Downstairs, he ignored Skinner's sneer and left the house in haste.

Crutched Friars, the street backing on to London's east wall by Aldgate, was in darkness. A few lights could be seen at the windows of large houses with walled gardens, the dwellings of noblemen and others of wealth and status. Marbeck knew which one belonged to Meriel's father: the city lawyer Thomas Walden, soon to be knighted it was said. Approaching the iron gates, as expected he found them padlocked. But there was a torch burning in a sconce on one of the pillars. He peered through the ironwork, scanning the house – and immediately he knew. A light showed at a window on the ground floor: she was there, looking out for him, because she knew he would come.

Stepping into full view before the gates, he stood motionless and waited. And in less than a minute, a door opened and a cloaked figure moved through the garden towards him. She reached the gate and stopped, putting a hand on the bars. For a moment neither of them spoke. In the semi-darkness he could barely see her face . . . He touched his hand to hers, taking her fingers around the cold iron. But to his surprise, she drew them away.

'This is no glad reunion, Marbeck.' Her voice was taut, controlled. 'I have news for you, and when I've delivered it you should leave and not try to see me again.'

He blinked. 'Your father . . .?' he began vaguely, but she cut him short.

'He's absent, else I could not come out here like this. I'm almost a captive.' She shivered suddenly; the night was cold. Drawing her cloak about herself, she added: 'No matter – it's best this way.'

'Best?' He stared at her. 'What can you mean? I know it's a good while since I sought you out, but you know what I—'

'It isn't that.'

She cut him off abruptly, avoiding his eye. Deliberately, he put his hand through the gate until finally – reluctantly, it seemed – she took it. He squeezed, but she did not respond.

'So, have you tired of me at last?' he asked quietly. 'Or of this intelligencer's life, which blights both of us? If it's the latter, I've a mind to throw it over and—'

'Oh, indeed – and how many times have you said so?'

She was sharp, even bitter. He pressed forward, forcing her to look at him in the gloom. Finally, eyes shining in the torch-light, she met his gaze.

'It's too late in any case,' she said at last, in a calmer voice. 'I've taken this chance, while my father is away, to tell you what's occurred since we last parted. The matter is, I'm to marry soon.'

Marbeck was silent.

'My husband-to-be is a lawyer – a widower, Richard Verney. He's a good man: a neighbour, and a long-standing friend of our family. I'll be mistress of my own home thereafter and put an end to this constant warring between my father and myself. It's the best way . . . You must see that.'

Still he said nothing. And when she spoke again it was too quickly, her words spilling over themselves in haste.

'We'll never have a life together! You live like a moon-man, riding who knows where, coming to me penniless and blooded like a beggar, as you did once at my sister's. You claim you've never lied, but you would if the need arose – I've seen it in your face, even as you lay with me. The scars you carry, within and without . . . Fine swordsman or no, one day it'll be your heart that's pierced—' She stopped, rather quickly, and pulled her hand away.

'Well,' he breathed. 'It sounds to me as if you've been saving that speech up.'

She made no reply.

'This Richard Verney . . . A widower, you say?'

'He's without issue – is that what you were going to ask?'

'No, it wasn't . . .' Taken aback by her sharpness, he stared, trying to frame questions; then it hit him. 'You're carrying my child.'

She looked at the ground.

'By the Christ . . . why did you not send word?'

He sounded angry; though what he felt, with a rush, was a mix of emotions in which anger was but a minor element. Gripping the gate with both hands, he said: 'You found me at that shambles of a bowling-house – you could have found me sooner! Do you think I wouldn't have come to you? That I'd abandon you like a trull—'

'Aye – perhaps I did!' Fiercely, she looked up. 'Have you ever used me otherwise? As you did the Lady Scroop – before she was widowed, and after – until she put an end to it? You, who could return to your family's estate, marry and live like a gentleman, yet choose to court risks like a fool, matching wits with your enemies – what does it avail you? Answer me now, while you have this chance!'

He shook his head, fumbling for an answer.

'See – you cannot!' Her tone was almost triumphant. 'Since you ask, it was Gifford who told me where you lodged, before he went away – how else could I know? And while I speak of Gifford, what was I to you but his cast-off, to be passed on like a suit of clothes? Yet you've known me better than he did . . . known my most secret parts . . . I even thought . . .'

Once again she stopped herself. She was as close to tears as Marbeck had ever known, which unsettled him almost as much as anything she'd said. But she spoke the truth, and both of them knew it. A bleakness rose inside him, borne of the knowledge of the past seventeen years, back when he had taken to the intelligencer's life with relish. Now, at thirty-five, he was no longer that strutting youth . . . He swallowed and found the words.

'I'll do it – I swear. I'll take you away, as far as you like . . . to the Indies, even. I'll tell Levinus Monk he can go hang himself – him, and his crookback master, and the whole whoreson Council. And your father, too . . .' He banged his fist on the gate, startling her. 'Your father, and your upstanding husband-to-be – this widower he's persuaded into taking you off his hands. How much is the dowry?'

She caught her breath, but made no answer; why should she, when the facts were plain enough? His chest rising, he thrust his hand out again, seeking hers; to his surprise, she took it.

'What else is there, Marbeck?' she said, weary all of a sudden. 'What other course do I have?'

Her anger had drained away, and in silence they gazed at each other. Somewhere nearby a watchman called the hour; the ringing of his bell was as the clang of doom. When, for some reason, her eyes strayed to the gate that stood between them, Marbeck said: 'We'll leave now, if you like. You think I couldn't pick a toy like this?'

He fingered the iron padlock, and for a moment Meriel looked as if she would laugh. It was almost reminiscent of happier times . . . but she shook her head sadly.

'You know it can't be. I won't fly like a fugitive. It may be my fancy, but of late I believe I've felt the child move. I will not endanger her.'

'*Her*?' His brow knitted. 'How can you . . .?'

'Call that my fancy, too. But Goody Joan says it's a girl . . . our oldest servant, who's given birth to seven of her own and claims she can tell. She'll be my midwife, when I'm confined.'

'But, how long do you think—?' Feeling utterly helpless, Marbeck broke off.

Meriel gave him her most brazen expression, letting him know that he could reckon the time well enough. 'Three months,' she answered finally. 'It will show soon, and then everyone will know. Hence, Richard and I will marry within a month. The first banns have been read.'

He let out a breath. 'You're resolved, then.'

She gave no answer.

'And you're certain of this?'

Their eyes locked, and for a fleeting moment his hopes rose . . . only to vanish at once. 'I have to be,' she replied. 'I want a good life for the child, and for those who might follow her. They will never know they are different—'

'What – so you too will lie, if need arises?' His anger erupted again. 'To your own children? Have you lied to Verney – no, of course you haven't. Widowed and childless – he and your father have made a fitting arrangement, and all of you will keep to the tale. Heaven forbid that anyone should know your child's true sire is a shiftless cove who serves their King in secret, for whatever payment he can wheedle out of the Council . . .'

'Marbeck, for pity's sake!'

He stopped, suppressing a curse. She bit her lip, looking at him in anguish – and in that moment he knew her feelings for him had not changed; if anything, they were even deeper. A few women had loved him, but not as Meriel did. And none had conceived a child by him; he was as certain as he could be. He opened his mouth, then saw her shiver again, quite violently this time.

'You should go inside,' was all he could say.

She gave a nod and wrapped her cloak tightly about her. 'Swear you will let it be,' she said softly. 'Whatever it costs you, it cannot be more than what it costs me. Swear now . . . I pray you.'

But slowly he shook his head. 'I can't.'

So she left him, swinging her body away without another word. Head down, she walked back through the gardens to her father's house.

He heard a door close, but didn't move. Instead he stood at the gates, hands on the bars like some Newgate felon. Soon he saw the light in the downstairs room vanish and knew she had retired for the night. Perhaps the matron Goody Joan was her chamber companion now. One thing seemed clear enough: never again would Marbeck share her bed.

He stayed there a while longer, long after the torch on the pillar had burned itself out. He heard a bellman call again, not knowing if it was the same one. Finally, numb with cold, he forced himself to turn away. In the pitch dark he walked off blindly, finding himself eventually in Aldgate Street, heading towards Cornhill.

His fingers had lost all feeling, but he didn't notice.

THREE

The skiff hit Parliament Stairs with a thud, prompting the waterman to let out an oath. Cursing his own clumsiness he swung the boat round, gripped the jetty post and threw an apologetic look at his passenger. 'Your pardon . . . 'Tis a fierce current today.'

The boat lurched as Marbeck stood up, and he had to grip the gunwale as he fished out a coin. The waterman took it and touched his cap. 'My thanks to you, sir . . . shall I wait for your return?'

He shook his head and clambered on to the stairs, slippery with mould. The morning was cloudy, with an autumn damp that seeped through his clothes. Once on the pathway, with Westminster Abbey looming ahead, he made his way to the Old Palace Yard. The Whitehall village, a community in itself, was astir with Crown servants and military-looking men, some of whom looked keenly at him. But he walked briskly on, past the Jewel Tower, before turning a corner and stopping at a low door studded with square-headed nails. He knocked in the familiar pattern and went in.

'Praise be . . . he's here at last.'

In the firelit room, its single window shuttered, Levinus Monk stood by a table strewn with papers. Five years back, Marbeck recalled briefly, this was how he would have met with Lord Cecil, when he was still plain Sir Robert and not the Earl of Salisbury, King James's chief minister and the most powerful man in England. Now the hawk-faced Monk was the new 'Martha', as his agents nicknamed him: a toiler, loaded with the murky business of intelligence. The man's shrewd gaze was undimmed, though he looked tired; tired and tightly-wound. Brusquely, he pointed to a sideboard where stood a jug and cups, but Marbeck declined. He'd put himself to sleep the night before with a mug of Skinner's cheap muscadine, taken from the deserted table while his landlord sported elsewhere; this morning, he could still taste it.

'Ah . . .' Monk peered at him. 'You wear that hangdog look, Marbeck. Have you come to disappoint me?'

'I lost Ferdinand Gower,' Marbeck said flatly. 'At the cockpit in Shoe Lane . . . I've no excuse, other than carelessness.'

The spymaster stiffened, but remained silent.

'I could find him again, I suppose . . . He makes little effort to hide his whereabouts. I think he knows he's being watched and doesn't care – even sees it as a mark of status.'

Monk appeared to weigh the matter.

'And besides . . .' Marbeck met his eye. 'I confess I can't see what it avails us: I mean, watching Papists like him. You can pick them up any time you choose, since everyone knows who they are and where they worship. As for the Recusants . . .' He shrugged. 'How many noble families are left, who can afford the fines for non-attendance at church? A dozen?'

'Fifteen, at the last count.' Monk's tone was dry. 'Is that all you have to tell me?'

He knew it wasn't, of course; this had become part of their ritual, before getting down to business. Despite his manner, Monk knew who his best intelligencers were and took pains to keep them. Soon he would speak of money and produce a purse, Marbeck knew. But today, even that seemed unimportant; he gritted his teeth, forcing down the memory of last night . . .

Monk broke the silence, eyeing him grimly . 'There's a difference, this year. They're more than restive . . . they're angry. It's been brewing since the last Parliament, when they finally realized the King's no Papist sympathizer, but had played them along from the beginning. Now their hopes of toleration are as dust, even their archpriest has spoken out, urging them to remain calm and obey the law . . . pin their hopes on God. The poor lambs.'

In some surprise, Marbeck returned his gaze; for Levinus Monk, staunch Dutch Protestant, such a comment was rare. 'Obey the law?' he echoed. 'Does he know something we don't?'

The other smiled, though it was more of a grimace. For answer he seized a handful of documents and waved them at Marbeck. 'More than likely, I'd say. Who would doubt it, when

I get reports by the day of fearful goings-on, from here to the Scottish borders? Someone called Woodrington, in the far north, is said to be able to muster two thousand men for the Catholic cause, at short notice. In the Midlands large numbers of horses have been seen, gathered in the stables of certain country manors. Store of arms, too . . . The swordsmiths have more orders than they can fill, apparently. Meanwhile, John Cutler says there's weaponry being shifted by night up the Surrey road – though I know of no one else who's seen it. So – what am I supposed to think?' With a look of exasperation, he dumped the papers back on the table.

Marbeck was frowning. 'Cutler? I thought he'd slipped away. Keeping bees somewhere, or—'

'Yes, the man's half-mad,' Monk broke in. 'Bees in his head, if you ask me – but I can't afford to waste even him. He's keeping an eye on the archbishop's palace in Croydon . . . We must leave nowhere unwatched.'

He fell silent, and all of a sudden Marbeck's own troubles appeared slight. There was always talk of rebellion – even of Spanish involvement, despite the peace treaty signed last year – but perhaps this year, as Monk had said, was different. Catholics were dismayed by their sovereign's betrayal, after the hopes raised at his accession. Instead of the promised easing of restrictions on their worship, laws against them had been strengthened to the point of brutality, as many saw it . . .

'Well, as it happens, Monk, I've more rumours to add to your store,' he said at last. 'One comes from among the Scottish loafers about Portpoole . . . It seems the Papists aren't the only ones who see themselves under threat.'

The spymaster looked dismissive. 'I know that. One man told me the Scotsmen would be blown back to their frozen lands soon. Barbarians, he called them. I mentioned that King James is a Scot, shrewder and better educated than most of the men on his Council, but I doubt he was listening.'

'And yet, there might be some substance to it,' Marbeck said, thinking of the dour-faced MacNeish. 'My source has always been a truthful man, with an ear to the ground. There's a stirring, as he put it. The Scots are afraid, and not merely of the rakes who assail them in the streets.'

There was a moment while Monk considered. But when he spoke again, it was on a different tack. 'You know that the opening of Parliament was prorogued,' he said with a frown. 'It will take place on a Tuesday, the fifth day of November . . . If the King returns from Royston in time, that is.'

Marbeck said nothing; today, his mind seemed to be drifting. All England knew that their monarch spent more and more time away hunting and hawking, leaving the Queen at home and the business of government to ministers. Even when at Whitehall, he was likely to be found at the royal cockpit or at the mews, among his falconers . . .

'Which is why . . .' With a stern look, Monk forced his intelligencer to give him full attention. 'Which is why I'm so hard pressed just now – forced to employ even a witless cove like Cutler. I have to treat every report – every rumour – with due seriousness.'

He paused, then: 'Your intelligence from France was useful. Since Henri lifted the ban last year, everyone knows Jesuits have been flocking to the new schools . . . though we had only a vague notion of their numbers. Small wonder that some say we're almost besieged by those people.' Irritably, he slapped the table. 'Do you know how many of their priests are believed to be at large now – I mean, not in France, but here in England? More than forty! Do you mark that?'

But Marbeck merely raised an eyebrow; the figure did not surprise him, after his sojourn among the eager students of the colleges in Northern Europe. For more than twenty-five years, since Robert Persons and Edmund Campion had first brought their Jesuit mission to England, the trickle of clandestine priests had increased, year by year; the threat of hanging seemed only to encourage them.

'Do you want me to turn my attention to them again?' he asked, without enthusiasm. Then, before the spymaster could answer, he added: 'First, perhaps you should hear my other intelligence that came from the same source. For if there's any truth to it, it's graver than anything else I've heard.'

Monk blinked at him, his beak-like nose almost quivering. 'What now?' he demanded. 'Are the Spanish in the Channel with a new armada, or what?'

'Not as far as I know,' Marbeck answered. As briefly as he could, he related Colum MacNeish's testimony of a perceived threat to the princes and princesses of the realm.

The spymaster listened, with growing unease – but when Marbeck spoke of Thomas Percy, kinsman to the Earl of Northumberland, he almost spluttered. 'Him! By the Christ, I wish I'd a crown for every man at Court that would like to see that fellow hanged. Why, I could—' With an oath, he broke off.

Half-amused, Marbeck spoke up. 'Buy yourself a knighthood? I hear the going rate is thirty pounds . . . Very lucrative for the royal coffers.'

He had overstepped the mark, but he knew Monk well enough. The man snorted and said something about treasonous remarks that got men imprisoned, before returning to the matter in hand. 'But see now, Percy's often about Westminster. As a Gentleman Pensioner, he has quarters here. How can your man be certain he watches the princes? And as for kidnap . . .?' He looked sceptical.

'My Scotsman says he got it from someone close by,' Marbeck told him. 'A servant to the Careys, named Prestall. He was drunk at the time, it seems, but . . .'

'I'll have him brought to me,' Monk said at once. 'Have you no further details?'

'Not at present.'

'Well, there's a new task for you. You may forget about Gower and watch Thomas Percy instead. He's not an easy man to lose.'

His spirits sinking, Marbeck looked away. But at least he could leave Skinner's and move elsewhere – whereupon, as if divining his thoughts, Monk asked him where he was lodging. When Marbeck answered, he added: 'It's best you stay there, isn't it? If you live too near the Palace, you may be noticed. You can remain Lawrence Tucker, turn up now and then and hang about with the rakes and gamesters. Percy has hired rooms close to the Lords' Chamber, though he's sometimes at Essex House – the earl's town residence. How you might gain access there, I don't know. But you'll find a way, Marbeck; you always do.'

The conversation was over, yet Marbeck stood his ground until the spymaster took the hint. He opened a small wooden chest, drew out a purse and, after weighing it in his hand, said: 'Now I think on it, will you undertake a journey before you seek Percy out? Go down to Croydon and find Cutler . . . See if he sticks to his tale about the mysterious goods that pass up the Surrey road by night. If it holds up, you might poke about a little. If it doesn't . . .'

In some surprise, Marbeck nodded; the purse, and the prospect of a ride in the country, cheered him a little. Taking his payment, he paused, then said: 'Croydon's a summer palace, isn't it? The archbishop won't even be there.'

Monk gave a shrug. 'My Lord Secretary has ordered it,' he said dryly. 'And who am I to question him?'

By midday he was ready. Managing to avoid Skinner, he left the bowling-house carrying a light pack and walked to the nearby stables to get Cobb. The place was small and mean, but discreet, kept by a taciturn friend of Skinner's named Oliver. At sight of Marbeck, the dour-faced man merely nodded and fiddled with his tobacco pipe, as he always did, before indicating the farthest stall. When Marbeck approached, his horse almost reared: he had been indoors too long. Once saddled and bridled he followed his master out on to the cobbles, head tossing. Within the hour they had crossed London Bridge and were cantering south, away from the noise and smells of the city.

It was a ten-mile ride along the old Roman Road, through the villages of Newington and Streatham. By late afternoon they were in the market town of Croydon, on the edge of the Surrey Hills. Wood smoke drifted on the wind and cattle lowed in the fields, ready to be brought in for milking. Walking his horse Marbeck entered the square, found a water-trough and dismounted. While Cobb drank, he looked about at the townsfolk who passed by before hailing one and asking for the whereabouts of John Cutler, who kept bees. The man nodded: Marbeck would find him at the last cottage on the Waddon road, below Dubber's Hill.

So, with the afternoon waning, he led Cobb to the edge of

the town, passed several thatched houses and stopped at the end one. Smoke curled from the chimney, and there was a faint light within. Leaving his mount at the gate he walked the few paces to the door and knocked . . . but when it opened, he took a step back: the man was a stranger.

'Your pardon . . .' Marbeck blinked. 'I'm seeking Master Cutler.'

Ruddy-faced, his features almost hidden by a heavy beard and a mass of unkempt hair, the cottager peered back at him. He was roughly dressed and none too clean; from inside the house drifted the bland odour of bean pottage. 'I'm Cutler.'

You can't be, Marbeck thought. But he said: 'Well then, you'll remember me – John Sands, servant to Lord Cecil?'

There was no reaction.

'Shall I try the names of a few others?' He was hungry and stiff from riding, and his patience was thin. 'Joseph Gifford, also known as Porter? Or what of Giles Winterburn—'

'Lord Cecil?' The other gave a start. 'You've come from him?'

'Not exactly,' Marbeck said – then suddenly, the other's face cleared.

'By the heavens . . . you're Marbeck.'

They stared at each other, whereupon recognition dawned on Marbeck too. The man's appearance had belied him: the John Cutler he remembered was a swordsman like him, athletic and alert. The one who stood before him was a stooped countryman in stained breeches and jerkin, wide-eyed and wild-haired . . . yet it was him, after all. Then, it had been well over a year . . .

'I am,' Marbeck replied, with some relief. 'I confess I didn't know you . . . You've altered somewhat.'

'Have I?' Cutler said vaguely. There was a look in his eye that made Marbeck uneasy. But he stepped back and drew the door wide. 'Well, come inside, won't you . . .' He glanced at Cobb and gestured towards the side of the house. 'That's a fine horse you have . . . Take him into the back garden. There's a lean-to, but I've no animal of my own now. Take care to avoid the skeps – the bees are asleep, and I don't want them roused.'

With a nod, Marbeck led Cobb round the back. He saw the straw skeps, a dozen or more, well-made and set out on wooden stands. But in the chill of autumn, no bees flew. The rest of the garden was overgrown; Cutler had let it run wild for the sake of his apian friends.

Having put Cobb under cover, he hung the nosebag about his neck and went to the back door. Inside the cottage he found Cutler stoking the fire. After swinging an iron pot back over the blaze, he straightened up. 'So, is it Levinus Monk you serve now?'

When Marbeck nodded briefly, he added: 'He sent me down here to bury me, you know. I doubt if he even reads the reports I send . . . Not that I send many. Where's the need, when the archbishop's palace lies empty, save for a handful of servants?' He gestured towards the window. 'It's across the road, beyond the trees . . . You could go and see for yourself.'

'In fact, that isn't why I'm here,' Marbeck told him. After stretching himself he looked round, saw an oak chest and sat down on it. 'Our master's more interested in the goods you spoke of, going up the road to London.' He raised an eyebrow, but Cutler looked blank.

'Goods?'

'Weaponry – isn't that what you reported . . .?' Marbeck paused. 'Carts passing by night?'

'No, no – they carried hides. Untanned hides and barrels of beer.' Cutler put on a lopsided smile. 'I remember now: I took a peek one night, while the carters watered their oxen. Lifted the covers, but there were only hides and kegs beneath them. The kegs reeked of beer.' His grin broadened. 'You've had a wasted journey. But no matter . . . You can sup with me and talk of other topics.'

A weariness settled upon Marbeck. For a moment annoy-ance rose, but he forced it down as Cutler bent down by the fire and began whistling to himself. Lifting the pot lid he peered inside, nodded in satisfaction and spoke over his shoulder. 'I've some sack to wash this down, and there's honey to smear on your bread. I sell it in the market – I could make my living doing it, you know . . .'

'By the Christ, Cutler.' Marbeck let out a breath and waited for the other to turn – which he did, reluctantly. 'I didn't know you when you opened the door . . . Now, I wonder if I do yet.'

Cutler opened his mouth, then closed it again. Seeing he wasn't about to speak, Marbeck pressed on. 'Will you think back to the old fencing hall, in the city? You and I had a bout there once. Your *stoccada* was perfect – you won ten crowns off me. You had a Toledo sword with a motto chased into it and a dagger to match . . . You lodged by Queenhithe, with Winterburn. He used to challenge you to drinking contests—'

'No, no . . .' Much too quickly, Cutler stood to his full height. 'I never did . . . I always lodged at the Irish Boy in the Strand.' To Marbeck's alarm, he threw up a hand as if to ward off a new thought. 'I hear Papists meet there now . . . Secret masses and such. Dark stuff. Best keep out of it, I say.'

Silence fell. His heart sinking, Marbeck gazed at him. Whistling once more, Cutler stepped to a shelf, took down a mug and stuck his nose in it. Then as Marbeck watched, he pulled out a dirty kerchief and wiped the inside busily. Finally, he looked round, grinning.

'I never use sugar – always sweeten my wine with honey. Do you know I keep skeps out the back? I fashion them myself – sell honey at the market. Why, I could make a living by it.'

He turned away again, polishing vigorously. And all Marbeck could do was regard the man who had once been John Cutler, crown intelligencer, and was now someone else who went by the same name: a bee-keeper of Croydon.

FOUR

He awoke early in the morning, in a hard bed in the Gun Tavern. Below him, the inn was stirring into life. Without thinking he threw the coverlet aside and sat up . . . then events flooded back.

He had a child unborn: a daughter, perhaps, who would never know him.

He stared at the floor as a wild scheme flew into his mind: of riding hard to London, going to the Walden house and carrying Meriel away by force. He could take her to his father's manor in Lancashire . . . He could play the prodigal son, swear he was a changed man who was eager to start afresh. But at that something welled up, to emerge as a bitter laugh.

The biggest fool is the man who fools himself . . .

His father's words rang in his head; the voice of Sir Julius Marbeck, Justice of the Peace, now in his seventieth year. Marbeck pictured the old man, a look of scorn on his face. Then he pictured Monk, wearing his most sardonic expression; the notion was absurd.

He stood up quickly and began to dress. Within the hour he had left the inn and was back in the market square, leading Cobb toward the London road. He was about to mount, then checked himself: the horse's gait was amiss. Carefully, he looked him over; speaking soothingly, he bent and lifted one front hoof, then the other, before setting it down.

Cobb had a shoe loose. Had he been fully alert last night, Marbeck told himself, he would have noticed it sooner. With an air of resignation, he went looking for a blacksmith.

In the forge, he stood by the open doorway and watched the man at work. At the rear the furnace roared, while a sweating boy worked the bellows. The smith himself, his hair tied back, plucked the glowing horseshoe from the fire with tongs and swung it round to his anvil. Expertly, he hammered away, punching a new hole in the iron, pausing now and then to talk. The coals he'd got of late were poor, he said. He preferred charcoal from his own parish . . . Did the gentleman know Croydon produced it? Mostly from willow and alder, but dogwood charcoal was best. It was hard to get just now . . . Evelyn took it all, down in Godstone.

To all of this Marbeck listened with half an ear, managing a nod from time to time. His thoughts were now on John Cutler and last night's frugal supper at his cottage. The man had chattered about his bees to the exclusion of all else; anything that might have passed for intelligence was gone to the wind, and Marbeck couldn't wait to take his leave. When he'd finally done so, his host hardly seemed to notice . . .

'He's a close one, sir – Evelyn, that is,' the blacksmith was saying. 'Took over the works after his father died – the family's held the patent from way back. Never short of business – you'd think we were still at war with the Spaniards, the way they turn the stuff out. Opened up the old nitre pits in the forest, I heard, because they can't get enough of it.'

Emerging from his reverie, Marbeck caught the man's last words and turned to him. 'What can't they get enough of?'

'Saltpetre, sir.'

The smith lifted the horseshoe and plunged it into a pail of water. There was a loud hissing, and steam filled the air. Marbeck tried to recall the rest of what he'd said, though without much success.

'You mentioned works, at Godstone . . .?'

'Gunpowder mills, aye – the Evelyn brothers.' The man drew the shoe from the pail, peered at it and nodded. 'This will serve. If you'll fetch your mount over, I'll fit it in no time—' He looked up, caught Marbeck's expression and broke off.

'Would you mind telling me again – about the gunpowder?' Marbeck asked.

It was another ten-mile ride, southwards down the old Roman Road through Warlingham and the Caterham Gap to Godstone. The village was tiny: a cluster of cottages with a church and an inn, surrounded by a patch of heath and, beyond that, dense woods.

Marbeck reined in by the horse pond, dismounted and let Cobb drink. At the Bell Inn he ate dinner, asked casually about the Evelyn brothers and received a ready response. The family were well-known in the area, the tapster told him: they owned the manor. There were four brothers, but Master Richard ran the mill. They employed local men, brought prosperity to the parish; Godstone was lucky to have such industrious folk. If the gentleman had business with them, they were easy to find.

And so it proved. In the early afternoon, Marbeck walked Cobb along a muddy cart-track through the woods until a wide clearing opened before him. Leigh Mill: a collection of sheds beside a brook, with a noise like a great drum roll emerging from one of them. There were storehouses, solidly built and windowless, with barrels stacked along the walls. Two empty carts stood nearby. Marbeck halted and found his pulse had quickened.

It was a whim, of course; but as so often before, his instinct told him he was on the edge of some discovery. Perhaps the visit to Cutler had not been wasted, after all. He'd been uneasy at the man's garbled account of carts rumbling through Croydon – and suddenly he realized why that was: there was a large tannery in the town. Why would anyone be sending untanned hides up to London – and by night? Was it really beer in the barrels Cutler had noticed underneath, or . . .?

'Good day, sir. How may I aid you?'

From a nearby building, a man had emerged. Broad-shouldered, he approached Marbeck and stood barring his way.

Summoning a faint smile, Marbeck drew breath; the situation called for swift impromptu. 'Master Evelyn, is it?'

'It is . . . and you are?'

'Thomas Wilders.' He used the cover name by which he was known on the continent, as a dealer in armaments. 'I do business with the Crown, now and then. I had a mind to see your workings . . . Word of your success has travelled far.'

But with a suspicious look, Evelyn took a pace forward. 'This land is private,' he said. 'I've no time for visitors.'

'A pity,' Marbeck said. 'I'm not unacquainted with weaponry . . . I trade in cannon sometimes. Does your powder go up to the Royal Ordnance, at the Tower?'

'If it did, I wouldn't be at liberty to speak of it.' Evelyn regarded him, his frown deepening. 'If you deal in armaments you would know that, surely?'

'I heard you have nitre pits, in the forest,' Marbeck pressed on. 'Difficult stuff to make, isn't it? No wonder it costs so dear . . . Fellow in Croydon told me you couldn't get enough of it.'

There was movement. Glancing aside, Marbeck saw another man emerge from the same building, followed by yet another. Both were in shirt sleeves and wore leather aprons. They looked hard at him, before moving to stand behind their master.

'Is anything amiss, sir?' one asked.

'No, nothing,' Evelyn answered, over his shoulder. 'This gentleman's been poorly advised, I believe.' He gave Marbeck a bland stare. 'You know your way back to the highway?'

'I believe so.' Marbeck returned his stare. 'Though I've a mind to exercise my mount first, in the forest . . . It doesn't all belong to you, does it?'

The labourers bristled, but Evelyn remained unmoved. 'Well, if you're so resolved,' he said smoothly, 'I'll send a couple of my men to accompany you, make sure you don't get lost.'

A moment passed. Briefly, Marbeck surveyed the surrounding buildings, but there was no need to look further: he'd seen the powder works at Rotherhithe by the Thames and knew what he would find. As for the nitre pits, they would tell him little. In any case the Evelyns held a royal patent, the tapster had told him, and made no secret of their business . . . Casually he shortened Cobb's rein, making ready to mount. 'I'll decline that pleasure this time,' he said. 'I wouldn't wish to take your men away from such important work.'

Without moving, the three watched him lift himself into the saddle, and they remained there as he rode away. At a bend in the track he looked behind and saw they still hadn't moved. With a cheerful wave, he turned and urged Cobb back towards Godstone.

But soon afterwards, Richard Evelyn might have been somewhat surprised to see Marbeck return to the Bell Inn, get his horse stabled and ask for a room overlooking the London road. How long he would be staying he was uncertain, he told the landlord; perhaps only one night, or even less. He paid the reckoning in advance and asked not to be disturbed. He had journeyed long and was tired.

Once in the best chamber, however, he ignored the ancient four-poster bed and took a stool by the window. Here, with a pie and a bottle of ale to fortify himself, he settled down to wait for evening. Thereafter he was prepared to watch all night, and if necessary the next one too. Any longer than that and he might have difficulty explaining his extended absence to Levinus Monk. But if his suspicions were correct, the intelligence he could take to his spymaster would justify everything.

As luck would have it, it was the second night.

Marbeck was dozing, his head resting on a cushion against the window-frame. He had slipped to the floor once, scrambling to his feet in the hope that no one had heard him. The first night he had dozed off twice before dawn broke, though he was certain no cart had passed through Godstone. Thereafter he had slept for much of the day, before taking supper and steeling himself to another night of surveillance; mercifully, his efforts had now borne fruit.

In fact, it was not the roll of wheels he heard first, but the grunting of animals, straining up the road towards the horse pond. In a moment he was alert, dropping to his knees and peering over the window sill. There was a cart, barely visible in the gloom, drawn by a pair of oxen. Two men sat on the driver's bench, hatted and muffled against the cold.

He allowed himself a sigh of relief, then got to work; he'd made his plans and was in no hurry. The teamsters would water their beasts, then move on up the highway; following them would be child's play. Marbeck's task was to stay far enough behind to observe, without being seen.

It took but a moment to dress, take up his pack and let himself quietly out of the chamber. It was barely midnight, he guessed, but he'd left payment for two nights on the bed. In the deserted downstairs room he waited in hat and cloak, his ear to the door, until he heard the creak of wheels. Then he was out in the sharp night air, moving silent and unseen towards the stables.

Now a long, cold ride loomed ahead: twenty tedious miles through Surrey, seven hours or more at oxen pace. It would be morning by the time they reached London, assuming that was the cart's destination. For some reason, Marbeck believed, Richard Evelyn chose to send consignments of gunpowder out under cover of darkness; he was certain now that Cutler had been mistaken about the carts' contents. And whatever lay behind it, he was very curious to know.

In the end, however, the journey took a little over six hours, and dawn was just breaking by the time the cart lumbered off the highway. The reason for it took Marbeck by surprise: the goods were not going to London. Instead, having passed through Croydon and Streatham, stopping only to water their animals, the teamsters left the highway at Newington and turned west, Marbeck trailing some distance behind. After moving along the Lambeth Road, with the lights of Lambeth Palace in view, they then turned south along the Thames Bank and drove another two hundred yards, before drawing to a halt.

Reining in, Marbeck dismounted and tethered Cobb to a sapling. On foot he moved forward, peering into the gloom. Now there were lights; the bulk of a large house loomed against the sky, and soon he realized where he was: the old Vaux Manor. He saw the carters dismount from their bench, rubbing their stiff limbs, their breath and that of the tired oxen steaming in the light of a lantern. And there were others now . . . two or three figures gathering about the cart; there was urgency in their movements.

His pulse quickening despite his own weariness, Marbeck crept closer. Finally, a dozen paces from the cart, he stopped and crouched beside the track. The men were talking softly, and it was impossible to hear what was said. But what he saw next was enough: a rain-sheet being untied and pulled off the cart, and one man clambering up. In the uneven light he saw what he assumed were the hides Cutler had spoken of, being thrown down. Then followed the real unloading: barrels – surprisingly large, needing three men to manoeuvre each one. Carefully, they were lifted down and set on the ground, perhaps half a dozen of them, until the cart was empty. Swiftly, they were taken away into the house, whereupon the lanterns disappeared and only one man remained. This one climbed back on the cart, and without any attempt at concealment cracked his whip, forcing his unwilling oxen to lumber into movement once again. Soon he had turned around a high wall and was lost to sight, prompting Marbeck to curse under his breath.

He had to know what was in the barrels: supposition and guesswork would be of no use to Levinus Monk. The manor was walled and gated, owned by the wealthy Vaux family . . . who, as it happened, were well-known Papists. And another memory sprang up: he recalled that the place wasn't used by them nowadays, but rented out, to persons unknown to him.

By the waterside, stiff, cold and dog-tired, he forced himself to decide. Trying to break in was out of the question: he had neither the means nor the energy, and there were people within. Only one solution came to mind: catch the teamster and force him to speak.

He stood up and began walking briskly. Reaching the wall where the cart had disappeared, he rounded it and stopped: there it was, at a standstill, but there was no sign of its driver. Then he heard the squeal of hinges as a gate swung open. A shadow appeared, moving heavily . . . and in seconds Marbeck had darted forward and seized him. The man yelped in fright as the ice-cold steel of a blade was pressed to his neck.

'Call out, and your blood will wet the ground,' Marbeck snapped.

His victim went rigid, but uttered only a whimper.

'This way.' Marbeck shoved him roughly, back around the wall to the riverside and out of sight of the house. Then, keeping his poniard tight to the man's skin, he kicked the back of his leg and forced him to his knees.

'That's better . . .' Catching his breath, he bent low and spoke into the terrified fellow's ear. 'You'll come to no harm, my friend – provided you feed me information. I know where you've come from, and I've an idea what's in those kegs you delivered . . . The question is, who are they for, and why all the secrecy? So, are you willing to spill your tale, or must I persuade you?'

FIVE

In the afternoon, having snatched a few hours' sleep, Marbeck took a boat from Blackfriars to the Parliament Stairs and went straight to the private room by the Jewel Tower. When he entered, however, it was not Levinus Monk who rose from the cluttered table, but another man: one whose presence made him tense at once. He took a moment to close the door, before turning round and meeting his eye. 'Deverell.'

The other barely nodded, not troubling to hide his own displeasure. The two of them rarely encountered one another, but when they did the feeling was mutual: a long-standing dislike.

'Well now . . .' William Deverell looked Marbeck up and down, his frog-mouth forming a fleshy smile. 'I was told you were likely to appear sooner or later, as a bad penny will.'

'Where's Monk?' Marbeck asked, looking round pointedly.

'He attends My Lord Secretary. I act in his place for the present . . . Did you wish to make a report?'

He took his time answering. The man before him was an experienced intelligencer, but better known as a zealous priest-hunter, a veteran of many recent searches. His harshness towards prisoners was notorious; something Marbeck had seldom been able to stomach. But then, perhaps this man's presence reflected the general mood just now . . .

'How much do you know about Robert Catesby?' he asked.

At once, Deverell gave a snort. 'A Papist, and a hothead. He spent time in prison for his part in the Essex rising, paid an enormous fine – do you mean to tell me you've forgotten?'

'He rents the Vaux Manor at Lambeth, does he not?'

'It's possible, I suppose . . . He's tight with the Vaux family.'

'Has anyone marked what he's been doing of late?'

The spymaster's deputy – since such appeared to be his role – allowed a look of pained amusement to spread over his

features. 'I hate to disappoint you, Marbeck, but you're somewhat tardy with your news. If you mean to tell me of the
horses Catesby has gathered at his manor in Northamptonshire,
or his store of powder and firearms at various places, I'm well
aware of them. The fellow's raising a regiment to fight in
Flanders. One of the Percy family is its colonel . . . Catesby
is to be lieutenant-colonel, I heard. He's recruiting other young
firebrands of his persuasion.' He gave a shrug. 'It's no longer
illegal, now we're at peace with Spain. Let them all perish in
the Catholic cause, I say – and rot where they lie.'

'Very well, but I followed a cartload of gunpowder,' Marbeck
said tartly, 'all the way from Godstone in Surrey to the Vaux
house. It seems it's one of several consignments that have
been taken there – by night, the kegs concealed under hides.
Does that not arouse your suspicion?'

'In view of what I've just told you, why should it?' came
the reply. 'It's natural that Catesby and his friends don't want
to draw attention to themselves. They hate the Crown . . . He
probably thinks we'll confiscate his powder.'

'Wouldn't that be best, in any case?'

'Should it prove necessary, it'll be done,' Deverell replied
brusquely. 'I must say, you've taken a deal of trouble to find
out something we already knew. As I understood it, you were
ordered to keep surveillance on another of the Percy flock –
Thomas, the Papist convert. I assumed it was he you wished
to speak of.'

Marbeck eyed him grimly. Not only did his efforts in Surrey
now appear to have been a waste of time, he found himself
being berated for neglecting his duties. Still weary from his
sojourn, he drew a breath and said: 'I'll watch Percy, have
no fears about that. But I'd prefer to report to Monk next
time.'

'Of course you would,' the other retorted. 'I hear you and
he enjoy the theatre together, at times. You should have a care:
two unmarried men, no longer young . . . People gossip, you
know.'

But to Deverell's obvious disappointment, Marbeck relaxed;
this was the man he remembered of old and could manage.

'They do,' he agreed. 'As they do about you and your wife.

I'm surprised you're here, given the tight rein she keeps you on. What did you have to do, to win her consent?'

Bristling, Deverell searched for a riposte, but Marbeck was already tired of the bout and turned to go out.

The spymaster said loudly: 'I'll speak to Monk – doubtless he'll be interested to hear about your holiday.' But as his fellow intelligencer was through the door, the last words were wasted.

Once outside, Marbeck walked past Westminster Hall, barely noticing the comings and goings of lawyers and courtiers. Standing in New Palace Yard beside the old fountain, he looked out across the river. On the other side of the Thames, the dull red towers of Lambeth Palace could clearly be seen. He thought of his long ride from Godstone, and the testimony he had forced out of the frightened carter early that morning: how Robert Catesby, and another man named Rookwood, were buying gunpowder and storing it in the cellars of the Vaux house under lock and key. What happened to it after that, the carter didn't know; he had sworn, and Marbeck believed him. His last act had been to order the man not to speak of his interrogation, though it was likely he would have blabbed the moment he was set free.

'By the heavens . . . Marbeck?'

Startled, he swung round to find himself facing a handsome man of about his own age, bejewelled and dressed in a slashed doublet with great padded shoulders, a cloak pinned to one of them. With the scent of musk perfume in his nostrils, Marbeck stared. 'Matthew Curzon . . .?'

'It's *Sir* Matthew now.' The other smiled and took his hand warmly. 'I thought I'd seen a phantom . . . Where have you hidden yourself all these years?'

For a moment Marbeck made no reply. As a rule he took pains to avoid his old university friends; it was impossible to speak of what he'd done since his time at Cambridge. Gifford knew, of course; but Gifford was an agent of the Crown too, unlike the man who stood here, his fine, silk-lined cloak lifting in the breeze. Curzon had been a dandy ever since he could walk, it was said. A delicate wit, who wrote poetry and spent lavishly on clothes, wine and entertainment, he'd been in debt from his first term . . .

'So, what do you here, Sir Matthew?' Marbeck asked with a smile. 'Palace business, or . . .?'

'Well, indeed, in a way.'

The man looked sheepish, he thought – and a suspicion formed. 'By the Christ, you're not going to ask me for a loan?'

'Why, shame upon you, sirrah!' Curzon assumed a hurt expression. 'How can you think it, after all this time? I was going to invite you indoors for sweetmeats and a cup of Alicante. I have use of a small chamber when the, er . . .'

'When the owner's away?' Marbeck ventured, though he was amused; he'd always liked Curzon. 'I'm pleased to accept your invitation. But tell me, when did you acquire your knighthood? Not purchased, I hope—' He broke off, for it was suddenly obvious: how else would a man like this have risen in rank?

'You mock me, Marbeck,' the gallant said ruefully. 'Then, you often did, back at St John's. In truth, I thought a title would be a useful investment . . . I had a sum from my father that was lying idle. In fact, it turned out to be the last sum he gave me . . . Ran out of patience, I suppose. I was knighted by His Majesty, for services to a boarhound. It gains me access to places, to certain circles . . . though when it comes to my debts, I find it's quite a different matter.'

His gaze dropped, but by now his position was becoming clear to Marbeck. Curzon was not alone in being a virtual prisoner inside the vast warren that was Whitehall Palace. While he was within its confines he was safe; the moment he stepped outside, he was liable to be arrested for debt. With a wry look, Marbeck placed a hand on his shoulder. 'Let me taste your Alicante, and you can tell me more.'

A short while later, having passed through various doors and corridors, they were in a small but elegant ground-floor chamber hung with tapestries. Seated at a table spread with a garish Turkey carpet, Marbeck sampled the good Alicante wine, knowing it wasn't Curzon's at all, but belonged to the usual occupant of the room.

Helping himself from a platter piled with sweetmeats, his old student friend relaxed and began to hold forth. 'It's a precarious life here, Marbeck. There are a few of us hanging about the place, risking a peep out of the gates now and then to see if bailiffs are lurking. The varlets even watch the river, so I can't escape by boat. They've been set on me by my jeweller in Goldsmith's Row – such a greedy man. I've written to him offering to return several rings, but it wasn't enough. For the past fortnight I've lived in fear of the sergeant-at-mace and his tipstaffs, prowling without the Court Gate. While here I'm at the mercy of others' generosity – and that of the Knight-Marshall. Should he decide to eject me, I could find myself seized and clapped in the Counter! Can you imagine such horror?'

Marbeck gave a sympathetic shrug. 'How much do you owe, in total?'

The other sighed. 'Close on two hundred pounds, I suppose.'

'What, to one creditor?' Marbeck exclaimed.

'Not exactly . . .' Curzon heaved another sigh. 'There's my tailor too, and a bootmaker in Holborn, and a hatter . . .' Seeing Marbeck's expression, he looked indignant. 'A man must own a decent hat in this climate! Would you see me freeze to death?'

'Have you thought of disguise?' Marbeck enquired. 'Borrow a servant's garb and follow some lord out of the gates?'

'Dress as a lackey?' The knight looked appalled. 'You truly think someone like myself could carry that off? Nor can I swim,' he added, 'if that's how your mind moves. I've contemplated trying to make a run for it, but I was never the athletic sort.'

'Well then, we must think of another ruse,' Marbeck said, suppressing a smile. He took a drink and thought for a moment. 'These places to which your new status has given you access – might Essex House be one of them?'

'But of course,' Curzon replied airily. 'I'm acquainted with the Earl of Northumberland . . . A true nobleman, if deaf as a post.'

'And his cousin, Thomas Percy?' Marbeck enquired casually. 'I hear he's in and out of there, too.'

At that, the other's face clouded. 'I rarely see him . . . He's away in the North a good deal. Moves in circles I don't care to know about.'

'Papists, you mean?'

'I assume so.' Curzon looked uncomfortable. 'Of course, anyone will tell you the earl's of the Roman persuasion too – it's an open secret. But he keeps to himself, pottering about with his scientific experiments at Syon House . . . There's no harm in the man, to my mind. The cousin is of a different stamp – not one I'd play at cards with.'

'And yet, I believe I've a notion to do just that,' Marbeck said, on sudden impulse.

Curzon eyed him. 'You're still a gambler, then? It's reassuring to find that hasn't changed. I confess I was taken aback when I first saw you. You look as if these past years have used you badly.'

'Too long a story,' Marbeck replied. 'Just now, I'm doing my best to devise a means of getting you out of here and evading the sergeant-at-mace. If I can do it, have we a bargain?'

The other blinked, whereupon Marbeck explained. 'I speak of a simple exchange of favours. I'll spring you from Whitehall and take you somewhere your creditors won't find you. In return, you take me to Essex House this evening – no arresting party would expect to see you there – and introduce me to anyone I ask you to.' He paused. 'And by the way, for reasons I don't care to discuss just now, I'm Lawrence Tucker, a landed gentleman from Hampshire. Are we agreed?'

So it was done, and for Marbeck it was easy enough. In the dozen or more years since he'd last seen Matthew Curzon he had become a master of deception, he thought fleetingly, while his friend was unchanged: a foppish fellow, but remarkably devoid of guile. Curzon was astonished at the ease with which Marbeck transformed him from a well-dressed nobleman into a prisoner in shirtsleeves, hands bound behind his back. His sword, it transpired, had already been pawned, but his poniard was taken from him. Leaving his fine clothes in a closet to be collected at some later date, he was obliged to step outside the Court Gate into the cold, head bowed in submission. But the most dramatic part of it was the performance Marbeck put on for the arresting party – a sergeant and several watchmen – who accosted them the moment they emerged into the thoroughfare by Scotland Yard.

Belligerently, hand on sword, Marbeck informed them that this man was in his charge, under arrest by order of the Privy Council. The Knight-Marshall would verify it, if they cared to enquire. It was a serious matter – and when he mentioned Star Chamber, even the suspicious sergeant-at-mace fell silent. The word *treason* wasn't mentioned, but the implications were clear. Whereupon, watched by the disappointed group, Curzon was marched away via Charing Cross to the Strand. There, having looked back to see they weren't followed, Marbeck steered him into a cut-through by Covent Garden, where he untied his hands before taking him to St Martin's Lane. Minutes later they entered Skinner's bowling-house where, with immense relief, Curzon sank down on a stool and gazed at his rescuer.

'Great God, Mar—' he began, then caught his breath. 'I mean . . . I thank you most heartily, Master Tucker.'

He was just in time: Skinner had appeared from somewhere in a rumpled shirt and was looking askance at them both. At once, Marbeck addressed him. 'Here's my friend . . . Knight,' he said briskly. 'He'll be sharing my chamber for a while, if you've no objection.'

'Objection?' Skinner's brow furrowed. 'Well, I might have—'

'We'll adjust the reckoning,' Marbeck broke in. 'He's very quiet and sober, is Master Knight . . . The perfect tenant. And you're not exactly overwhelmed by applicants, are you? I wonder if word's got round about the state of the timbers.'

His landlord scowled. 'That's slander, that is – and how do you know I haven't got other applicants? Many would be glad of a big, fine room like that!' His frown deepened. 'And now I think on it, there was half a pint of muscadine on the table the other night that had disappeared come morning . . .' But he stopped, seeing Marbeck reach for his purse.

'Will a half angel cover it?' he asked. 'That, and the rent?'

Skinner put on a glassy smile.

Essex House fronted the Thames by the Middle Temple: a rambling mansion where the late earl of that name had once plotted against Queen Elizabeth, before his folly led to his own downfall. Various people lodged here, or came and went as they pleased; the Earl of Northumberland, into whose hands it had fallen, was immensely rich and a generous host. Though he was often at his country seat at Syon House, people mingled, dined and entertained in his absence. Here, after night had fallen, Marbeck arrived with Matthew Curzon and was admitted without difficulty.

The clothes helped, of course; he wore his best doublet and cloak, and had borrowed some of Curzon's jewels: his friend had been adamant about not leaving those behind and had made his escape with them rolled in a cloth inside his breeches. Curzon himself was decked in clothing Marbeck had picked up from a fripperer's stall that afternoon, and though they were inferior to his own, they would serve.

Adopting the swagger that came naturally to him, the newly-dubbed knight threw his gloves to a footman and strolled across the hallway. Marbeck hung back, taking stock of the place. Music came from nearby, a small consort playing, while laughter and voices drifted from other rooms. Finally, he made his way into a great chamber overlooking the river, where well-dressed men and women were stood or seated in conversation while attentive servants moved about. A curly-haired gallant posed by the doorway, hand on hip to display his gold-embroidered suit: he would do.

'Is there a primero game afoot anywhere, sir?' Marbeck enquired with a sniff.

The man turned and took stock of him, taking his time answering. 'I expect there is, sir . . . Are you of a mind to play?'

'Perhaps. Would you care to direct me?'

'Up the stairs,' came the reply. 'The blue chamber . . . You'll find Heywood, among others.'

'I thank you . . .' Marbeck made as if to move off. 'Is there anyone else there I might know?'

The gallant raised an eyebrow. 'Since I ken you not, sir, how might I answer that?' he demanded. 'But if you're acquainted with the earl's rent-collector, will he serve?'

Marbeck kept his face blank. 'Do you mean Thomas Percy?'

The other flicked a mote of dust from his sleeve. With a

thinly-disguised sneer, he said: 'As far as I'm aware, His Lordship has only one rent-collector in his family, sir . . . What did you say your name was?'

But Marbeck was already out in the hallway, his pulse quickening. The opportunity was too good to miss.

SIX

Wearing his most impassive face, Marbeck stared at his cards, holding them in a firm grip.

He held a *fluxus*: a deuce, a four, a seven and a knave, all of the same suit. It was worth a bluff, even if he were down to his last few pounds. Most of his money was in the middle of the table, along with that wagered by the other three players. But they were wealthy men who could afford to lose; Marbeck could not. The situation demanded nerve and his blandest expression.

'Well, sirs, will you vie?'

The speaker was the host of the primero game, a bluff, white-haired man named Heywood. Seated opposite him was a young gentleman who, Marbeck guessed, suspected he was out of luck and would soon withdraw. But it was the fourth man he was interested in, which was why he took care to pay him least attention. For as fate would have it, he found himself facing none other than his new quarry, Thomas Percy.

Florid and powerfully-built, with a broad beard, Percy was taller than Marbeck expected. After throwing a glance at Heywood, he spoke up. 'I will vie, if our new friend Master Tucker will dare to lead?' He looked coldly at Marbeck.

'As you wish, sir,' Marbeck answered amiably. 'I hold a *supremus*: a high three-flush, and an ace from outside. What say you?'

The other players maintained their impassive looks. A *supremus*, worth fifty-five points, was the highest hand possible next to *primero*. If this were a bluff, it would be a bold one. The young gallant on Marbeck's right blinked.

'A *supremus*, eh?' Heywood echoed. 'Does fortune smile on this man?' Keeping his own cards low, he looked to the stack of coins by his elbow, took two and placed them on the pile. 'I'll add a trifle, just to sweeten the pot,' he said. 'Percy?'

Percy was frowning, and Marbeck sensed his aggression.

Not only was this a man who must win at all costs, he decided, he was one of those who liked to grind his opponents down. His eye on Marbeck, he said: 'Well now, I've a mind to test Tucker's nerve.' He fingered a small column of gold coins, then pushed it forward. 'There's ten pounds . . . More than I pay my gardeners in a year. Who'll match it?'

There was silence as the tension rose. Several other people who had been standing about the blue-painted chamber were moving round to observe the game. Out of the corner of his eye Marbeck saw a woman enter the room, splendidly attired in red and silver, her hair elaborately dressed. Lowering his eyes, he focused on the table and was not surprised when the young man on his right let out a heavy sigh, leaned back and showed his cards. It was a poor hand: three and six of clubs, plus an unrelated four and a queen. Accepting defeat with a wry look, he threw them down.

'Not worth a straw,' he murmured. 'I must withdraw from the game.'

Now three card-players remained. Heywood was concentrating, head down, but Percy fixed Marbeck with another stare, daring him to act. Whereupon Marbeck moved the last of his coins to the stake and said: 'I can't meet your ten pounds, sir. Here's all of my purse . . . Will you take my bond for the rest?'

'What . . . do you mean to match me, or outbid me?' Percy snapped. There was colour in his cheeks, or that part visible above the thick beard. Like the others he had partaken freely of the host's wine, but it had little to do with his manner. He was kinsman to the earl, whose house this was, and would brook no defeat. And yet, along with hostility, there was a hint of uncertainty in his eyes; Marbeck saw it, if the others did not.

'To outbid you, of course,' he answered. To Heywood he said: 'I believe fortune indeed smiles on me, sir. I felt it as soon as I awoke today . . . I'm a man who trusts his instincts.'

Heywood grunted; he was looking less then pleased. Finally, aware of the antagonism brewing between Marbeck and Percy, he gave a sigh and turned his own cards about. Marbeck hid his relief, for the man held three hearts including a knave: a *numerus*, which would have beaten his own hand. Thus far, his bluff held.

'You yield too easily, Richard,' Heywood said to the young man opposite him. 'And yet I find myself following suit . . . Perhaps I grow cautious in my latter years. But I dislike the way this game moves.' He looked deliberately at Percy, then at Marbeck. 'I also dislike it when a man claims his purse is empty and speaks of bonds or promissory notes. You're unknown to me, Master Tucker . . . hence, what security can you offer, to match Percy's bid?'

All eyes were on Marbeck now. Yet, try as he might, he could not fail to be distracted by the woman, who was now moving to stand behind him. Keeping a level tone, he turned slightly to reveal his basket-hilt rapier in its scabbard.

'This is a good sword,' he said. 'Well-tempered steel, with a chased silver pommel. I forget what it cost me, but—'

'It'll serve.' Percy's voice was sharp. In a disdainful tone, he added: 'I'd thought of ordering a new blade myself soon – this will save me the trouble. And I don't fear your *supremus*, Tucker, for I hold one of my own. The question now is, whose cards are the higher? Or perhaps I should say, whose nerve is the stronger?'

They eyed each other, and now the silence was such that music and laughter could be heard from downstairs. Here in the blue chamber, two or three men had moved behind Percy: Marbeck caught their expressions and felt his left hand stray towards his dagger-hilt. He had a fleeting notion, should he win the game, of finding himself followed out into the street . . . though at least, he thought, he would still have his sword. As for whoever now stood behind him: he heard the faint rustle of silk and caught a whiff of civet perfume.

Placing his free hand on the table, he said: 'That is indeed the nub of it, Master Percy. We've seen a knave and a queen thus far – where do the other court cards lie, I wonder?'

They locked eyes; but while Percy was controlling his hostility with an effort, Marbeck felt elation. This stage in a game always excited him: the moment it narrowed to a duel, when nerve and the ability to bluff were the best weapons a man had at his disposal. He bided his time, his gaze flickering to his cards and back. Percy bided his, too . . . until, at last, a shade of doubt showed. It was gone in a second, but Marbeck saw it and breathed in silent relief; perhaps the man was a blusterer, after all.

'Do you own a good horse, sir?' Percy demanded suddenly.

In some surprise, Marbeck confirmed that he did, then added: 'Yet he's precious to me and not part of my wager. I'd rather lose my clothes and step into the night barefoot than lose him.'

'What a pity,' Percy replied with sarcasm. 'I merely wished to raise the stakes . . . In fact, I'll do so anyway.' Whereupon he took another column of coins and pushed it to the centre of the table. There was a stir from the watchers.

'Well, what will you do?' Percy wore another look of disdain. 'You won't wager your horse, and we can't have you go home naked. Why, your extreme parts might shrivel to nothing.'

There were smiles from his friends, and suppressed laughter from some of the onlookers – but what happened next caught Marbeck unaware. He gave a start as a hand was placed lightly on his shoulder. Whereupon a low female voice, with a heavy accent, spoke above his head.

'I will partner the gentleman. He's a man of worth, I believe. We match your sovereigns, Master Percy . . . and bet a further twenty.'

A murmur of surprise followed. Percy looked up sharply, while Marbeck turned in his chair to see who had spoken and found himself looking into a pair of dark eyes that carried a meaning no man could mistake. Getting up to make his bow, he smiled and said: 'Lawrence Tucker, madam . . . who, I confess, is both at your service and at a loss.'

The lady inclined her head. 'I am Charlotte de Baume. Pray continue your game . . . Whatever the outcome, we may speak of it later.' Shifting her gaze to Percy, she added: 'Are you content, sir? Or did you wish to raise the stakes even higher? And before you ask . . .' She arched her brows. 'I have not looked at your opponent's cards. I know you and I have had only short acquaintance, yet surely you will not doubt my word?'

It was a challenge, but one to which Thomas Percy would

not rise. He swallowed and said thickly: 'Of course not, madam. I accept your bet.' He faced Marbeck, who had resumed his seat, and pushed the last of his stake across the table. There was a tense moment, but Marbeck held the man's gaze and allowed a faint look of triumph to appear before quickly suppressing it. It was his final bluff, but it worked.

Stifling an oath, Percy looked at the substantial sum of money that now lay on the table. For a moment he wavered, then with a gesture of irritation threw down his cards. People craned their necks, and a few whispers followed. But Marbeck kept his own cards close; and this time, it cost him considerable effort to conceal his relief.

Percy had not bluffed at all, but had truly held a *supremus* – one that would have beaten even Heywood's hand. The host, surprised at the turn of events, peered along with everyone else at the three matching cards – an ace, six and seven – and the king of spades. Had the game continued Percy could have swept the table, and Marbeck would have lost everything. Feeling eyes upon him, he waited until his opponent looked up, before finally laying his own hand out.

A collective gasp followed. The other players – or rather, Heywood and the younger gentleman – stared in disbelief, while from the onlookers came spontaneous applause. With a mere *fluxus* – almost the poorest hand he could have held – this stranger had outfaced them all. Such a bluff took courage, someone murmured. Someone else dared to make a jibe at Percy, but when the man's friends looked angrily at him, he dropped his gaze. Marbeck, meanwhile, remained calm and reached out to take his winnings. But glancing up, he stiffened: Thomas Percy's expression would have quelled most men. His face twitched, and his fingers worked as if he were itching to draw sword. But it was impossible, of course; a gentleman accepted defeat with grace, as he would greet victory with humility.

'I thank you for your forbearance, sir,' Marbeck said. 'And your kindness, in accepting my sword as potential payment. Now I'll feel safer as I journey homewards.' Deliberately, he turned to face his rescuer, who had pledged twenty pounds so readily. He'd assumed she was still behind him, but she wasn't.

'Madame de Baume . . .?' he began, whereupon a bystander touched his sleeve and pointed. Swinging round, Marbeck saw only the lady's back, and her elaborately styled head of hair, as she swept out of the room.

'So, Master Tucker: you appear to have won the day . . . and by sheer guile, at that.'

Unhurriedly, Marbeck faced Percy again. The man was sitting back, regarding him coolly. Someone had placed a goblet in his hand, from which he took a sip. 'It's odd we haven't met before,' he went on. 'Where is it you hail from?'

'Hampshire . . . near Fareham,' Marbeck told him. There was a pause while he took up his winnings. Heywood and the young player had risen without further word and moved off, nursing their defeat. Others drifted away, leaving the two men alone.

Percy watched Marbeck fill his purse until it bulged, then said: 'In that case you'll know Lord Pavey . . . a good friend of mine.'

'I've heard the name,' Marbeck said. He threw a glance at the other's followers and saw they were still close. As he rose, he gave a polite nod. 'Now, with regret, I must take my leave. My compliments to you for your indulgence . . . We must play again.'

'Indeed we must,' Percy said, his voice low. The warning in his eyes was stark, but Marbeck ignored it. He turned from the table to walk out, whereupon one of Percy's friends stepped towards him and took his sleeve.

'My master's a generous man,' he said gently. 'Yet if you care to take my advice, sir, you'll not set foot here again.'

But Marbeck merely looked down at his sleeve until the fellow let go and drew back; something told him this man would be more than his match.

Once downstairs he looked for Curzon and found him in the room where the consort played, in conversation with another dandyish figure. As Marbeck came up, his friend beamed at him.

'My dear fellow!' He raised a silver cup and took a slurp. 'See, I've run into an old acquaintance – a poet, like myself. We've much to speak of. Were you in haste to go, or . . .?'

'Lawrence Tucker,' Marbeck said emphatically, with a brief bow to the other man. While with his eyes he reminded Curzon not only of the name he was using, but of the circumstances in which they had met that day.

Taking the hint, his friend gulped. 'I'll not be returning to . . . to my lodging this night,' he said hastily. 'This gentleman has invited me to stay with him and read his new work . . . Mayhap we'll meet again tomorrow?'

Marbeck shrugged, remembering that in any case the city gates would now be shut. He was about to take his leave, then paused. 'Do you happen to know a Frenchwoman, by the name of Madame de Baume?' he asked casually.

But both men looked blank, and Curzon shook his head. So, with a nod to the poet, who was looking somewhat the worse for drink, he went out. As he moved into the hallway, he wondered how much the hapless fellow would have loaned Sir Matthew Curzon before the night was over.

In the wide entrance hall, he paused to collect himself. His task was to watch Percy from now on, while somehow keeping out of the man's sight, which wouldn't be easy. It had been rash of Marbeck, of course, to meet him face to face, let alone beat him at cards. And yet he couldn't help feeling pleased; it had been an exhilarating experience. Suppressing a grin, he passed a group of chattering gallants and walked towards the doors . . . only to stop in his tracks.

By the doorway stood Charlotte de Baume, looking directly at him. A servant fussed about, arranging her outdoor cloak, but she ignored him. With a polite smile, Marbeck walked forward and made his bow for the second time.

'I've not had the chance to thank you, madam,' he said. 'For your timely generosity, as well as your courage . . .' He raised his eyebrows. 'Assuming, that is, that you hadn't had sight of my cards, as you told my opponent?'

The lady smiled slightly. 'So . . . unlike Master Percy, sir, you would doubt my word?'

'Heaven forbid,' Marbeck answered. 'Or the weight of my winnings would prick my conscience.' He touched his purse briefly. 'As it is I leave here a contented man, thanks to you.'

A moment passed. The servant, a swarthy-looking man,

finished his task and stood back respectfully, whereupon Charlotte de Baume waved him away. Then, catching Marbeck unaware, she moved so close to him that they were almost touching and lowered her voice.

'My coach is outside. I'm staying at a house in Hampstead village – will you accompany me? I have a fear of highwaymen on the heath . . . and my servant is such a milksop.'

He met her gaze – and at once, a warmth swept over him. It began in his loins and spread through his entire body, while in the same moment his mind was filled with relief. Opportunity was not done with him yet: here was an invitation to forget all else, for one night at least, and be nothing more nor less than a man: a man with appetites that were no different from any other's.

'It would be an honour and a pleasure,' he replied.

Whereupon, as if any shred of doubt remained, Madame de Baume ran a hand quickly down his thigh before turning to the doors. Her servant at once leaped forward to fling them open.

And as he passed outside, Marbeck could not fail to catch the man's expression: one of contempt, compounded with what looked like sheer envy. This was no milksop, he reflected; but then, as excuses went for wanting his company, he'd heard worse.

SEVEN

She was from Paris: a widow, she said, related to the wife of the French ambassador, Monsieur de Harlay. The ambassador was leaving London soon, yet Charlotte had decided to stay for a while. The Paris court was so tiresome, she maintained: a hive of intrigue and base treachery, where men and women alike preened and jostled for power or preferment at any cost. She told Marbeck this in the morning, as they lay between silken sheets in her ornate bed with its tasselled canopy. But if Marbeck appeared to listen attentively, his mind was elsewhere: on Meriel, whose body he had pictured at times throughout the night, while he and this voluptuous woman had coupled like satyr and nymph.

'Whereas England . . . England, *c'est charmante*,' Charlotte said. 'I even like the rain . . . and here on the hill the air is fresh. One may live freely – as I perceive you do. Or am I wrong in that?'

She had rolled on to her side to look at him. With an effort, Marbeck pushed his thoughts away and faced her.

'Wrong . . . in what sense?'

'In assuming you are a free man. Or, have you dependants? Wife, children—'

'No.' He gave a quick shake of his head. And though his heart sank, he forced a smile. 'I'm a restless fellow, who travels a good deal. When in London, I like to gamble.'

'That much I know,' she replied. 'As I know you have a taste for danger . . . or you would not have dared to wager all your money on such a weak set of cards.'

His smile faded. 'So you saw my hand, after all . . . and hence, you knew my strategy. Were you so eager to see me beat Percy that you would not only risk your money, but also tell an untruth?'

'An untruth!' She laughed, more harshly than he expected. 'If you mean *un mensonge*, why not say it? I was eager, perhaps, but merely to see the game finish. I was tired of the company in that house, and by then I had made my plans.'

'You mean, plans to spend the night with me?'

'You, or another,' she teased. 'In France, widows like me are less constrained in satisfying their needs . . . as by now you have learned. As I have learned things about you.'

'What might those be, madam?' Marbeck enquired. Outwardly, he appeared playful, but in his mind a faint warning sounded. Reaching for her hand, he drew it from beneath the covers.

'*Des choses grandes et petites*,' she murmured, squeezing his hand; she'd learned that he understood French. 'One is that you have a paramour somewhere.' And though he tried not to react, she put on a knowing smile. '*Voilà* . . . I knew it.'

'If I did, would it matter?' he enquired.

'Of course!' She retained her smile, but he believed he saw through it. There was a possessiveness about her, he suspected; likely, this woman was a jealous lover.

'I regret I must leave you soon,' he said, after a moment.

'Indeed? And where must you go?'

'Business, in the city . . . A dull matter.' He leaned forward and kissed her, but was unprepared for the reaction. With a rapid movement she threw the sheet aside and raised herself, her loose breasts brushing his chest.

'And it cannot wait – not even for another hour?' she cried.

He blinked. 'Well, perhaps . . .'

'*Donc, coîtes-moi! Sinon, allez!*'

Shocked by her vehemence, he was silent. Her anger had burst forth in a moment . . . but almost as quickly, she turned it into pouting indignation. Reaching down, she tugged his beard, hard enough to make him wince.

'Perhaps I have misjudged,' she said. 'I thought we would make sport once more, then dine together. I have a splendid cook . . . He would delight to make you breakfast, no matter what the hour.'

'It's most tempting,' Marbeck said. But a wariness had come over him, more intense than before. In any case, he had things to do, following Thomas Percy being the chief one. Monk would expect results – and Deverell, he knew, would not be slow to report any slackness on Marbeck's part. Sitting up, he took Charlotte's face in his hands.

'I promise we will dine together, as soon as I can arrange it. But there are matters I must attend to. Can you not forgive me?'

A moment passed, in which he sensed the effort she was making; clearly, she was a woman used to getting her way. But finally she let out a breath, took his hands away and placed a hard kiss on his lips.

'*Alors . . . tu m'a apaisé*, Lawrence – for this once.' She lay back with a deep sigh and deliberately covered herself. 'Be sure to visit me soon . . . or you may find I have changed my mind and followed *Monsieur l'Ambassadeur* back to Paris.'

In some relief, Marbeck promised. Whereupon, taking care not to show undue haste, he arose and dressed, and soon left the house of Charlotte de Baume.

It was a five-mile walk from Hampstead back to London. Hungry and footsore, he entered the city by Aldersgate, mingling with the throng. He made his way to Skinner's where he found the man at his table, talking business with a fellow as unsavoury-looking as himself. But as Marbeck made for the stairs, his landlord stayed him.

'There's one above, waiting for you. He's been here for an hour and wouldn't say what it was about. The cove's as close-mouthed as you are.' Seeing Marbeck's questioning look, he added: 'It's not your friend Knight. Seems to me you're using this place like Paul's Walk – if you're expecting any more visitors, I think I ought to hear about it.'

'I'm not,' Marbeck said. But as he made his way up the creaking stairs, his resolve grew firm: the dwelling was no longer safe, and he would quit it soon. Outside the upstairs chamber he listened, loosening his sword in its scabbard. But the moment he placed his hand on the latch the door was opened abruptly. There stood William Deverell with a frown on his face.

'At last . . . I was about to give up. This is the foulest lodging I've ever had the misfortune to be in. I should have sent word and ordered you to Whitehall – but the task won't wait.' He stood back to allow Marbeck to enter.

'What task is that?' Marbeck enquired. He would have mentioned Percy, assuring Deverell he had him under surveillance, but observing his manner he hesitated. Was it agitation, or mere impatience that gripped the man? Then he caught the fierce light in his eye, and a suspicion formed.

'I'm about to make a search,' Deverell said. 'In Essex, on good intelligence. I've gathered a company of men together at short notice, and I need you too. Believe me, you're not my first choice, however no one else with your skills is close at hand. Will you get your horse? I want to be on the road before noon.'

'The road to where?' Marbeck asked. A gloom was descending upon him: the last thing he wished for, now or at any other time, was to accompany Deverell on one of his passionate hunts for a priest-in-hiding.

'Great Willoughby, a manor near Romford,' came the reply. 'It's twenty miles, or thereabouts.'

'What of Thomas Percy?' Marbeck began, but the other swept the question aside.

'He'll wait – will you ready yourself?'

The party thundered along the East Road: twenty-five men or more, with Deverell at their head. A Puritan zeal was upon him: an unquenchable desire to root out the people that many considered to be servants of the anti-Christ, who would convert all England to Papistry if they could. Some of his men had tools strapped to their saddles: crowbars and pickaxes with which to tear down partitions, rods to measure the thickness of walls. All were armed, some with pistols and calivers as well as swords. Marbeck, armed as usual with rapier and poniard, had paused only to shed his clothing from the night before and change into plainer garb. He had also taken a moment, while Deverell waited impatiently in the street, to hide his winnings from the primero game.

Having no enthusiasm for the task ahead, he rode near the rear of the party, the breeze whipping through Cobb's mane. There had been a frost in the night, and the fields still glistened.

When they stopped in the early afternoon to eat bare rations and water the horses, he took the opportunity to question the spymaster, only to receive a cool response.

'I sense your unwillingness, Marbeck,' he said. They stood apart from the other men, who were huddled in groups, talking low. 'If I didn't know better, I might think you'd some sympathy for these Catholic devils yourself. Have you forgotten the Smithfield fires and the hundreds who perished under Queen Mary's tyranny?' When Marbeck made no reply, he added: 'One of my uncles was among them . . . a humble rector who did naught but good, yet dared to stand against them in the name of God.'

'Then, is it vengeance that drives you?' Marbeck asked.

'Perhaps it is!' the other threw back. 'I'm no saint, any more than you are – yet I know where my duty lies. I've had reports of Masses being said at Great Willoughby. The place has been searched before, but it was a hurried affair – I intend to remedy that. It appears there was a good deal of toing and froing around the Feast of St Luke – that's the time the Jesuits renew their vows. I'd not be surprised if the house was a meeting place for some of them, before they scattered again to spread their poison elsewhere.'

Marbeck said nothing, and Deverell paused, as if aware how bitter he sounded. 'The Warlake family pretend to be moderates,' he said, in a more even tone. 'The sort who attend church when they must and stay out of trouble. Yet my informant tells of a secret chapel, and of a stranger who's been there for weeks, keeping within the house. The man's a Jesuit, I'd swear to it. And when we get there I will know – I'll smell him.'

He turned away, leaving Marbeck to walk back to Cobb. Soon he was again in the saddle, following the party eastward through the Essex countryside. And less than two hours later, guided by a man who knew the area, they turned from the Romford road into a lane between hedgerows. Here at last Deverell called a halt. Great Willoughby was but a few hundred yards off, he said, surrounded by pasture and woodland. As soon as the house came into view they would divide into two groups and spread out to surround the manor. No one would be permitted to enter, or to leave: not the lowliest servant, and especially no one who claimed to be merely on their way there from somewhere else. Catching Marbeck's eye, he beckoned him forward.

'Stay alongside me. And sharpen up your Latin, will you? I may need a scholar to decipher papers.' And a few minutes later they were riding through a gateway into a wide courtyard, with the manor of Great Willoughby towering over them.

They reined in, conscious of the silence. There was an air of deep tranquillity about the house; smoke rose from chimneys, a solitary horse stood in the paddock, and there were sheep in the fields beyond. But nobody appeared, nor was anyone seen at the windows. After a brief look round, Deverell dismounted and strode towards the imposing entranceway. He tried the doors, rattled them, then turned in triumph.

'They're barred!' he called out. 'It's a delaying tactic, to allow the black-robed devil to hide himself . . . Hurry!'

Two other men had accompanied the spymaster beside Marbeck, the others having dispersed to encircle the manor. Quickly they got down, while Marbeck followed suit, boots crunching on the gravelled forecourt. Deverell was hammering on the doors, which were of oak and very solid indeed. But when the others came up he gestured to them to wait. Stepping back, he raised his head and shouted at the top of his voice.

'Thomas Warlake! I hold a warrant from His Majesty's Privy Council, to search these premises for seditious persons! Open your doors forthwith, or face summary arrest!'

The answer was a resounding silence. Marbeck glanced about, as did the other pursuivants. He thought he could hear noises from within, but they were faint. Despite his dislike for Deverell, however, he knew the man was right. The priest, assuming there was one, was getting himself into a well-prepared hiding-hole, having also concealed his vestments, portable altar and other trappings. Meanwhile, the family and their servants would be scouring the house for any tell-tale sign of their guest's presence . . .

'Break in!'

Deverell's voice cut through his thoughts like a whip-crack. While his men went to unpack their tools, he turned to Marbeck and said: 'I look to you – to those keen eyes of yours that

Monk always crows about – to spot anything amiss. A servant who looks more nervous than he should be, a fire that's been doused in haste, a floorboard that sits oddly – anything at all. We'll search the ground floor first, while others guard doors and windows . . . Do I need to add anything?'

With a shake of his head, Marbeck looked away and focused on the doors. There were marks, he saw, that spoke of a previous attempt to force entry. He was musing on this when there came a sound that made both he and Deverell start: that of a heavy bolt being drawn. The other pursuivants, carrying a crowbar and a sledgehammer, stopped in their tracks. The next moment one door swung inwards to reveal a small woman, middle-aged and soberly dressed, standing on the threshold. Placing her hands demurely before her, she gazed at Deverell with apparent calm.

'You pardon, sir . . . I was upstairs and have only just come into the hall. I walk slowly . . . An old ailment. The servants have orders not to open to strangers without my leave . . .' She looked at the men with the tools and raised her brows. 'By all that's holy: surely you didn't intend to break down my doors—?'

'You're Mildred Warlake?' Deverell broke in. The lady indicated that she was, whereupon, containing his anger, he mounted the lower step. She, however, did not flinch.

'I've no time for tales,' he snapped. 'Where's your husband?'

'Thomas is away,' came the reply. 'He has other estates to manage. If you'd made enquiry in advance, I could have saved you a wasted journey.'

'Oh, believe me, madam, it will not be wasted.' Even on a lower step, Deverell loomed above her. 'I ask you to stand aside and let my men do their work. And in case you didn't hear me earlier: I have a warrant to search the house, for as long as it takes. While we proceed, no one may enter, and none may leave: not you, your family, servants – not even a dog.' With a grim smile, he added: 'Call it a whim, but I've seen hounds used to carry messages. By the way, I hope you are well provisioned: I've known some searches take weeks. Do you have questions?'

But Mildred Warlake made no answer. Impassive and

dignified, she refused to be cowed. And if she were afraid – as well she might be, since the penalty for harbouring a Jesuit was most severe – she gave no sign of it. Instead, she turned round and walked into the house, leaving the door ajar.

As she went she glanced from Deverell to Marbeck, who caught her eye for a second. In that instant he marked her courage, along with a faith that sat deeper than any man could dislodge, and could not help admiring her for it.

But it was of no use. Forcing his feelings aside, he followed Deverell into Great Willoughby, to share in the grim task of tearing the huge house apart from attic to cellar.

EIGHT

The search had lasted for three days, and by the end of the third one, Deverell and his company were still no nearer to finding the mysterious priest.

Patience had worn thin, on both sides. Walls had been broken through, floorboards lifted, closets turned out. Brickwork had been prodded, timbers sounded and masonry dislodged, all to no avail. Even though the tiny, private chapel had long been discovered, and found empty, some of the searchers had begun to wonder whether there had been a priest here at all. Meanwhile, somewhat bizarrely, the business of the household went on around them as if everything was normal. Servants came and went, eyes lowered, while Deverell's men tore away finely-carved panelling, smashed chimney-pieces and regarded everyone with suspicion. Mess and disorder were everywhere, but no one was permitted to clear up. Through it all, Mildred Warlake spent most of the time in her chamber, once it too had been thoroughly searched. The only revelation had come on the second day, when an old hiding-place was discovered behind a false wall in the main downstairs chamber. But the tiny alcove, barely high enough for a man to stand in, contained nothing but a thick layer of dust.

Finally, seething with frustration, Deverell ordered Mistress Warlake to be brought to him in the same room. Outside dusk was falling, and candles had been lit. The lady arrived, accompanied by an elderly woman-in-waiting. They found the master of the search on his feet, pacing restlessly. Men stood about, while others were still at work, knocking and hammering. Marbeck, tired of the whole affair, leaned against a wall and watched as Mildred Warlake entered, composed and silent. When Deverell gestured to a chair, she ignored him.

'There's a simple way for this to end, madam – as you know perfectly well,' he said finally. 'Accept defeat with grace, tell us where the priest is hiding, and I'll speak in mitigation at your husband's trial. Meanwhile, your household may put the manor back in order. Hasn't there been enough disarray?'

The doughty little woman eyed him, with something akin to scorn. 'You dare speak to me of grace, sir?' she replied. 'I need no sermon from a man like you. Do your worst – take a month or more, if you will. We'll celebrate Christmas at Great Willoughby as we always have. I've told you, many times now, that no seditious person is concealed here, yet you choose to disbelieve me. As for my husband, he will return soon, and he'll be most displeased. He's not without influence. You may need to look to your own future—'

'Enough!' His temper frayed, Deverell frowned at her. 'My future's not your concern. You'd best look to your own, once we find the whoreson Jesuit who's hiding somewhere within these walls – for make no mistake, find him we will! In fact, I've barely started – there's still the roof space to open. Let's hope it doesn't rain, shall we?'

The lady of the house, however, kept her composure. The woman-in-waiting, made of weaker stuff, flinched; the search had taken its toll, and she looked close to tears. Marbeck pitied her, as his admiration for her mistress merely grew. If there were some way to bring this sorry business to an end, he heartily wished he could discover it.

There was a crash from the room directly above that made even Mildred Warlake start. Eyes strayed to the ceiling as dust floated gently down. The men listened, but no shout of discovery followed. Soon knocking resumed, while below the tension remained.

'Come . . . this is foolishness!' With an effort, Deverell took a step towards the lady. 'I know without a doubt what your religion is, madam, as does everyone else here. I also know you act out of loyalty to your husband – I might even commend you for it. But you must know there can be only one outcome: sooner or later, the fugitive must emerge. I could leave men here for months, if need be, until the priest is starved out or loses his mind. How long can he thrive, in whatever hole he cowers? If you care not for yourself, then think of him.'

But even this tactic, Marbeck knew, was fruitless. He watched as Mildred Warlake drew herself up and met Deverell's eye. 'Do your worst, sir,' she repeated, 'and may God have mercy on you. Now, if you've no further need of me?' With that she turned and stalked out of the room, her woman-servant following. In the passage outside voices were heard, but quickly stifled.

A silence ensued, until Deverell let fly an oath, span on his heel and walked across the room, to the huge fireplace with its carved pilasters. Without troubling to hide his weariness, he leaned on the stonework and let out a long breath.

'Can't we stop work for today, sir?' One of his pursuivants spoke up. 'The men are all spent. Yet supper and a mug of beer, followed by a night's rest, may do wonders . . . What say you?'

'Yes . . . yes, very well.' His commander turned to him. 'We'll recommence tomorrow. But let no man mistake: I'm not done. There are corners we haven't prodded, and I mean to sound every one of them.' He looked at Marbeck. 'Have the stables and outbuildings been searched?'

Blank-faced, Marbeck gave a nod. 'The woods too, as well as the nearby farm . . . There's nothing untoward.'

A moment passed until, at a nod from Deverell, the other men began to leave, their relief plain to see. When only he and Marbeck remained, the Crown's eager priest-hunter moved to a chair and sank down. 'Don't let me keep you,' he muttered. 'Go, eat and drink with the others . . . bed a wench, for all I care. One of the maids looks willing enough.'

'Have you given thought to the fact that, when all's said and done, you could be wrong?' Marbeck asked, after a moment. 'That the priest – assuming he was here – got clear before we arrived? The barred doors, the attempts to delay us . . . they could have been merely a cover, to let the man get further away—'

'Of course I've thought of it!' Bleary-eyed, Deverell glared at him. 'I know every trick they use – and besides, I told you I can smell them. Who do you think it was, who found two of the devils crouched in a hole in Berkshire last summer? They'd lived like rats for almost a fortnight, breaking a loaf into scraps, sharing water to the last drop. One even drank his own piss – they couldn't walk when we dragged them out.

Yet they gave thanks on their knees . . . Martyrdom lay ahead, and they rejoiced!' Lowering his gaze, he lapsed into silence.

Marbeck said nothing, but let his eyes stray to the gaping hole beside the chimney, where the hiding-place had been found the previous day. How any man could spend days, let alone weeks, confined in a dark, airless space like that stretched his imagination to its limit. And yet in France, in the Jesuit schools, he had seen the rapture that drove men to endure, to spare no effort in spreading their mission throughout the world.

'You should sleep,' he said finally, setting his dislike of Deverell aside. For there was no denying that this man's faith, misguided or not, was real too. There were some crueller than he, who seized the chance to torture Papists. Deverell was a hard man, but he took his satisfaction from the pursuit and discovery of outlawed priests. Like Marbeck, Monk and all of those who made up the Lord Secretary's intelligence service, he would serve the Crown unto his own death.

'I will.' Too tired to argue, Deverell was looking at him. 'And you? There's a fire in the chamber overlooking the paddock. Most of the men will bed down there again.'

'I think I'll sleep here tonight,' Marbeck said, on impulse. 'I prefer a cold room . . . and my own company.'

'As you wish.' The other stood up, stretched his limbs and went out. Upstairs, the noise of searching had at last ceased, and for the first time that day a kind of peace reigned at Great Willoughby. Marbeck looked absently at a pile of stone flags that had been lifted from a section of the floor – pointlessly, as he'd suspected from the outset. Then he too went to supper, with the gloomy prospect of another day's search ahead.

But that night, everything changed, and it was Marbeck's decision to sleep in a room that had already been searched that brought it about.

He woke, as he often did, just before dawn. His bed was hard, and there was a smell of plaster dust . . . then he remembered where he was: on the floor, with his folded doublet beneath him and his cloak for a coverlet. Raising his head stiffly he peered round, making out the contours of the large room with difficulty. The house was quiet, occupants and occupiers alike sleeping. With a yawn, he lay down again . . . then froze.

It was barely audible: a scuffle or a scratch that could have been made by a small animal, or even a mote of falling masonry. He listened intently, but no other sound followed. Feeling another yawn coming on, he was on the point of dismissing it – then the next moment he sat up, fumbling for his poniard.

Unlikely as it seemed, the noise had come from near the chimney: from the old hiding-hole that had already been exposed. On his feet at once, Marbeck padded silently across the floor in his hose and peered inside. There was no tell-tale chink of light, nor any further sound. And yet he waited, for at least a minute, his ear turned to the fireplace . . . until, at last, his suspicions proved correct. His pulse rising, he leaned forward, poking his head into the dark alcove until he heard a faint rustling – and now he was certain: there was a second hiding-space beyond it.

Drawing back, he collected his thoughts quickly. He was loath to leave the room, for there could be an escape route somewhere that was yet to be discovered. The second hiding-hole, he guessed, bent round behind the fireplace. No fire had been lit here for days: the searchers had observed that from the start. Once the first hole had been found, however, they'd lost interest and moved elsewhere. Marbeck needed to get Deverell here . . . but first he needed light.

Moving carefully about the room, he found a candle in a holder and got out his tinderbox. Carrying the light, he returned to the hiding-place and stepped inside it. He raised the holder, and at once the flame wavered. Holding up his palm, he felt for the tiny draught: as he'd suspected it came not from the chimney-stack, but from the rear of the hole. Putting his ear to the wall he listened – and caught his breath.

On the other side of it, someone was praying.

Breathing slowly, Marbeck stepped away from the alcove. Setting the candle on a side table, he moved to the doorway and out to the hall. One of the pursuivants, supposed to guard the front entrance, was asleep on a bench. But when Marbeck shook him roughly, he awoke with a cry.

'Rouse Deverell. Get everyone up – bring lights to the main chamber, and quickly.'

The man scrambled to his feet and stumbled towards the

stairs, rubbing his eyes. Marbeck returned to the room and hunted for more candles. By the time Deverell appeared, tousle-haired and clad only in shirt and breeches, the place was lit well enough. Other men followed him in, while footsteps thudded overhead and on the staircase.

'Behind the hole,' Marbeck said, pointing. 'There's another chamber – dust was laid in the first one to trick us.'

Without hesitation Deverell strode to the chimney wall, calling over his shoulder for men to bring hammers and pick-axes. Marbeck took a light and followed him. Soon both of them were peering into the space, scanning the brickwork beyond . . . whereupon Deverell gave a cry of triumph.

'There – it's a feeding tube! Do you see?'

Marbeck stared and saw what looked like a quill, protruding barely an inch from the masonry. It was narrow, but not so narrow that liquids couldn't be poured through it into the space behind. There were no other tell-tale signs, nor was there any discernible chink in the wall, but all was becoming clear.

His face aglow in the candlelight, Deverell turned to him. 'I should have known. I've seen it before, in Warwickshire . . . The first hole's a decoy. He's been there all along. He could have heard every word we've said in here and laughed at us!'

'What of the space on the other side of the chimney-wall?' Marbeck wondered. 'There must be another way out . . . The kitchen's beyond there, isn't it?'

'No matter.' In some triumph, Deverell smiled. 'I'll set men all round, while we break in from this side. Indeed, it may not even be necessary . . .' With a sudden movement, he banged on the wall with his closed fist and shouted into the gloom. 'You are discovered, priest! We're about to break in, so why not reveal yourself? Are you mortared up in there? Either way, it's all over . . . Best stand clear of the wall, if you have the room!'

Marbeck stepped back as men came hurrying in with tools. Grey fingers of dawn were poking through the curtains, and he moved across the room to draw them back. He was hoping he wouldn't be needed, now that the hunt was almost finished. Having little relish for what might follow, he found his shoes and sat down to put them on. Fully dressed, he stood by as work proceeded: a hammering and gouging that raised clouds of dust from the hiding-hole.

Deverell watched closely, then turned to a man who stood by. 'Gather the servants, have them keep to the kitchens. And send word to Mistress Warlake . . . though I wager she's up already.' Briskly, he addressed the others. 'I want every ground floor room guarded, and the cellars beneath. There might be a concealed stair, or a hole big enough for our rat to crawl through. Watch the outside, too. Cover every door and window – I don't intend to lose him now!'

It was done swiftly, pursuivants moving off through the great house. Doors banged, and from the stairs came the shriek of a frightened servant girl. But when Marbeck moved, as if to join the others, Deverell beckoned to him.

'Come over here, for I may need you.'

So Marbeck was obliged to join him, and to watch the operation proceed to its close. It didn't take long: in a matter of minutes, two men had knocked a ragged hole in the second wall, revealing another dark cavity behind. Now there came the unmistakable smell of a candle, recently snuffed out. And there was another smell, too, far less pleasant . . .

'By the Christ!' The man wielding the hammer drew back, bumping into his companion. 'The bastard's filled his chamber-pot – how long has he been in there?' He wrinkled his nose, but there was humour in his gaze. Like his master, he relished his task now that success was near. Having dealt a few further blows, he nodded to the second man. This one hooked a pickaxe in and dislodged more bricks, narrowly avoiding them as they fell. Dust flew everywhere, prompting a few coughs.

Close by, Deverell stood impassively, but Marbeck saw the controlled anger in the man's eyes and knew what would follow. He was about to turn away – then he gave a start. So did the men, the one with the pickaxe jerking back in alarm.

Like some ghost in the half-light, a figure had appeared on the other side of the opening. Bending down, the man showed his face: pale, and grimed with dust. His spade-shaped beard was silver-grey, his hair cut to little more than a stubble, while a black skullcap was set tightly on his head. In the shocked silence that fell, he eyed his discoverers, then spoke in a soft voice.

'Permit me to spare you further effort, sirs. I have no other means of egress, since you appear to have blocked it off. If you'll be good enough to assist me, I will come to you.'

They stared at him, as if at some inhabitant of another world – as in a way he was, Marbeck thought briefly. Glancing at Deverell's men, he saw unease on their faces. Perhaps it was the fugitive priest's dignity, or the gentleness of his tone that had startled them . . .

'Bring him out, and keep a firm grip – likely, he's as slippery as an eel!'

Deverell's voice was harsh, and at once the spell was broken. Dropping their tools, the men bent forward. Slowly and stiffly the priest raised a knee, pushing his dusty black robe up his bare thigh as he did so. With difficulty he was manhandled out of the hiding-place, the two men gripping his upper arms. His skin was scraped by the rough edges of the brickwork, drawing blood, but he made no sound. Finally, somewhat short of breath and smelling like a horse, he was pulled from the hole into the room . . . whereupon he stood to his full height, prompting a collective intake of breath. At more than six feet tall, he dwarfed those around him.

'Well, sirs, I thank you.' Calmly, he surveyed his captors, settling finally on Deverell. 'No doubt this has been an ordeal for all of us . . . Might I beg a cup of water? My throat is somewhat parched.'

But Deverell eyed him, shaking his head. 'Neither food nor drink shall pass your lips,' he said in a voice as hard as flint, 'until you've told me what I want to know.' He faced Marbeck. 'Will you find a suitable place in which to question our friend? Meanwhile I'll get myself dressed . . . Do you want to take breakfast with me?'

With a heavy heart, Marbeck turned away.

NINE

I t was a cellar: cold, dank and windowless, heavy with the smell of apples laid down for the winter. Lanterns had been brought in, and a space cleared. The prisoner was bound to a central pillar, hands behind his head, which obliged him to stoop slightly since the ceiling was low. Two men stood guard, even though escape was impossible. When his interrogator, as Deverell had become, descended the staircase with Marbeck, the priest barely glanced at them. At once the spymaster approached him, while Marbeck found a seat by the wall.

'Your name,' Deverell began without preamble. 'Who are you?'

'I am Ralph Cornford, of the Society of Jesus.'

'Are you alone? If there are others of your order concealed here, speak and spare them further hardship. For they'll be found in time – you know it well enough.'

'There are none here, save me.' Father Cornford gazed steadily at his captor. Though weak from his confinement, and no doubt hungry as well as thirsty, he appeared resigned to his fate.

'And who sent you?'

'Sent me?' The priest raised his brows. 'I'm an Englishman, born and bred. Do I need leave to travel in—'

'You know what I ask,' Deverell broke in. Since dawn he had appeared satisfied with his success and was trying to be patient. 'Who sent you over here, to this country?'

'Well then, the superiors of my Society,' Cornford replied. 'If that's what you wish to hear.'

'Why?'

'To bring back wandering souls to their maker.'

'No . . .' Grimly, Deverell shook his head. 'You came here to seduce people from the King's allegiance to the Pope's – and to meddle in state business.'

'You're mistaken, for I've no interest in that,' came the firm reply. 'The head of our order has spoken against such policy – my concern is with matters spiritual, and nothing more.'

'If you mean Claudio Aquaviva in Rome, I curse him,' Deverell said contemptuously. 'He's a heretic, with no dominion here. Now, tell me how long you've lived in this house.'

But at that the priest hesitated, and those watching knew why: by admitting he'd been sheltered by the Warlake family, he would condemn them.

Deverell, however, was having none of it. 'Forbear to waste my time,' he snapped. 'Your hosts will answer for their actions, come what may. My reports suggest you've been here for at least a month, so speak.'

'Then, does it matter what I say?' Father Cornford sighed. His discomfort was great, but he bore it with stoicism. 'I came here of my own free will, under no man's persuasion. What more can I tell? Have I held Masses since I arrived in England? Yes, many. Yet I ask not the names of those who seek me out.'

Deverell thought, then unexpectedly turned to Marbeck. 'Do you have questions for him?' he asked sharply.

Taken aback, Marbeck met his eye; the man was drawing him in deliberately, forcing him to take part. Concealing his reluctance, he got up and came forward. 'Which part of England were you sent to minister to, Father Cornford?' he asked. 'The Eastern Counties? Or have you journeyed here from elsewhere?'

There was no answer at first. The priest was in difficulties, with the awkward posture he was forced to adopt. Finally, he returned Marbeck's gaze and said stiffly: 'I'm always travelling. There isn't a county I haven't visited . . . What does it matter where I lay my head? My work is the same, wherever—'

'Your work!' In spite of himself, Deverell's impatience was growing. 'Twisting men's hearts and minds, spouting Roman poison? That's over – as your miserable life will be soon, on the end of a rope . . .' With an effort, the spymaster checked himself. Whereupon, as if he hadn't heard, Marbeck resumed.

'You must tell of the houses where you've lodged,' he said.

'And give the names of those who've harboured you – or you may be taken elsewhere and forced to speak. It's but a matter of time, for even you will testify in the end. Everyone does.'

But even as he spoke, he saw Cornford's resolve hardening. This man was well aware of the risk of torture; likely, he had been preparing himself for it from the time of his discovery. He paused, working his dry mouth, then said: 'Take me away then, and do what you will. My future is in the hands of a power far greater than yours.'

'Your future?' Deverell was struggling to contain himself now. 'You have none! Once you've been stretched until your limbs tear out, you'll give full testimony – and wish there were more you could tell. What can this stubbornness avail you?' He paused, then levelled a finger at his captive. 'Or must I have others brought here to join you – servants, even your gentle hostess? Do you think her resolve will prove as strong as yours?'

It was an empty threat; Marbeck and the other watchers knew it. But a shadow passed across the priest's face. He swallowed, then in a hoarse voice answered: 'Their fate, like mine, lies in God's hands . . . and in His name, I pity you.'

'You do *what*?' The effect on Deverell was striking. With an oath he darted forward and seized the man's dirty cassock, pulling it tight about his neck. 'You whoreson wretch . . . You think to set yourself above me? I serve God and my King – not the demons of Rome! I've a mind to treat you as I would any low villain that's been taken in felony—' In a fury, he broke off and looked at Marbeck.

'Help me strip him to the waist,' he ordered. 'You . . .' He turned to one of the other men. 'Find a switch, or a horsewhip – a belt, even! I've a mind to administer a flogging and see how his pride stands after that!'

Without a word, the pursuivant went to the steps and ascended. The other man stood stock-still, but Marbeck caught the look in his eye: the fellow liked this no more than he did.

'It isn't in our warrant,' he began, taking a step forward – but Deverell turned on him.

'I told you to aid me,' he snapped. 'No matter: my nerve won't fail me, even if yours has.' With that he drew his poniard.

Instinctively, Marbeck moved to stay him, but Deverell shifted the weapon to his other hand. Using it like a butcher's knife, he slashed Cornford's cassock from neck to shoulder. Then he dropped the dagger, gripped the thick cloth and, to the alarm of his victim, began to rip it apart. In a moment he had torn the robe roughly from the man's body, peeling it downwards. Then as Marbeck stood by, restraining himself with difficulty, the spymaster seized the hapless priest by the shoulders and turned him about. The man cried out as his arms were twisted violently . . . and then, a silence fell.

It was so intense that the only sound was that of Father Cornford wheezing in pain. The three other men stared at the priest's exposed torso, before beginning to stir. The pursuivant, who had come forward, took an involuntary step away. After a moment Deverell too backed off, dropping his eyes. But Marbeck remained where he stood, gazing at the priest's bare back. From neck to waist, it was a mass of bruised and scarred skin: old wounds that had healed but were yet livid; others that were raw, even fresh. From some abrasions blood welled: the result of Deverell's action, which had raked the scabs off. Even for men used to violence, it was a sobering sight.

Finally, since even the spymaster seemed lost for words, Marbeck spoke. 'How does your notion of dealing him a flogging stand now?' he enquired, keeping emotion from his voice. 'For it looks as if someone has gone before you – the prisoner himself, I'd say.'

Deverell made no answer, and to Marbeck's surprise, there was shame in his eyes. So without a word Marbeck drew his own poniard and, standing on tiptoe, reached up to cut the priest's bonds. The dagger's edge being somewhat blunt, it took a little time. But finally, with a groan, Cornford was able to free his arms. At once he sank to the floor and began gathering his tattered robe about himself, to cover the evidence of his own self-scourging. Breathing hard, he looked up at Marbeck.

'My thanks to you, sir.'

But Marbeck turned on Deverell. 'With your leave,' he said, in a voice that suggested he didn't care whether he received it or not, 'I'll get someone to tend the man's hurts. He can hardly travel to London like this, can he?'

For a moment Deverell looked as if he would offer a retort, but instead he wavered. 'Find a healing-woman, then,' he said in a tired voice. 'I've done my part here.' He glanced round as footsteps sounded on the stairs.

The pursuivant appeared, a switch in his hand. But on reaching the floor, he stopped.

'We won't be needing that,' Deverell snapped. 'Bring bread and water for the prisoner instead.' And when the other showed surprise, he allowed his anger to resurface. 'Are you deaf? Go – and have the lady of the house attend me again.'

Finally, he faced Marbeck and spoke low. 'We return to London at midday, with the prisoner. I'll leave men to keep Mistress Warlake under house arrest. Let Monk take the matter further. I've other business to deal with – as do you.'

He moved off, instructing his follower to remain and guard the priest. Others would be sent to the cellar too, Marbeck heard him say; as if the black-clad figure, still slumped on the floor, were capable of flight. He was on the point of following Deverell up the stair, when something made him hesitate. Looking round, he found the priest gazing at him.

'Is there aught else you need?' Marbeck asked, for want of something to say.

'No . . . and again, I thank you,' Cornford answered. 'Or rather . . .' He hesitated, then: 'In the place where I was you'll find certain objects, one of them a bible. I would beg you . . .'

'I'll fetch it,' Marbeck said at once.

Upstairs the house was filled with activity, Deverell's men moving about at their various tasks. The hayloft had been sorely depleted, he heard one say, as well as the larders, so it was as well they were leaving. Meanwhile, the servants were still penned in the kitchen, no one having bothered to ask what should be done with them.

Deverell was in the downstairs room, waiting impatiently for Mildred Warlake to be brought to him. When Marbeck entered and made for the priest-hole, he frowned. 'Leave everything there as it was,' he ordered. 'The chalice, the pyx and the rest – they're evidence.'

'He asks for his bible,' Marbeck replied. 'I didn't think it could do any harm.'

'Then find another one.'

So Marbeck looked about the house, moving through the destruction wreaked by the searchers, and finally came upon a small bible in a case of books. Learning, with some relief, that Deverell didn't need him when he confronted Mistress Warlake again, he returned to the cellar.

Two guards stood at the foot of the stairs, but on seeing who it was they moved aside. Father Cornford was now seated on a box and seemed to have regained some composure. When Marbeck approached him with the bible, he even managed a wan smile.

'Once again, sir, I'm in your debt,' he said. Taking the book, he pressed it to his chest. 'Might I know your name?'

'Tucker,' Marbeck said – then stiffened; the look on the other's face showed that he didn't believe him.

'Master . . . Tucker.' Cornford met his eye. 'Would you deign to spend a moment with me?'

But Marbeck raised a warning hand. 'I can't – I'd have to fetch witnesses. You won't be left alone again – at least, not until you reach prison. There you may be allowed to join others of your faith . . . though I couldn't swear to it.'

'I understand, but—' The priest broke off.

Marbeck caught a different look in his eye and found himself frowning.

'The matter is, I know I haven't long to live,' the other told him. But again he wavered, and Marbeck thought he understood.

'If you wish to make confession to another priest, that too must wait,' he said – whereupon Cornford shook his head.

'No . . . you misunderstand me.' In some agitation he looked to the guards, who had seated themselves on the bottom stair. Eyeing Marbeck again, he said softly: 'It's another matter . . . one that troubles me greatly. Yet, for the reason you've touched upon, I may not speak of it.'

Marbeck narrowed his eyes; there was something in the priest's gaze he couldn't fathom. Perhaps the man's composure – formed, he'd assumed, of an unshakeable faith in the life to come – was but a veneer after all. Instead, he saw a look that allowed for another interpretation: one of underlying anguish.

'If . . . What if I told you that there is something fearful
. . . a terrible fate, set to befall certain people within a matter
of days?' the priest said haltingly. He was forcing the words
out; Marbeck saw he clutched the bible so tightly, his knuckles
had paled. Involuntarily, he moved closer, whereupon the prisoner leaned towards him and whispered urgently.

'I was told of it under confession . . . do you see? Whatever
they may do to me in London, I cannot break my vow. I'll
die with the knowledge – but so will others, because of my
silence . . . It's a weight I've found impossible to bear. God
forgive me, I've begged for guidance, yet none comes.
Someone must act, or cataclysm will follow – a slaughter of
innocents!'

There was a stir from across the room: Marbeck glanced
round and saw the guards watching him. Blank-faced, he
walked over to them and spoke softly. 'The prisoner spins his
tale,' he said, forcing a grim smile. 'I've resolved to listen and
see what he may let slip. Give me time, will you?' And when
the men nodded, he returned to Cornford.

This time he knelt on one knee. He believed the priest, he
realized: something told him the man's fears were not for
himself, but for others. Though what the terrible event he'd
hinted at might be, he couldn't imagine. Bending close, he
said: 'You're amiss if you think I can betray my fellows – I
should report anything you say. The man who questioned you
doesn't bluff: he could have you put to hard question until
you tell of this matter, whether it breaks your sacred vow or
not . . .'

'Please – you must listen.' Despite the chill of the cellar,
sweat stood on the priest's brow. With almost a sob he put a
hand out, his desperation such that he seemed to have forgotten
the circumstances.

But Marbeck shook his head. 'If you want me to act in this
matter, you've picked the wrong man,' he said wearily. 'I've
no powers . . . I'm a Crown servant who—'

'Your King: would you not try to save him?' Cornford whispered hoarsely. Then, as Marbeck gave a start, he dropped his
gaze. 'There – I can say nothing more; indeed, I've told enough
to condemn myself already. But if you believe in the power

of mercy, sir, and in hope, I urge you to try. Think on what I've said, and follow your heart. I believe you're a good man . . .' But with that, he choked on his own words.

As Marbeck watched he bowed his head, trembling slightly in the cold room. And for some reason, he found his own hand reach out to touch the tormented priest's shoulder. But Cornford didn't seem to notice, and he soon let go.

As he left the room, he glanced down from the stairway and saw that the prisoner hadn't stirred. Whereupon he turned away and ascended, knowing in that moment that interrogation, even under the worst torture, would be merely a waste of time and effort. The man he left was broken already, and beyond anyone's help in this world.

The knowledge stayed with Marbeck, hours later, when the party at last rode away from Great Willoughby, the manacled prisoner in their midst. Nor did his feelings alter when, as the day waned, they passed through Aldgate and made their way through the busy streets of London, with people stopping to stare. And as word spread quickly others came running, to shout angrily, and to wave fists, at the sight of one more captured Jesuit being conveyed to his doom.

But for Marbeck, something greater filled his mind, which seemed to swell with each hour that passed. There was a terrible danger, he had been told, aimed at the King and perhaps others too; yet he had no inkling where it came from, nor what he might do about it.

TEN

The next morning, Marbeck and William Deverell stood face to face in the room by the Jewel Tower and railed at each other.

'You took it upon yourself to question that devil in my absence, without authority!' the spymaster shouted. 'I should have known better than to let you take him a bible. The varlet was manipulating you like a puppet, sowing doubt for his own wicked ends, and you believed him! What in heaven's name possessed you . . . No, I'll answer that myself: Popish lies, dripped into your ears like poison!'

'Then you're content to dismiss every word he said?' Marbeck threw back. 'The King could be in danger, yet you refuse even to consider the notion? Meanwhile you busy yourself arresting people like the Warlakes, whose only real crime is their faith—'

'Enough, damn you!' Red-faced, and still tired from the exertions of the past days, Deverell glared at him, then turned abruptly away. In the cramped chamber, each could hear the other's breathing. Marbeck stood rigid, his thoughts in a whirl. Faces crowded his mind: John Cutler, Thomas Percy, Mildred Warlake, Father Cornford. . . then, for some reason, MacNeish's flew up to displace the others.

'And what of Prestall?' he said abruptly.

'Who?' Frowning, Deverell swung round.

'He's a servant to the Careys – an informer passed on his intelligence to me. Monk said he'd question the man.'

'I've no knowledge of it,' came the retort. 'And why do you raise it now – to divert me from your foolishness?'

'The kidnap threat,' Marbeck said sharply. 'If you refuse to hear me out concerning Cornford, then think on this. Prestall told my informant about a scheme to kidnap one of the royal children. That's why I was told to watch Percy . . .'

'Then why don't you do that, instead of coming to me with your Popish nonsense?' Deverell's shoulders were tense as a bullock's, his fists clenched.

In spite of everything, Marbeck almost laughed. 'By the Christ, is it a fight you want?' he asked. 'Or would you prefer to fence? I'm willing if you are, though I doubt it'd prove much.'

There was a moment, until with an effort the other mastered himself. Deliberately, he stalked to the side cupboard and poured himself a drink, without offering one to Marbeck. Moving to the table, he sank down on a stool, his eyes flitting over the untidy mass of paperwork. The actions were trivial, but to Marbeck's eyes they conveyed a good deal: at the final turn, this man was not up to the tasks Monk had laid upon him.

'I knew about the rumour of kidnap,' Deverell said finally.

'Did you, indeed?'

'Monk spoke of it briefly, before he left for Salisbury House. I thought the notion absurd . . . The royal children are never unguarded, day or night. But since he appeared to think the threat worth investigating, you'd better follow his orders. Percy's another Papist dog, when all's said and done, and not to be trusted. As for this fellow Prestall, I've no idea whether he was questioned or not. Do you wish me to find out?'

'It's your affair.' Marbeck was weary of the room and of its occupant. 'Best you leave me to my own devices. Monk usually does – as the Lord Secretary did before him.'

'I'm well aware of it,' Deverell said scathingly. 'You've always been one of his favourites, have you not?'

'You think so?' Marbeck enquired. A memory came up then, of Lord Cecil lying in the healing waters at Bath, more than a year ago, telling him that he considered him an accessory to murder, and hence at his – the spymaster's – mercy. It was a sobering thought, which checked him whenever he harboured ideas of quitting his life as an intelligencer.

'I've always thought so.' Deverell grunted. He took another drink and lowered his gaze. 'But as to matters now in hand, I've no authority except to bid you follow Percy as you were ordered. Anything more you can take to Monk when he returns – whenever that may be. He's told me precious little.'

The meeting was over, fruitless as it had been. And something else occurred to Marbeck as he took a last look at the man who sat regarding him over the rim of his cup. At best, he thought, Deverell was little more than a lackey himself: of small importance except as a diligent seeker-out of hidden priests. He was here merely to mind the shop, while his master was away.

Without further word Marbeck went out. And as he'd done the last time, he walked by the river to gather his thoughts. There had been a shower of rain in the night, and the paths were wet. He thought briefly of Curzon, whom he'd left that morning, asleep on a straw pallet in his chamber: Skinner's sole concession to his new lodger. Recalling the springing of his friend from Whitehall, he had a sudden notion to find his way to Lady Carey's rooms and enquire for himself about the servant Prestall, the man who appeared to have started this rumour of kidnap. Perhaps there was little substance to it after all, he mused, and MacNeish had merely embellished the tale to winkle payment out of him; it would not be unlike the man. Somehow, the thought offered a crumb of comfort.

Assuming an air of brisk authority, he entered the palace by a side door and tipped a servant to point him to the apartments of Duke Charles. Drawing near, as expected he was soon stopped by armed guards and asked his business. On enquiry, however, he learned that the infant prince wasn't there, but at St James's with his brother. Whereupon, with a casual air, he asked after a man named Prestall – only to receive a curt reply.

'Gone . . . Dismissed,' the guard told him. 'Are you a friend of his?' And when Marbeck let him understand that he was, the man's face hardened. 'Then I'd keep quiet about it, if I were you.' Raising a gloved hand, he pointed. 'That's the way out . . . You wouldn't want to linger hereabouts.'

So he left Whitehall and made his way back to Parliament Stairs. He was uneasy now. Swiftly, he ran the events of recent days through his mind, yet could make little sense of them. But then, like it or not, he had a task just now that he must fulfil. With a sigh he drew his cloak about him, stepped on to the jetty and waited for a boat.

By the evening, however, he found himself thwarted. After some tedious hanging about as Lawrence Tucker, cadging information in the vicinity of Essex House, he discovered that Thomas Percy had left London. The man had ridden north, he was told, to collect rents from the Border properties of his cousin, the Earl of Northumberland. He would be three hundred miles away, and it was not known when he would return. Hungry and dispirited, Marbeck trudged into the city by Ludgate and made his way to the Pegasus in Cheapside.

It was not a regular haunt, but it was big and noisy, which suited him well enough. Once in a corner booth he called for a hot supper and a jug of claret and set about consuming both. Whereupon, a good deal later, with the tavern roaring about his ears, he lifted the jug and found it almost empty. Somewhat fuddled, he looked round to see the inn glowing with the light of candles and darkness outside the windows.

'Can I fetch you aught, sir?' A portly drawer stood over him, his hands full of empty mugs. 'A boy with a torch to light you home, perhaps?'

'Why . . . is it so late?' Marbeck peered up at him.

'Nay, 'tis approaching nine of the clock. Time for another mug, if you've a mind.' But the man raised an eyebrow, his meaning clear enough: he doubted the gentleman needed any more.

'Don't trouble yourself,' Marbeck said, picking up his cup and gazing into it. 'I've a mouthful here yet . . . and with your leave, I'll take my time in finishing it.' But when the drawer seemed to be taking his time moving away, something came from his lips unbidden. 'Do you have children?' he muttered.

The other blinked. 'I do, sir – a son and two daughters.'

'And do they delight you?'

'Delight me?' The man's brow creased. 'I'd not put it

so. The boy's a trial at times, but the maids – those two would drive a man to distraction.' No doubt thinking he'd gossiped long enough he turned to go, but Marbeck caught his arm.

'I have a daughter,' he said. 'And you're the first man I've told of it . . . Here: take this for your girls, with my blessing.' He put down his cup, produced his purse and tugged it open. When a handful of coins fell into his palm, he poured them into one of the mugs the drawer held. The man stared in astonishment.

'That'll be all,' Marbeck told him and lifted his cup again. Without another word, the other turned and left.

A while later, he stood outside in Cheapside and let the cold breeze blow the fumes of ale and tobacco from his clothing. There was noise and laughter, with night-time revellers passing to and fro. A bellman passed nearby, calling the hour . . . and that everyday sound was all Marbeck needed to shape his intent. But then, he'd formed it an hour ago, in the tavern; it was foolhardy, even desperate, but he no longer cared.

Turning eastwards, he began walking along Cheap towards the Stocks Market. There he veered into Lombard Street, finding strength as he went. By the time he had walked the length of Fenchurch Street and turned into the narrow way that led to Crutched Friars, he was more sober, but not very. Had he been clear-headed, he would have stopped himself from doing what he was about to do.

He reached the Walden House and found it in darkness. As before, the iron gates were padlocked, but this time no torch blazed on the gatepost. On peering through the bars, however, he saw lights in the big house, on the upper floors. A warning sounded in his head, but he ignored it. Instead, his breath clouding in the cold air, he reached in a pocket and drew out the tailor's bodkin he always carried. Two minutes' work on the lock was enough to force the tumblers aside, until with a loud click the hasp sprang free. His fingers stiff from the task, he wrenched the padlock from the bars and, with some vehemence, threw it over the wall. A moment later the gates were open and Marbeck was striding through the garden towards the main door. On reaching it he halted, raised his fist and hammered.

At first nothing happened. He hammered again, whereupon an unwelcome noise came from within: the bark of a large dog. Breathing hard, he fumbled for his sword-hilt. Then above his head, a casement creaked open and a male voice called out angrily.

'Who's there? Show yourself!'

Marbeck took a backward pace and looked up. The room above him was lit, and a face peered out: that of an elderly man wearing a night-bonnet. 'Who in God's name are you?' he demanded. 'The hour is late . . . and how did you get in?'

'Thomas Walden?' Marbeck called. 'I'm a friend to your daughter . . . It's her I seek, not you.'

The man gave a start. Other sounds came from beyond the door: voices, and the growling of the dog. But a recklessness was upon Marbeck that would not be quenched. On occasions, in desperate fights both here and abroad, a disregard for his own safety had saved his life; now it served a different purpose.

'I beg your indulgence and ask you to send her down,' he said, raising his voice. 'She'll come to no harm, I swear. But I must speak with her—'

'You shall not!' the old man roared, in sudden outrage. 'Whoever you are, you're an intruder with no business here! I've servants enough to overpower you – and a pistol too! I'll call the watch and have you taken away in chains—'

'Send her down,' Marbeck broke in, his voice hard as steel. 'Or I'll force my way in!'

But his reply was a muffled oath and the thud of the casement being shut. Shifting his gaze to the door, he prepared to draw his sword and face whatever resistance Thomas Walden could muster. He glanced to right and left, half-expecting someone to emerge from a side door, but no one appeared. Meanwhile, he grew aware of voices: an urgent debate on the other side of the door. In frustration he banged his closed fist on the heavy timbers, making them tremble.

'Open up!' he yelled. Then, throwing any last scrap of

restraint aside, he grasped his sword-hilt and drew. Steel rang in the crisp night air – and now another dog barked, from some house nearby. Soon, he thought grimly, he would rouse the whole street. Using the pommel of his rapier, he banged ferociously on the door again, then gave a start. A bolt was being drawn . . .

The door opened a short way, and Meriel's face appeared. 'Go – I beg you!' she said, in a voice that shook.

'I can't.' He dropped his sword on the flagged path with a clang and took a pace forward, but she gripped the edge of the door tightly.

'Please – it's no use. My father doesn't lie: he has a pistol. I promised him I'd get rid of you . . .'

She was trembling, and at once shame welled up inside him. All else became indistinct, except her face. In the light that spilled from within, she seemed to glow . . .

'The gates are open,' he said, struggling to sound calm. 'Come with me now, as you are. I can get you to a safe place, and in the morning we'll ride. Here . . .' He tore off his cloak and held it out. 'I know your feelings for me haven't changed . . . In the name of our child—'

'There is no child!'

It was almost a scream, and it cut him to the bone. Rigid, he stared at her, and the cloak fell from his grasp. He was barely aware of the door swinging inward, and of the figures that crowded the entrance; her words rang in his head, rendering him numb. And only then, with alarm, did he see her face clearly: drawn and pale, with lines of pain that weren't there, more than a week ago . . .

'The baby is lost,' she said, in a tone that left no room for doubt. 'There's nothing for you to do here . . . Go while you can.'

But he couldn't move . . . until a thought sprang up that almost made him stagger. 'Was it my coming here . . .? Did I cause you such distress . . .?' he began, but she didn't answer. Instead she was pulled aside, out of his sight. The door flew wide, and in her place stood her father in a heavy gown, his arm levelled; Marbeck was looking down the muzzle of a pistol.

'Get you gone, or I swear I'll shoot!' Thomas Walden snapped.

A moment passed. Drained of anger, Marbeck stared into the gun-barrel. He smelled the whiff of sulphur and knew the weapon was primed and ready. Yet still he didn't move. Just then, he realized, the solution to all his troubles was before him; all he need do was make a sudden movement. Then, as if from a fog, he saw the faces of Thomas Walden and his male servants appear, a mixture of anger and fear upon every one of them. He grew aware of the dog too: a great mastiff, growling balefully at him, held on a chain by a nervous boy. Whereupon, forcing his limbs to move, he took a step back. For a moment those in the doorway seemed to think he would fall, but he didn't. Instead, he half-raised both hands.

'Your pardon,' he muttered, feeling utterly broken. 'I came to the wrong house.' Slowly, he bent down, picked up his sword and turned away.

In some surprise, and no small relief, master and servants let him go. Finally, as he neared the gateway and vanished in the gloom, Thomas Walden gave brisk orders for his men to follow the madman as far as the end of the street.

But when they did so, making as little haste as they could, there was nothing to see: the wild-eyed stranger, who dressed as a gentleman but had the manner of a cut-throat, was gone. Soon they returned to the gardens, inspected the gates and found that the padlock too had gone.

Marbeck, meanwhile, was standing near the corner of Aldgate and Poor Jewry, looking up at a niche in the city's east wall known to many, but used by few: a place where, if a man were bold enough – or desperate enough – he could climb up by using ancient footholds in the stonework. A few minutes later, seen by no one, he had scaled the rampart and let himself down on the outside, dropping into a back garden in the Minories. He climbed a fence, then began walking doggedly by Houndsditch and Bishopsgate Street, until at last he could turn off the roadway into open fields.

It took him almost two hours in the pitch dark, but he

was in no hurry. By the time he reached Hampstead Village he was almost frozen. Only then did he recall that he'd left his cloak behind, on the pathway at Walden house.

But along with everything else, it had ceased to matter.

ELEVEN

There was a distant voice, calling to him. But the name wasn't his . . . Someone must be in error. Dismissing it, he tried to burrow into the space he'd been in, which was warm and inviting. But the voice grew louder, until in irritation he was forced to address it. Turning sharply, he flung out a hand – and woke at once, with someone shouting in his ear.

'Lawrence! *Mon dieu!*'

Charlotte de Baume was bending over him, her hair loose, wearing an elaborate morning-gown. When recognition dawned, Marbeck fell back on to the pillow. He was sweating, his mouth was dry and his limbs ached . . . Unable to summon a word, he gazed at her.

'Do you not know me?' she asked, her large eyes peering into his. 'You seemed to remember last night, when you fetched up at my door like a ghost . . . What has happened to you?'

But the only response was a barely audible groan as things came into focus. Frowning, he closed his eyes.

'Don't shut me out . . . It is most unkind.' Charlotte shook his shoulder, rather sharply.

When he opened his eyes again, she was wearing a look of concern. 'Your pardon,' he murmured. 'I . . . I promised to come and dine with you, did I not?'

'Indeed, so you did!' Charlotte arched her brows. 'Yet I see you have been occupied in some questionable business. You came here like a fugitive, Lawrence. Was it sanctuary you sought? If so, you are too late – the ambassador is gone, and I have no influence.'

For a moment he didn't understand; then it dawned. 'You mean Monsieur Harlay?' He shook his head. 'No, it wasn't that kind of sanctuary I sought . . .'

'Only that of my body, perhaps?' A smile was forming.

'Well, that was on offer last night. But there was such a weariness upon you, it could not be assuaged. In short, you forbore to touch me, and I let you slumber.'

He frowned, remembering at last. 'How long have I slept?'

'Many hours – the sleep of *un cadavre*. It is morning, and now you should eat. Look – see what has been brought.' Her smile broadened. Drawing back, she gestured to a table across the wide room, laden with silver platters, jugs and cups.

Marbeck took one look, caught the fatty odour of roast meats, and averted his gaze. 'Your pardon once again . . . You're most kind, but I've little appetite.'

She froze, and almost at once he feared a repeat of the last time he'd been here and witnessed her explosion of anger. Once more her dark eyes flashed as she struggled to master her temper.

Raising a hand, he put it to her cheek. 'Forgive me, I'm not myself. I should get some air . . . though I'd welcome a drink. Is there something weak on that tray?'

It did not placate her. Her chest rising menacingly, she took his hand away and gestured impatiently to the table. 'Weak? Indeed . . . as weak as you are today, *monsieur*. There is juice of pomegranates . . . Most difficult to obtain just now, I might add. I would have mixed it with wine, with my own hand, and served it to you. But first I meant to disrobe and climb in beside you, that we may delight in each other's bodies again. Instead, I see you devoid of that appetite, even now!'

She fell silent and turned her back on him, her voluminous gown swirling. She wore stockings of fine lawn, and no doubt little else beneath the robe. But it was true: bodily desire had deserted him. All he could see was Meriel's careworn face, telling him there was no child . . .

'I'm a fool, and a milksop too,' he said finally. 'No man in his senses would refuse you . . . I can but ask pardon again.'

Somewhat shakily he roused himself, threw the covers back and stood up, whereupon she turned to face him. He was in shirt and hose, still damp with sweat. His outer clothes lay upon a nearby chest, where no doubt Charlotte had placed them. He forced a smile, and quickly her manner changed.

'Lawrence . . . forgive my harshness, pray. Will you not sit with me and try to eat something? You need to regain your strength.'

So they sat down at the table, close together, and at once she became talkative. Though she avoided speaking of the manner in which he'd arrived at her house, which was a relief. Soon, while he inspected the dishes laid before him without enthusiasm, he managed to change the subject.

'Will you not speak of yourself?' he murmured. 'Do you still plan to remain in England, or return to France?'

'That would be telling,' Charlotte teased. 'I am in no hurry . . . though there's no lack of men in Paris who would like to hasten my return. While here, others would prefer me to stay . . .' She arched her brows. 'Some have been insolent in their approaches – as if I were no better than *une putain*. The kind of men you mix with too, perhaps, at Essex House . . . Do not deny, Lawrence. You were eager to bed me on sight, as you would a Bankside trull.'

'As you were me, Madame de Baume,' he answered after a moment. 'I hope, in that respect at least, I gave satisfaction.'

She laughed at that, with a coquettish air that seemed somehow false. Then she softened and bent forward deliberately, allowing him a clear view down the front of her loose gown. 'Indeed you did,' she murmured. 'Or I could not contemplate the things I wish to do with you soon, in my bed. As I trust you will delight me, as you promised . . . but first, will you take a little wine mixed with pomegranates, as I promised you?'

He nodded. The meal set before him was too sumptuous, though most of it was familiar enough to an Englishman: veal and eggs, broth, roast neat's tongue. But first, Charlotte insisted, he must take some oysters.

'They are my delight,' she said, opening one with the aid of an elegant silver knife. 'And they warm the blood, Lawrence . . . A prelude to love.'

To please her he ate one and signalled his approval. She

was eager to press more dishes upon him, which he tasted sparingly. Try as he might to put other thoughts aside, the events of last night preyed upon him. Finally, it became obvious to Charlotte, who put down her knife somewhat sharply.

'Lawrence . . . this is too unkind. Today you are in my house. Forget the world outside, as well as your troubles, and give yourself to me. What must I do, to fix your attention?' She smiled archly. 'Lower my gown and dine bare-breasted, like a tavern coquette?'

She put out a hand, which he took. Though a fire had burned itself out in the grate, the bedchamber was warm enough. Feeling tense, Marbeck wondered how he might take his leave, when, as if sensing it, Charlotte spoke up.

'See – I spoke of my promise!' She withdrew her hand and tapped him playfully on the wrist. 'Here is a delightful Romney wine . . . You must taste it, Lawrence.' Whereupon, taking up a silver jug, she half-filled a cup. Then she lifted another jug and poured the deep red juice of pomegranates in with the wine. Smiling archly, she dipped her forefinger into the mixture and swirled it about.

'Did I not say I would serve you with my own hand, Lawrence?' And with that, she took her finger from the cup and put it to his lips. 'Now – taste!'

So to please her again, he touched her forefinger with his tongue and tasted the mixture, which was sickly sweet. Managing a look of approval, he took the cup, sipped, and made a show of savouring it. 'You're a good hostess,' he said. 'But are you not going to partake with me?'

'Of course.' Charlotte smiled and half-filled her own cup with wine. She raised it, regarding him over the rim. 'Now I will confess something: I knew nothing of this Romney wine, until a friend told me of its special character. That is the reason I had my servant search for it, after your last visit: he would be refused entry to the house, I told him, until he'd found some.' Her smile widened. 'Do you know what property I speak of?'

He hesitated. 'Is it a cure for melancholy?'

She blinked, her smile fading; then seeing that he was

jesting, she gave one of her pouts. 'Lawrence, you torment me! You know what I speak of . . . This beverage, my friend assured me, is . . . how shall I say, *pour encourager l'amour*?'

'I follow you, madame.' He raised an eyebrow. 'Though it's the first time I've heard that. I fear your friend may have spun you an old wives' tale. But no matter: I toast your kindness, as well as your determination.' He took another sip, then saw that Charlotte wasn't done with pretending offence.

She tapped him again on the wrist and said: 'Determination? How like a man, to think in such fashion! You think I am so starved of love that I must take measures to secure your presence in my bed?' Her eyes widened. 'Men have fought duels over me, Lawrence . . . Do you doubt my word on that?'

'How could I?' Marbeck said. 'I can imagine such. But you know you've no need to seduce me – you knew it after our first night together.'

'Our first night?' Charlotte arched her brows again. 'You mean our *only* night together, *monsieur*. Yesterday you came as a fugitive and forbore even to touch me.'

He took a breath. He was eager to leave her and this house, to be alone. But as he was seeking the words, quite suddenly an odd feeling stole over him . . . a touch of dizziness. Blinking, he lifted his cup to drink again . . . then as it touched his lower lip, he froze.

Charlotte, he saw, wasn't drinking. In fact, he realized with a shock, she hadn't even tasted her own cup. With an effort, he set down his drink carefully and forced a smile.

'Forgive me. I must to the jakes,' he said. 'A man's weakness, first thing of a morning. If you'll direct me to it, I'll make haste to return, that we may finish our breakfast together.'

He was acting: his intelligencer's instinct kicking in at once, for the purpose of self-preservation. Yet his smile was such that it worked: even on this woman who, he had learned in that moment, meant to poison him.

He stood up, trying not to appear hasty, and saw her gazing fixedly at him. 'There is a good-sized jordan in my closet, and it is unused,' she said gently. 'Pray, avail yourself of that.'

But as she gestured, he shook his head. 'I thank you, but I need some air, too.'

There was a moment, and once again that warning flash of mingled anger and impatience showed in Charlotte's gaze. Then to Marbeck's relief she flicked a hand dismissively, and gave a shout of laughter.

'Pah, you Englishmen – so particular in your privacy! In Paris a gentleman would step aside from his salon conversation, summon a servant with a *urinoir* and relieve himself then and there! But go . . . descend the stairs and follow the passage to the rear of the house, where you will find what you need. Then hurry back, for I mean to test your stamina.'

So he went from the room, still in his shirt and hose. Having descended the staircase to a dimly-lit passage, he quickened his step and found a back door, barred from within. A moment later he was out in the cold morning air, striding through a walled garden. He didn't trouble to find the jakes: instead, by the far wall he bent over, thrust two fingers hard down his throat and vomited into a flowerbed.

Bring it forth . . . Make the yellow fountain . . .

They were his father's words, half impatient, half-amused, from far away and long ago, in a nobleman's garden in the Ribble Valley. There he had scolded his twelve-year-old son, who'd drunk copiously and foolishly, as boys will. How many times since had he repeated that experience?

The memory vanished as he breathed in the still October air, gagging and retching. Up came the undigested oyster, along with the liquids he'd drunk. Especially the mixture of Romney wine and pomegranate juice; that had an under-taste he hadn't noticed – until he'd smelled a faint aroma that made him uneasy. Yet it wasn't that, so much as the look he'd caught in Charlotte's eye – that, and the fact that she was so eager for him to drink while she took not a sip.

He stood for several minutes to regain his strength, shivering slightly. He had ceased making himself vomit: there was nothing left, apart from a soreness in his stomach. He had acted quickly enough, he believed; had he taken one more mouthful of the wine . . .

He needed water, to flush out his innards. He straightened

up, looked towards the house and saw a rainwater-butt. Stumbling over to it, he shoved his face under the ice-cold surface, through a layer of leaves and algae, and filled his mouth. Then he drew back, swallowed the foul-tasting water and bent double. This time he had no need to force himself: up it came, along with the last trace of scarlet juice. Coughing and gasping, he sat down at last on damp flagstones with his back to the barrel . . . only to become aware of a figure, drawing close.

He looked up sharply and saw Charlotte's servant: the one who had fussed about her at Essex house and stared so brazenly at him; the same one, he now recalled vaguely, who had admitted him the night before.

'Are you ill, sir?' the man enquired – in a thick accent that wasn't French, but Spanish, which set a warning bell clanging in Marbeck's head. 'Pray, let me help you to rise . . .'

He bent forward, stretching out a hand – but he wasn't quick enough with his other hand. The blade flashed, only to be turned aside as Marbeck grabbed his forearm. There followed a crack as the bone was shattered, then a yelp of pain . . . and the man reeled backwards, his own poniard protruding from his neck. He fell heavily, choking, his blood gushing on to dew-soaked grass.

On his feet and panting, Marbeck whirled about, alert for further danger. But there was only a light wind, and the distant call of crows. With a glance at the assassin, who would never pose a threat to anyone again, he took a moment to gather his wits. Then he went back into the house, closing the door behind him.

In the gloom he stood and listened, but heard nothing. Moving soundlessly, he passed a door that must lead to the kitchen, then softly ascended the stairs and approached the bedchamber where, as far as he knew, Charlotte still waited. He hesitated, whereupon there came a sound from behind the door. He had tensed in every muscle, but just then one desire overrode all others: to confront the woman who'd tried to poison him and find out why. Steeling himself, he drew a breath, then thrust the door open – to be greeted by a thud and a cry of alarm: Charlotte had been listening on the other side.

Thrown backwards, arms flailing, she tripped over her gown and, with a shriek, fell on to her back. For a moment she lay on the floor, eyes wide, before finding voice. 'Lawrence – you frightened me! What is wrong? Why do you look at me so?'

'Have you more than one servant?' he asked, his voice flat.

She stared at him. 'No, only Miguel . . . Why—'

'Why do I ask? Because he's dying, or dead by now. Was he under orders to kill me?'

Breathing hard, Charlotte struggled to sit up. 'I don't understand . . .' She caught her breath. 'He's dead . . . Miguel is dead?'

Marbeck merely eyed her. A long moment passed as she returned his gaze . . . and saw not only that he didn't lie, but that he also knew what she'd tried to do. In silence, she seemed to be weighing her choices – until she sensed he knew that, too. Whereupon not fear, but a look of uncertainty appeared.

'Won't you at least help me up?' she asked finally.

He reached down, took her hand and pulled her to her feet, letting her feel his strength. When she stood before him, her chest rising and falling rapidly, he gestured sharply. 'Sit,' he ordered.

She moved to the table and sat down, then spoke up quickly. 'There's my maid too, I should say. She will raise the alarm—'

'You're lying,' he snapped.

She fell silent.

'So, who are you, then?' Moving suddenly, so as to startle her, Marbeck sat down in the chair he'd occupied earlier, pulling it closer. 'For I'd wager you're not Charlotte de Baume,' he continued. 'Nor, I suspect, are you related to the wife of the French ambassador.'

When she refused to speak, he leaned forward. 'As for that . . .' He indicated the jug of Romney wine. 'What was your intent – to despatch me once I'd drunk enough to lose my senses? Was Miguel waiting to finish the task – or did you send him outside in haste, because you feared I'd guessed what was afoot and intended to make my escape?'

'This is nonsense . . . You have lost your wits!' she exclaimed. But she refused to meet his eye, gazing down at the table. Whereupon Marbeck, angry as well as relieved at having spoiled her plan, picked up his cup and brought it to her lips.

'Drink, then,' he said. 'Prove that you weren't trying to kill me with this wine, that you'd have me believe would serve *pour encourager l'amour*. The wine you sweetened so liberally with pomegranates, to disguise the taste of poison.'

She caught her breath, but made no move.

'Must I force you?' he went on. 'You know I could, as you know there's no one here to help you—'

'*Con! Frai du diable!*' Her rage welled up at last. Eyes blazing suddenly, she bared her teeth and spat out a stream of French obscenities . . . whereupon, to her evident chagrin, Marbeck relaxed.

'So you are truly French and not Spanish . . . It's useful to know. Now I'd like to know who sent you. And more . . .' He raised his brow. 'Was it your intent to snare me that evening, back at Essex House? In which case, how did you know I'd be there?' He frowned. 'Unless you were watching me . . . you, or someone else.'

She merely glared at him, then looked away.

So he put his hand behind her neck, pressing her head forward. 'Drink,' he said. 'Or must I compel you?'

Breathing hard, she clamped her mouth shut.

'Do you not see?' He forced her to meet his eye. 'Your servant is slain. Nobody knows I'm here: I could deal with you as you would have done me. So, will you tell me things I can believe, Charlotte? I'll call you such, until I learn your real name—'

She moved then, so suddenly that he was caught unawares. Dashing the cup aside, sending it flying from his grasp, she snatched a knife from the table and lunged at him. He had barely time to avoid the thrust, though the flimsy weapon could have done little harm.

Recovering quickly, he gripped her wrist and twisted, forcing her to drop the blade. But she was on her feet, grabbing for other implements, before he was finally able to overpower her and force her back into the chair. Whereupon, all restraint gone, she thrust her face out and screamed at him.

'I *am* Charlotte de Baume! I've no need to hide behind other names, like all you cowards! I am Charlotte de Baume, of noble blood. And I know full well who you are – *Monsieur* Marbeck!'

TWELVE

Charlotte's mask was gone, and she seemed almost relieved to have put it aside. Remarkably composed, she sat at the table and now admitted what Marbeck suspected: that she was one of a team of two who had been ordered to kill him. And after some thought, he began to guess more.

'I've heard of women like you in Paris,' he said. 'Yet you seem young, for one of those . . . Shall I speak of the former *escadron volante*?'

She did not deny it, and, on his feet now, he began to piece it out even as he spoke. Long ago Catherine de Médicis, Queen Consort and mistress of intrigue, had put together her notorious company of female spies: young, pretty women who would seduce men of power in order to learn their secrets. The flying squadron, they were nicknamed by some; by others, less charitably, a stable of unscrupulous whores. How effective they had been while Catherine was alive, few people knew for certain. What seemed bizarre was that one of them should arrive in London to kill Marbeck, so many years after the death of their notorious queen.

'Let's come to it, then,' he said dryly. 'I want to know who hired you – for it wasn't your former mistress, from beyond the grave. Nor was it usual, I recall, for women like you to operate outside France. As for keeping a Spanish servant . . .' He frowned, and suspicions arose . . . but when he looked at her again, he saw a different expression.

'I can offer a bargain,' she said, without lifting her eyes.

Slowly, Marbeck shook his head. 'I think not, madam.'

'But you *should* think so. For this is not some tiresome matter of state intelligence; the man I serve has little use for such.'

She looked up then, and for a moment he almost swayed where he stood. He was struck by the glow from her eyes, and by a jolt of unseen power that shot through his vitals like a current. Whereupon, very deliberately, she put her hands to her gown and pulled it low, to expose both breasts.

'We are the same, Marbeck,' she said softly. 'Why should we pretend? If ordered, or if forced by one who had the means, you would kill me too; as you killed Miguel, you say – and I believe you. In any case, I was told something about the man I came to seek out . . . I, and my helper.' She gave a shrug. 'Miguel was never a servant, or only as long as appearance counted: he was sent to make sure I did as I was ordered. After that—' She broke off.

He sat down then, somewhat heavily. Realization had been just beyond his consciousness, he realized: ever since he'd overpowered her and heard her shout his real name. Perhaps he should have guessed sooner; as it was, for a time he was lost for words. Finally, he let out a breath. 'You work for Juan Roble.'

Her silence was answer enough.

'Does he hate me still, that he takes such pains – spends so much, merely to destroy me?' he went on. 'Five years, since . . .'

He stopped, almost in disbelief. Juan Roble, a man he'd never seen: the former Spanish spymaster he had once humiliated, and who, it seemed, could never forgive the slight. The same man who was now a renegade, a commander of murderous corsairs who spread terror throughout the Mediterranean Sea . . . Marbeck shook his head. 'Did someone aid you, when you reached London?' he asked finally. 'Or does that man know so much, that you were able to find me with ease? If so, his reach is long indeed.'

'His reach is long,' she answered, speaking low. 'Yet even he cannot know where you live, since you move about so often. Yes, I had help . . . poor men, who blow with the wind. I will not say more. You know there are always people who can be bought.'

He stiffened; something else had just fallen into place, which shook him more than he would show. 'No, you needn't say more,' he said, after a moment. 'And I'll have a reckoning soon, with one of those I think you mean. Yet now, one question remains: what must I do with you?'

'Indeed, I see your dilemma.' She smiled then, as if growing in confidence. 'There are rumours, or so I'm told, that you're dissatisfied with your life. You were offered riches once, were you not? Yet you remained loyal to your masters and to your country. I admire that – even if men like Juan Roble scorn such sentiment. Even I served France, Marbeck . . .' She stopped, with another look of uncertainty, for his anger had risen with sudden speed.

'You served France?' he echoed, on his feet again. 'Perhaps you did, at one time, in the only way you could. But what happened afterwards, when Catherine was dead? Were your skills no longer needed – were you even despised? You were no longer the young coquette you'd been . . . Was it then you were tempted, by a man who offered wealth beyond your dreams? That's what one of his minions offered me, in a dark room by the Thames: the chance to live under balmy skies like a pasha, with a harem. Is it possible for a woman to live so, in certain places? Even to keep a harem of men – a stable of your own?'

Angrily, he stood over her – but she laughed in his face. '*Mon dieu*, Marbeck, what a puritan you can be!' she cried. 'Are you truly such *un moraliste*? You've played a wicked game yourself: lied and deceived, fought and killed – for what? Your enemies are not only overseas, but also here, in your own country! I ask again, what is it for? One day you may falter, and it will be you who dies before your time. What does it matter then, if you are slain by a lord or a lackey – a prince, or *une putain*? For who will care? Your father, your ruthless brother . . . your paramour, whoever she is?'

She sighed, giving him a look almost of pity . . . then quite suddenly, she began to speak in a different tone. 'Think what we can do together, you and I! When I report your death, I mean – and that of Miguel, who is nothing to me. I can explain the loss of a servant, in a way that will satisfy El Roble. Then, with the payment he promised, you and I can go away, make a home wherever we choose. What could be better than to live free of restraint, delighting in our senses? Come – speak plainly: do you not yearn to fall on my body, even now?'

They gazed at each other: she smiling, Marbeck bewitched;

or at least, that was what he would think, much later. For just
then, he saw the truth in her words. There was little difference
between the two of them, in the end . . . and a very short
distance physically. The easiest thing for him to do was to go
to her, as she clearly expected; yet he hesitated.

'I did as I was ordered, Marbeck,' Charlotte said finally.
'As do you, every day. I told you: we are the same.'

'No . . . I don't believe that.' He drew a long breath and
forced himself to turn away – and when he faced her again,
the spell was broken. She saw it too, and would have spoken
had he not forestalled her.

'We could do as you say, easily enough,' he admitted.
'Between us, we may bend matters to our will . . . and for a
time, things might even be as you describe. But how could
we trust each other? You would tire of me before long, perhaps
before I tired of you – and what then?' He nodded towards
the spilled cup of wine she'd knocked from his hand. 'How
long would it be before you picked your moment to unburden
yourself of my company?'

After that there was silence between them, until finally she
turned aside and covered herself, pulling the gown about her
shoulders brusquely. When she faced him again it was with a
sullen look.

'Do your will, then,' she said. 'For I tire of this.'

He paused, thinking of her servant Miguel, who had offered
to help him before pulling a dagger; he thought of Charlotte
seizing the table knife and attacking him; then he glanced at the
jug of Romney wine, still more than half-full. He lifted it, picked
up the overturned cup with his other hand and filled it.

'Drink,' he said, placing it before her. 'You know how much
to take, I suspect, to make yourself sleep. Whether you choose to
drink more, I leave to you. Either way, I'll be gone.'

She stared, not understanding. 'You won't force me? Why,
when you could do so?'

Marbeck didn't answer.

'Why?' she repeated angrily. 'Do you wish me to live, or
do you expect me to take my own life? Is this mercy,
or vengeance? If the latter, I refuse you: you'll have to kill
me with your own hands, for I'll not do your work!'

But his response was a bleak smile. 'I'm tired of killing, Charlotte,' he said. 'I leave you to deal with *El Roble*, for I can hardly be of service there. I expect he'll find out, one way or another, that you failed him.'

She was rigid, sitting like a figure of wax. When he crossed the room to collect his clothes, she made no sound. He glanced back once and saw her gazing at the cup, but making no move to take it. So he left her and went outside to dress himself.

It was raining now: not a sweet refreshing shower, but an autumn drizzle that soaked his clothes. His face set tight, Marbeck reached London by early afternoon, walking doggedly. But instead of returning to his lodgings he went straight to Fleet Street, turned into Shoe Lane and arrived at the cockpit.

For a moment he stood outside, hearing the familiar noises from within. Men of all classes were passing in and out, winners and losers distinguishable merely by their manner. Nearby a ballad seller did brisk business, selling broadsides. Marbeck eyed him absently and asked what news.

'No sense in asking me, sir,' the man replied breezily. 'I don't read well, myself. Here, buy a sheet and read a ballad – the ink's barely dry, I swear it.'

'When I come out,' Marbeck said, nodding towards the cockpit.

The other groaned. 'Nay, sir – I pray you, buy now! Or you'll emerge with an empty purse, and I'll make no sale.'

But Marbeck shook his head and moved off. At the doorway he stiffened, placed a hand on his sword hilt and went inside. A short time later, having surveyed the crowd, he found the man he was seeking and approached him from behind.

'Good-day, MacNeish.'

There was a grunt, and the big man stiffened like a board. Once again, Marbeck smelled the familiar odour of coarse wool and leather. He waited for what seemed a long time until MacNeish turned, whereupon the look on Marbeck's face was enough to unsettle him.

'Good-day to you, Sands . . . Are ye come to make a wager? Yon snow-white cock's the new champion.' The Scotsman appeared affable, though his mouth was tight. When Marbeck merely eyed him he added: 'I've not seen ye in a while—'

'Indeed,' Marbeck broke in. 'What's the word in Little Scotland now?'

The big man managed a shrug. Over on the brightly-lit platform, a bout was drawing to its close, men shouting and bawling. Beneath the din the squawking of gamecocks could be heard, along with a frantic beating of wings. Finally, unhurriedly, Marbeck fixed his informant with a cold eye and said: 'I can't hear myself think in here. Will you step outside?'

MacNeish swallowed. His eyes went to Marbeck's hand, resting lightly on his sword-hilt. 'Have I a choice?' he muttered.

Outside, they stood in the same spot they had occupied many days ago. The big man's cloak lifted in the breeze, revealing a thick leather belt with a dagger in its sheath. Marbeck barely glanced at it before coming to business.

'Since we last spoke I've thought on what you said,' he began conversationally. 'I've also met Thomas Percy. But in the matter of your friend Prestall, I was unlucky. He's gone from Whitehall – dismissed, I was told.'

'Then my source of palace intelligence is gone too,' MacNeish said, somewhat quickly. 'It'll be the strong wine that did for him . . . The man never could stop himself.'

'What of Percy?' Marbeck asked sharply. 'Not someone you'd want to wrangle with, was my impression. He's away now on business for the earl . . . Is there more you could say about him?'

'There is.' MacNeish grimaced. 'Then, so could any Scotsman who remembers the days before King Jimmy took the English throne . . . when Percy was in and out of Holyrood, up and down betwixt Edinburgh and London. He it was raised the Papists' hopes, appointing himself messenger, telling of joy and toleration to come – all of it lies, but mayhap he was as eager to believe them as any of his kind. Now . . .' The big man shrugged and seemed to acquire a sudden eagerness. 'Now he's one of those seethes in private, I'd say – mixes with other Papists, angry fellows who cast about for other ways to advance their cause. The real firebrand among them is Robert Catesby, they say. A born leader . . . and if I'm honest with ye, John Sands, he's the man I'd be watching instead of Percy.'

'The name interests me,' Marbeck said, managing a casual tone. 'I believe he rents a house at Lambeth: the old Vaux manor. Have you heard that?'

'No . . . I canna say I have,' MacNeish replied.

'What of the other matters you told me about?' Marbeck persisted, leaning forward deliberately. 'The plan to attack the Scots was one – but what of the rumour of kidnap?'

MacNeish was tense now. 'Mayhap I spoke somewhat rashly,' he said. 'When I mulled it over later, I doubted anyone could get near the Royal children . . . not even Percy.'

'Even though he's a house at Westminster, within a stone's throw of the Palace?' Marbeck said dourly. 'As well as the right to come and go as he pleases?' And when the other failed to reply, he pressed him harshly. 'As for Catesby, you're right in a way. He's gathering a regiment to fight in Flanders, they say. Men like him can't very well take up arms for Popery here, so they take their fight abroad instead.'

'Fools,' MacNeish grunted, with forced vehemence. 'Let 'em drench the Dutch fields with their blood, for all the good that'll do!'

Marbeck said nothing, but looked pointedly at the big man. A moment passed, until finally the Scotsman could stand it no longer. He was about to take a step back, but Marbeck laid a hand gently on his arm.

'How much did the lady pay you, MacNeish?' he asked. 'Or was it her servant who came to seek you out?'

THIRTEEN

There was a long moment, while MacNeish gazed at Marbeck. Finally, seeing that dissembling was pointless, he spoke up.

'He was a foreigner,' he admitted, with a glance at Marbeck's hand, now on his sword-hilt. 'Spanish or Portugee . . . Claimed he had important news for you – a warning, he said. He knew we'd done business, off and on – the Lord knows how, but he did.'

'As *you* knew he was lying,' Marbeck said gently. 'About wanting to warn me, I mean.'

MacNeish gave no answer.

'In fact, it hardly matters, for he's dead now,' Marbeck told him. 'Or at least, the odds on that are better than you'll ever make in there.' He nodded towards the cockpit.

Still MacNeish was silent. Finally, he heaved a sigh and said: 'What will you do then, Sands? I've no head for guesswork.'

'But one for gathering scraps and rumours and knitting them into something you can sell,' Marbeck said coolly. 'Fool I may have been, but I thought you sold them to me and others like me, rather than to the one with the fattest purse.' Seeing the other about to speak, he lifted a hand briefly. 'I know – you're a poor man. The lady I spoke of told me: she tried to kill me, just this morning.' In a harsher tone he added: 'That's how I guessed it was you who gave me away: you're the only one who knew I lodged at Skinner's.'

Uneasily, MacNeish rubbed his beard and focused his gaze on the broadside seller – whereupon Marbeck seized the edge of his cloak and made him turn.

'Would you have seen me despatched so readily?' he demanded. 'You knew the people who sought me had some evil intent . . . Were you indifferent to it?' He waited, then: 'Or am I just another Englishman – little better than the Swaggerers who assail you in the street? What's one less?'

Another moment passed, in which the other man's silence was confirmation enough.

His mind busy now, Marbeck spoke quietly. 'You couldn't be everywhere, so I'm guessing you've had me watched,' he said. 'Indeed, I had a feeling I was being followed a while back . . . I should have paid more attention to it. How else could the lady have known I'd be at a certain house, at a certain time? Was it one of your friends from Little Scotland?'

The big man swallowed, but kept silent.

'You'd best answer me, MacNeish,' Marbeck said. 'Or I've a mind to turn you over to my masters . . . They'd hang you up by your wrists, simply on my word—'

'Enough, damn ye!' For a moment, the Scotsman's eyes flashed. But seeing Marbeck's expression, he let out a sigh; he was powerless, and he knew it. ''Twas Blue Donal watched ye,' he admitted, in a bitter tone. 'The wee man's family are near starving. They – the lady and her man – agreed to cut him in. That way I could help him, as he's helped me in the past – more than a man like you would know!'

After that, there was little left to say. The noise from the cockpit ebbed and flowed, while the broadside seller, having sold his stock, was walking away briskly.

'So you may do your worst, Sands,' MacNeish murmured, with a bleak look. 'I took the money for my wife and for others worse off than us . . . Believe that or no, as ye will. But you're right: you mean naught to me, when all's said and done. You serve a King who was my King too, but who's turned his royal back on folk like me. To the devil with him – and with you.'

There they stood: intelligencer and informant, who had once shared a bond of sorts, or so Marbeck had believed. Now, like so much else, he saw it was false. Yet despite everything, he felt no anger: only the same emptiness that had come upon him at Thomas Walden's house, when he had dropped his sword on the path.

With a last look at the Scotsman he turned and strode away, following the broadside seller back towards Fleet Street.

*   *   *

The afternoon was waning when he finally returned to the bowling-house. Skinner was nowhere about, so he ascended to his room and, with some relief, found that Curzon, too, was absent. Having checked that his winnings from the primero game were safe under a floorboard, he took some of the money for his purse and set about peeling off his damp clothes. A short while later, dry and newly attired, he was ready to go to supper . . . but suddenly checked himself as other events flooded back.

Heavily, he sat down on his bed and faced the truth: that Meriel was lost to him, and her child too; so was his informant . . . All at once, he realized just how alone he was. Moreover, he seemed reduced to wandering about London like an idler – or a fugitive, as Charlotte had described him. It struck him then that even a year ago he wouldn't have lost a man like Ferdinand Gower so easily – nor let himself be dogged through the streets by a poor Scotsman named Blue Donal. He recalled him vaguely: a nervous scarecrow of a man, sometimes seen at the cockpit – and the sort who, as Charlotte had also put it, could easily be bought.

And once again, Marbeck found himself underused, as he had been ever since the Lord Secretary had started to distance himself from the day-to-day work of his intelligencers. Now, fraught with difficulties as it was, the thought of quitting Cecil's service resurfaced with a vengeance. Had he simply lost heart? he wondered. After all, what was there to keep him in London – to keep him in England?

Restlessly, he stood up and paced the big empty room, boards creaking beneath his feet. Perhaps the doomsayers were right: the eclipses of sun and moon were portents. It had been a bad time for Marbeck, ever since he'd lost his wager at the cockpit. And despite beating Percy at cards, his actions since now looked like wasted time . . . Whereupon, at last, an image arose that he had done his best to push aside: the anguished face of Father Cornford, telling him of a disaster that was somehow imminent.

That, he realized, still troubled him: not merely Deverell's refusal to take the threat seriously, but the fact that Marbeck had failed to act on it. Then, all at once, a thought flew up that almost made him stagger. Frowning, he moved to the bed and sank down again. What if . . .?

No . . . it was ridiculous.

He gazed at the stale rushes on the floor, at Curzon's unmade pallet by the wall, then down at his shoes. The matter had irked him for days, he realized: like a toothache that wells up now and then, to remind the sufferer it needs attention. He thought again of Cornford's desperate testimony, of Deverell's scorn, and of MacNeish's dour face as he spoke of *something stirring* . . . in that matter, at least, he believed the man had spoken the truth. Then he thought of Percy, gazing at him over the rim of his goblet at Essex House. And at last he thought of John Cutler, babbling about his bees and the carts he'd seen: carts containing not barrels of ale, but gunpowder, taken to Catesby's house in Lambeth . . . which lay across the river from Westminster, within a few minutes' boat journey of Whitehall Palace.

Still he gazed down, forcing himself to countenance it. Wild thoughts sprang up of hurrying to Deverell and airing his suspicions – whereupon the man's face arose, filled with contempt. He could guess what the reaction would be. Well, then – he could go to Salisbury House and demand to see Monk, or even the Lord Secretary himself. If his fears proved groundless, he would at least have done right – Cecil would know that, whether others did or not.

On his feet again, he took up his sword and buckled it on. This could be his last act as a Crown intelligencer, he thought – in which case, whatever the outcome, he would do his utmost. Quickly, he went to take down his spare cloak – only to spin round as the door burst open and Curzon strode in.

'My dear fellow – you're here at last!' he exclaimed. 'I've been at a loss without you . . .' A sly grin appeared. 'Were you planning to go out to supper? I'd be honoured to join you. As you know, I'm somewhat short of funds, however—'

'Your pardon, Matthew,' Marbeck broke in. 'But I'm busy.'

His friend's face fell. 'Ah . . . an awkward time, is it?'

'I fear so. But here . . .' Unlacing his purse, he found a half angel and threw it. 'Go and dine, with my blessing.'

Curzon's hand shot out, but he missed the coin. Bending to

retrieve it, he muttered his thanks . . . then straightened up with a look of surprise; Marbeck was already gone.

It was almost dark, but mercifully the rain had ceased. Walking briskly through wet streets, he arrived at Paul's Stairs and found a boatman lighting his lantern. When Marbeck clambered aboard, rocking his skiff, the fellow looked round sharply. 'Steady, sir . . . Seat yourself. Where can I take you?'

Marbeck was about to name Salisbury House, but hesitated. Arriving unannounced at this hour, he realized, could be unwise . . . Monk might not even be there. And no matter how urgent his business, there was no certainty Lord Cecil would see him; the man would be surrounded, as always, by important people. Thinking fast, he looked out across the rain-swollen Thames, at the bobbing lights of small craft, and made a decision.

'Take me across to Lambeth – to Stangate Stairs.'

The current was strong, and the crossing took longer than he liked. But night had come, which was to his advantage. At the stairs he paid off the waterman and walked southwards along the path, hurrying past the well-lit entrance to Lambeth Palace. A few minutes more, and he was drawing near to the Vaux Manor again, slowing his pace. The big house was in darkness; he saw the outline of the wall where, six nights ago, he'd forced a terrified carter to tell him of the barrels stored in the cellar. Now, his mouth tight, he saw only one course of action: he would have to break in and see for himself.

He looked around swiftly: the path was deserted, while across the Thames the lights of Whitehall showed. Keeping low, he hurried forward and rounded the wall. There was no one about . . . He peered up at the house, but not a window was lit. Moving silently, he found the gate and climbed over it. He was in a stable-yard, where he paused to let his eyes adjust to the gloom. But there was still no sound: he saw a dog-kennel, yet no animal was tethered. So he moved to the main building and stopped at a rear door. Putting an ear to it, he listened, then tried it and found it locked. Finally, he knocked, darted back into shadows and waited. He waited a minute, and another, before he was satisfied: for some reason, the manor appeared to be unoccupied.

At the rear door again he hesitated; was there not even a servant within? But since events seemed to be on his side now, he pushed the thought away: breaking in had suddenly become a lot easier. Leaving the door, he worked his way round the walls and found a suitable window. Thereafter, with his bodkin and poniard, it was short work to force the casement open. A minute later he was inside the manor, moving cautiously through dusty rooms. By the time he'd found his way to the kitchens, and thence to a cellar door, all was clear: the house was deserted.

The cellar door was bolted, but the bolt was well-oiled, Marbeck found. Easing it aside, he fumbled for his tinderbox and lit a flame. By its faint light he descended the stairway into a low space that reeked of wine, smoked meat and onions. Whereupon one look round was enough: there were only two small kegs in the room, which, when their lids were lifted, proved to contain rancid bacon.

He searched, poking into every corner, but his first deduction was correct: there was no sign of the barrels he'd seen brought by night from Godstone. Peering at the floor, however, he found marks of recent activity. The barrels were here and had been moved, he was certain . . . and where else to, but across the river?

He left the cellar, bolted the door and extinguished his flame. Having left the house by the means he'd entered, he crossed the yard and climbed the gate, to stand once more on the river-bank. Here he drew deeply of the cold air and faced the appalling truth. For, why else would Catesby bring the gunpowder here – and why would he abandon his rented house, unless the stuff had now reached its intended destination?

Desperate – nay, preposterous as it was, Marbeck let the scheme unfold before him, in all its fearful dimensions. Angry Catholics like Catesby, with wealth and means; the cover story about gathering horses and armaments for the Flanders regiment; the secrecy, and the hostility displayed by Richard Evelyn at the powder mills; Cornford's anguished testimony of the tale given him under confession; the rumour of a kidnapping of one of the royal children, perhaps by Thomas Percy – another Papist. Something was indeed stirring:

rebellion. An heir to the throne taken hostage, perhaps, while well-laid plans were put in place for a new government. Which meant, of course, that the old one was first disabled, or even destroyed . . .

Only then did he recall Monk's words of more than a week ago: of two thousand men standing ready in the north.

But it was another of the man's phrases that sent him hurrying back along the riverside path towards the jetty. *Parliament prorogued . . . The opening to take place on the fifth of November, a Tuesday . . .*

The Tuesday in question, Marbeck realized, was but five days away. Today was Thursday, the last day of October: the night of Halloween.

FOURTEEN

I t took him almost an hour to hail a boat, and by the end of it he was as tense as a bowstring. The night had deepened and lights were few along the river, but at last a waterman answered his call and rowed to the landing. Concealing his agitation, Marbeck told the man to drop him at Parliament Stairs and wait there. Soon afterwards, splashing through puddles, he was making his way across the Old Palace Yard, only to be confronted by a burly sentry with a halberd. Realizing some serious bluffing was required, he assumed his most authoritative manner.

'I seek the house of Thomas Percy,' he snapped. 'I understand it's hereabouts – he's a Gentleman Pensioner.'

'I know that, sir.' The guard peered at him. 'Yet he's absent . . . Who are you, and what's your business?'

'John Sands, servant to the Lord Secretary. I've orders to go to Percy's dwelling . . . There's a message.' Marbeck tapped his pocket briskly.

'Very well, but I've told you he's not here,' the other said. 'You may look for yourself . . . The door's over there, close by the Lords' Chamber. In any case, the place isn't Percy's: it belongs to Whynniard, Keeper of the Old Palace . . . He rents it.'

With a word of thanks Marbeck moved off, but paused when the other called after him. 'Have a care, sir . . . If his servant's within, he may take you for an intruder.'

He raised a hand casually, then walked the short distance to the door, taking care not to hurry. Above him, the great stone bulk of the Lords' Chamber rose against the sky: the hall where the state opening of parliament would soon take place. But here in the yard there was an untidy huddle of smaller buildings: storehouses and lodgings for officials and servants, some of them little more than huts. At the low doorway he stopped and knocked loudly, then knocked again;

there was no answer. He knocked a third time, and still there was nothing . . . whereupon he realized his hand was on his sword.

Someone was there: he was sure of it. His old instincts, his nose for danger, hadn't deserted him. There was neither light nor sound from within, yet he knew. Glancing round to see that no one was about, he lifted the latch and, as he expected, the door didn't yield. There was one window, firmly shuttered. Glancing up he saw another, but climbing was out of the question; guards patrolled the Palace and its environs at all hours. His spirits flagging, he was considering his next step when the door opened.

In the gloom stood a tall figure, surveying Marbeck in silence. The man carried no lantern, and though there was a dim light from within the dwelling, his face was in shadow. Marbeck glimpsed the outline of a heavy beard and felt a pair of sharp eyes upon him. Drawing a quick breath, he spoke up. 'I give you good evening . . . Are you servant to Master Percy?'

'I am, sir,' came the reply. 'He's away just now and unlikely to return soon . . . May I know your business?'

His accent surprised Marbeck: as a northerner himself by birth, he recognized the Yorkshire brogue. 'My name's Sands, servant to the Earl of Salisbury,' he answered. 'May I come in?'

A pause, then: 'Do you need to do so, sir? If there's a message I may take it and give it my master when he returns.'

'Why – is there some reason you don't wish me to enter?'

'No . . . none at all.'

And yet the occupant of the house stood his ground. Marbeck gained an impression of a powerfully-built man, one who was not easily cowed; for a servant, his manner was odd. Then, glancing aside, he caught sight of something else. 'Are you aware that you break the law, wearing that?' he asked gently.

'You mean my sword? I wear it to guard my master's house. Thieves may come . . . and others, perhaps, with yet darker motives.'

A moment passed . . . and now Marbeck felt the other's will, bent forcefully against his. A lesser man might have stepped back . . . whereupon realization dawned. 'Well now, where did you soldier?' he asked, forcing a casual tone. 'Ireland, the Low Countries – or was it further afield?'

'I served God and my sovereign in Flanders, sir.'

The tone was friendly, but false: Marbeck sensed danger and remained on his guard. 'Indeed?' he answered. 'Who was your commander? It's possible I may know him.'

This time there was no reply – but something fell into place. The man had been a soldier, that much was obvious; what few would have suspected was that he'd fought not for his own country, but against it. Catholic gentlemen, as a rule, kept Catholic servants; this man was a Papist like his master, Marbeck guessed . . . and just now, he was assessing how to deal with an intruder who wouldn't go away.

At last, the man spoke up. 'My commander is dead, sir, and it unsettles me to speak of him. But I'm remiss . . . Won't you come in and warm yourself before you go? It's mighty cold out . . . and you may give me your message.'

He stepped aside, yet for Marbeck his change of manner made no difference. Ready for whatever might come, he walked past the servant into the dwelling. But once inside, doubts arose: the place was tiny.

There were just two floors; the one above was a box-like sleeping chamber, while the one below, though comfortably furnished, was devoid of anything that resembled a barrel. Nor was there any other door save the one by which he'd entered. Standing in the middle of the stuffy room, which was lit by a very small fire, he glanced at the shuttered windows that defined three sides, then at the other wall. There was no need to wonder what lay beyond that: the Lords' Chamber itself. Finally, he turned to Percy's servant and found the man smiling broadly at him.

'It's like a rabbit-hutch, sir, is it not?' he said. 'Then, 'tis but a place to sleep. My master must stay close to the Palace and his duties. His proper residence is by Holborn.'

'Of course.' Marbeck managed an air of unconcern. 'And I won't detain you longer . . .' He paused. 'What's your name, pray?'

'It's Johnson, sir – John Johnson.' The other raised his brows. 'Now, you spoke of a message?'

'Ah yes . . .' Marbeck appeared to recall it. 'My Lord
Secretary asks your master to attend him before the opening
of Parliament. He has a matter to discuss . . . What it is, I'm
not privy to.'

'Very well.' John Johnson kept his smile, but there was a
smirk beneath it: not only did he not believe a word Marbeck
had said, it seemed to say, but he also cared not a jot that
Marbeck knew it.

So he took his leave, allowing this stolid Yorkshireman to
close the door behind him. He looked back once, at the poky
little dwelling crouching beside the Lords' house. Then, with
a sigh, he walked back to the riverside.

But the night of Halloween wasn't done with him yet.

Finding his boat waiting as ordered, he had the waterman
row him downriver to Paul's Stairs, from where he walked
back to St Martins. He'd drawn a blank, both at the Vaux
Manor and at Percy's lodging, yet still the notion wouldn't
go away: somewhere, he knew, there was a large quantity of
gunpowder hidden, intended for a sinister purpose. And
though all Marbeck had was a jumble of half-truths and
suspicions, he believed that the danger was real. Just five
days hence, the King and his Privy Council, together with
the Queen and perhaps the young Prince Henry, a dozen
bishops, forty lords, courtiers and a host of lesser individuals,
would all be gathered in one place. What better opportunity
could arise to wipe out the Protestant rule of James Stuart
at one terrible stroke?

He walked faster, by Knightrider Street and Old Change,
head down. Soon he was in Martins Lane, close to his lodging,
where he slowed and finally stopped. He'd puzzled over the
matter long enough, he realized: he must go at once to Salisbury
House. Since the city gates were shut, he would return to the
river and get a boat.

At the door to Skinner's he halted, on the point of turning about . . . when something stopped him. He listened,
glancing about sharply, but saw no one. Yet the feeling was
there, once again – the sense that he was observed. At once
MacNeish's words sprang to mind: his admission that the
slippery Blue Donal had been following Marbeck. Surely,

he reasoned, by now the man would know that matters had changed? Or, perhaps he didn't . . .

He looked up at the tumbledown bowling-house. All seemed quiet, with a feeble light showing through the dirty window. Why, then, this strong sense of foreboding? He looked round again, saw the street was empty. Likely, Curzon was still out, making the most of the half-angel Marbeck had given him. Finally, he opened the door and went in, finding the downstairs room deserted. There was a guttering candle on the table, but no sign of the landlord, which was unusual at this hour . . .

'Skinner!' His voice rang to the ceiling. 'Are you here?'

No answer came, so Marbeck crossed to the stairs. Hearing nothing from the floor above, he turned impatiently and retraced his steps. He was almost at the door when he heard a faint sound from behind – and ducked instinctively, whereupon something knocked his hat off. He whirled round and saw them: three men, their faces covered with black scarves, bearing down on him.

The one with the billet, which had missed Marbeck's skull by a fraction, cursed and veered aside – but he wasn't quick enough. Marbeck's rapier flew from the scabbard, its blade glinting in the candlelight. He dealt the man a deep gash to the upper arm, causing him to cry out. But even as the billet fell from the fellow's grasp, Marbeck was crouching to face the others. Both men had swords, one already raised. Marbeck lifted his to meet it, the hilts clashing. He whipped his poniard from its sheath and took a swift back-pace, eyes darting from one to the other. Mercifully, the first assailant was down, and he could disregard him. That meant a sword-bout, one man against two – but here at last, he thought suddenly, was something he could do.

With relish, all cares forgotten, he levelled sword and dagger and prepared to fight, and if that meant death, so be it. And it was that resolve, of course, that saved him, as it had done so often. The physical advantage was with his masked opponents – but mental attitude was something apart. And quite soon, when they sensed that they faced not only a skilled swordsman, but one who seemed indifferent to his fate, their purpose began to waver.

At first the two men darted back and forth, making thrusts and feints, but each time their blows were parried. And every time Marbeck won a stroke he wielded his poniard, forcing them to dodge sharply. The blade of his rapier was soon dulled, yet his strength took both assailants by surprise. Soon there were muttered oaths and grunts of frustration . . . then came the first cry of pain as one man's shoulder was pierced. Blood showed on his coat as, panting, he lunged again, but found the stroke deflected. And another disadvantage soon told: in their increasingly desperate efforts to down their victim, each man at times got in the other's way.

For Marbeck, who seemed not only to anticipate their moves but also to adjust his tactics by the moment, their difficulty begged to be exploited. Seizing a chance, he made what looked like a clumsy stroke, uttering a curse. Whereupon one of his opponents hurried to make a counter-thrust, exposing his side . . . which was enough.

Marbeck's poniard sank between the man's ribs, deep into his vitals. He wrenched the blade free as, with a spluttering cry, the fellow sank to his knees. His accomplice wavered briefly, but that too was enough. Knocking his sword aside, Marbeck lunged again, thrusting hard into his stomach. With a great gasp the man sat down heavily, staring at the blood that spurted forth. At which point Marbeck lowered his own sword and, with a rapid movement, leaned down and tore the scarf from his face.

But the assailant was a stranger, the sort that could be seen in London streets at any time: just another discharged soldier, a victim of the King's peace with Spain, who had no skills for hire save his fighting ability. Leaving him, Marbeck stepped over to the other man, who lay on his back, and saw at once that his wound was fatal. He bent and removed the scarf, to reveal a grey-faced ruffian of similar stamp, staring up in fear.

'Good Christ . . . you've gone and finished me,' he muttered.

'As you meant to finish me,' Marbeck said.

He was breathing fast, but growing calmer. The exhilaration of the fight was fading, to be replaced by a cauldron of feelings: relief, anger, curiosity – and unease as the other events of the day came flooding back. Whereupon, remembering the third man, he swung round – and found him gone.

Scanning the room, he was about to go to the door when he heard a groan from the other side of the table. He moved around it and found his first assailant – the only non-swordsman – sitting with his back to a table-leg, nursing his arm and shaking. His sleeve was soaked with blood, while his eyes, wide with terror, gazed into Marbeck's . . . and then, the penny dropped.

'Skinner?'

In amazement, and with rising anger, Marbeck dropped to one knee beside the man. He seized the edge of his scarf and pulled it down – to reveal the face of his landlord, milk-pale beneath his unkempt beard. For a moment neither spoke, and the only sound was that of the other injured men, one wheezing, the other moaning pitifully. Then Skinner's tongue appeared, to wet his dry lips. With a sickly attempt at a smile, he said: 'You wouldn't, would you, Tucker? Those bastards threatened me . . . I'd no choice!'

'How much did they pay you?' Marbeck asked dryly.

'Nothing!' Skinner shook his head quickly. 'D'you think I'd have taken it, if they had? You're my tenant—'

'Oh, I think you took it,' Marbeck broke in. 'And I doubt you needed much persuasion.' He peered into his landlord's eyes, making him flinch . . . and a suspicion rose. 'Who else have you given my whereabouts to, lately?' he asked. 'It's plain that some people knew where to find me – even though you and I had an agreement, remember? No questions, private stabling for my horse, and a handsome rent for that shabby room . . .'

'Why, yes!' Skinner nodded eagerly. 'And I swear on my beloved's life, I've told no one. I said naught even when your friend Knight came here, though it's plain as daylight he was running from something. The only ones who've come are that boy with the message and that flabby fellow who waited for you, a few days back . . .'

'What about those two?' Marbeck indicated his assailants.

'In God's name, Tucker, I never set eyes on 'em before,'

Skinner told him. 'They came a couple of hours back . . .' He hesitated, but seeing Marbeck's suppressed anger, he began to babble.

'See, now, I meant no evil . . . Very well, I'll confess they paid me to knock you over the pate. But they swore there'd be nothing worse than that . . . They had a bone to pick with you, they said – money owed. They were going to take you away. They even had a warrant—'

'Did you see it?' Marbeck snapped, to which the landlord's expression was answer enough. 'No – you didn't ask to. But then, you've wanted rid of me for some time, haven't you? So when you saw the chance to do it, and earn a sum into the bargain, you grabbed it. You're a consummate grabber, Skinner.'

He drew a deep breath and stood up, while on the floor Skinner quaked. But when Marbeck stepped away to survey the scene of carnage, his landlord spoke up again quickly. 'See . . . why don't you go, and I'll say nothing? You weren't here – I never heard of you. I'll tell the constables these coves came to rob me. They can't counter that, can they . . .? Not if you finish 'em off.'

Slowly, Marbeck turned to look down at him. 'Finish them off?'

'Aye – why not? They're murderers, aren't they? Though I didn't know that . . . I swear I didn't!' Skinner was wheedling, desperation in his gaze.

Marbeck eyed him without expression. 'So: I end their lives, and you spin a tale about robbery, is that what you propose? How then would you explain their deaths? Claim you defeated two sturdy swordsmen, all by yourself?'

'No . . . I've another idea!' With a groan, Skinner raised himself and managed to stand up. Leaning against the table he faced Marbeck, clutching his wounded arm. 'We can blame Knight – arrange matters so they tell a different tale. I know how to make it stick . . . Come now, what say you?'

Yet still Marbeck stared, until the other looked away. 'I've met some miserable wretches in my time, Skinner,' he said finally. 'But you take the prize. Do you think I'd wait for my friend, kill him, then arrange his body to look as if he died fighting . . .?'

'No, no!' Skinner cried. 'You don't have to ki—' He caught his breath, clamping his mouth tight, and tried to turn it to a cough. Bending low, he hawked over the table-top, but the performance was wasted.

Marbeck stepped forward and seized his wrist, making him grunt with pain. 'Where's Knight, Skinner?' he breathed, bending close. 'What did you mean, I don't have to kill him?' And when his only reply was a whimper, he grabbed the other's upper arm and squeezed it.

This time Skinner screamed in agony. Veering aside, trying vainly to loosen Marbeck's grip, he squirmed like a rabbit. Finally, he was in tears, the pain too much to bear. 'He's upstairs!' he yelled. 'They did for him first . . . They thought he was you. I tried to tell 'em, I swear I did . . . For God's sake, Tucker – spare me, please!'

The last word became a cry as his arm was released at last. Slumping to the floor, he wept pitifully, while Marbeck turned away silently, walked to the staircase and ascended.

But even before he reached the half-open door of the chamber they had shared briefly, he knew what he would find. So it was more with a crippling sadness than with shock that he entered and approached the pallet beside which Matthew Curzon, recently knighted, lay in a bloody heap.

All debts are paid . . .

The phrase came to mind as he looked down at the handsome face of his friend, peaceful in death. Then, with dismay, he realized something else: Curzon had possessed no sword with which to defend himself, nor even a dagger. The one had been pawned somewhere, while the other was in a closet in Whitehall Palace, where he'd left it when Marbeck took him to freedom.

FIFTEEN

It was the first of November, a bitter morning, and Marbeck seethed with anger. Though one thing, at least, was in his favour: it wasn't Deverell he faced in the chamber by the Jewel Tower, but Levinus Monk, who had returned at last.

The spymaster was subdued, even contrite; he had grace enough for that. But the air of harassed impatience, which seemed to be part of his nature these days, was unchanged. He sat by the table, with its mass of papers that had also become a permanent fixture, eyes lowered. Marbeck stood over him, controlling himself with an effort.

'It's most regrettable, about Curzon,' Monk said.

Marbeck said nothing.

'I'll have the bowling alley cleared,' the other added. 'There's a solution: the place will burn down, destroying everything in it. It'll probably be a blessing, even to its owner . . .' He looked up. 'What did you do with him?'

'I left him – alive,' Marbeck answered. 'But Curzon's body is in the upper room.'

'It'll be taken to his father,' Monk said quickly. 'There was a fight, over debts unpaid . . . He'll believe that.'

'Very tidy.' Marbeck's voice was flat.

'It has to be.' There was warning in the other's tone. 'And it's not I who's been remiss here, I might add.'

'There's no need to add anything,' Marbeck said. 'Even you couldn't load me with more remorse than I have already.'

Monk sighed. 'Let's not tread this path,' he said wearily. 'You know the hazards, better than most. Our work's too important for sentiment when the safety of the realm is at stake—'

'Ah yes . . . the safety of the realm.' Marbeck looked coldly at him. 'Well, I've told you all I know: given a day-by-day account of all I've done since I saw Cutler – and yet, you seem ready to dismiss my intelligence once again.' In this, however, he was being less than truthful: he had left out the business of Charlotte de Baume and the ease with which she'd located him. That, something told him, was best left for another occasion.

'Of course I don't dismiss it,' the spymaster said testily. 'Do you think I've been idle myself, this past week? I've hardly slept – nor has My Lord Secretary. Now that the King's returned from Royston, his shoulders are loaded with business. The welfare of the monarch and his family is paramount – do you doubt that?'

'I do not. Yet what of the gunpowder? What of the actions of Catesby and his friends—'

'What actions?' Monk retorted. 'As far as Catesby goes, there are none that surprise me. Today is the Feast of All Saints – Papists everywhere will celebrate it in secret. Yet wherever they do so, one or more of our people will be hidden among the worshippers. Hence, has it not occurred to you, Marbeck, that if men like those were planning anything as cataclysmic as you suggest, someone might notice it?'

'For all I know they have done,' Marbeck replied. 'I've had no opportunity to ask, being somewhat busy . . .'

'Indeed?' Monk's mouth flattened into the familiar thin line. 'Then what of Thomas Percy – the man I told you to follow? Or were you merely going to tell me that he's on business in the North for his lord, the Earl of Northumberland?'

'I did know that – as you suspected,' Marbeck said, after a moment. 'And in view of all else, Percy's movements seemed of lesser import. I ask again – what of the gunpowder?'

'Well, what of it?'

Summoning what patience he retained, Marbeck spoke levelly, spelling it out for the second time. 'I followed it from Godstone to Lambeth, to the house rented by Catesby. It was stored in the cellar: not one cartload, but half a dozen, accumulated over weeks, according to my informant. That makes thirty barrels at least, by my reckoning. Now it's gone – all of it. And here we are just across the river, a short boat journey away in Westminster . . .'

'Where you have failed to find it. And I haven't noticed a heap of barrels lying around anywhere, now I think upon it.'

Monk wore his driest expression. 'What do you propose – that we cordon off the entire district, Palace and all, and search every room? That would cause fear and outrage . . . The Lord Secretary wouldn't countenance it, let alone the King.'

Marbeck drew a long breath; Monk could be immovable at times. But there was something else in the man's manner, he sensed: could it be unease?

'Would a discreet search not be wise?' he said at last. 'Just to be certain, at least in the Lords' Chamber and its surrounds. In view of the magnitude of the risk . . .'

'You speak of risk now?' Monk broke in. 'By the heavens, Marbeck, you've a nerve. My life revolves around risk – as does My Lord Secretary's. Not for himself, but for our country: its King and Council, and all who are loyal. Anyone who might pose a threat to the realm is being observed. Your task is to watch Percy – and I'll take neither advice nor instruction from you.'

Silence followed. Angry yet helpless, Marbeck was on the point of abandoning his efforts when a notion came up that he couldn't resist airing. 'Might I ask where you were back in 1587, Monk?' he enquired gently.

The other frowned. 'What do you mean?'

'I was at Cambridge . . . A youth of seventeen. London was far away then, yet I still recall the news that brought alarm, even to our cloistered little world. That was when we heard of a wild scheme to blow up Queen Elizabeth with gunpowder, placed in a room below her private chamber. Do you recall it?'

And when Monk refused to answer, he added: 'Hence my suggestion of a discreet search . . . I leave the notion with you. Now I'll locate Percy and watch him like a hawk; at least until the opening of Parliament is past and all is well. Thereafter my work will be done, won't it?'

Turning abruptly, he went to the door, half-hoping that the spymaster would call him back. But no word came, and he was soon outside.

The cold enveloped him, the air as heavy as lead. But he walked, as always, to work off his anger and to reflect. He had begun the day in temporary lodgings, hired late the previous night in a room above the Duck and Drake in the Strand; spending another night at Skinner's was impossible. He'd had hopes when he rose, of being believed; now desperate notions flew into his mind, only to be dismissed. Monk's intransigence not only infuriated him: it also dismayed him. The man was shrewd enough, as calculating at times as Lord Cecil himself . . . Why, then, this reluctance to give Marbeck's suspicions due credence?

Quickening his pace, he strode along King Street. To his right sprawled the Palace, an untidy jumble of buildings large and small. On his left were houses and cottages, the Royal Cockpit and the King's Head alehouse . . . He halted. And because no better idea occurred, he left the road and went to the inn. Frequented by Whitehall servants and hangers-on, it offered a temporary refuge. Soon he was in a corner nursing a mug of spiced ale, and at last he sagged, staring down at the scarred table.

'Well . . . what sorry sight is this?'

He looked up to see Deverell, a mug in his fist, gazing sardonically at him. Without replying, he resumed staring at the table. But seeing the man was about to take a stool beside him, he said: 'I don't want company.'

'I see that,' Deverell said, and sat down anyway. After a short silence, he added: 'Can we at least drink and share our troubles?'

'My thanks, but no,' Marbeck answered. 'And I wouldn't try using your authority just now . . . I'm in a poor humour.'

'You and I both,' the other said. When Marbeck ignored him, he added: 'Are you thrust on to the sidelines, too?'

Lifting his head, Marbeck eyed him. 'Don't pretend you don't know it already. You're Monk's lackey, when all's said and done. Is that why you're here? Now that he's back, has he thrown you out of his cosy little chamber?'

'Out of the chamber, and out of office,' came the reply. 'In short, Marbeck, I've little authority to wield. I'm supposed to kick my heels until there's another priest to find, or some such.'

In spite of himself, Marbeck's curiosity surfaced. 'What happened to the one from Great Willoughby?' he asked, after a moment. Once again, the haggard face of Father Cornford rose in his mind.

Deverell grimaced. 'He's in the Clink for the present, with others of his kind. It's a haven for Papists; they celebrate Mass, hear confessions, dine like princes. Too many people on the outside to succour them, send in food . . . even money.' He shook his head.

'No doubt you'd put a stop to that, if you could,' Marbeck said, but the other refused to rise to the bait. Instead, to Marbeck's discomfort, he laid a hand on his arm.

'Did you find that fellow Prestall? The Careys' servant?'

'No, I didn't,' Marbeck replied, remembering. 'He's been dismissed . . . Too fond of the drink, I heard.'

'Then you heard wrongly.' Deverell spoke low. 'He's dead. He was found floating in the river, his head caved in. They say it was a fall, but I'd wager it wasn't.'

Marbeck frowned. 'Would you, indeed?'

'So, what might you think?' Deverell let go of his arm.

'I'd think that, having a loose tongue, he could have posed a risk to someone,' Marbeck said, after some reflection. 'In which case, mayhap you should reconsider the kidnap threat.'

'I've done that,' his fellow-intelligencer said. 'I was poking around, making a few enquiries . . . until our good master returned and trampled all over my efforts.'

His hostility gone, Marbeck stared at him.

'And so, you may have been right all along,' Deverell went on, 'even if not about young Duke Charles. It seems our friend Thomas Percy stops often in the Midlands, at the houses of men of his faith. For some reason he often lingers by Coventry: close to Coombe Abbey, the seat of Lord Harrington – where lives a certain royal princess.'

'That could fit,' Marbeck said, with growing unease.

'And now that he's returned to London,' Deverell began, at which Marbeck blinked.

'He's back here, already?'

'Along with everyone else of any rank, in time for the opening of Parliament,' Deverell replied. 'Since he's a Gentleman Pensioner, such an action is perfectly normal.'

'And yet . . .?'

'And yet something stinks, like a dockside shambles. You smelled it first, but I wouldn't listen to you.'

In surprise, and no small relief, Marbeck met his eye. 'Then, would you care to listen now, to what I told Monk less than half an hour ago?'

Deverell nodded.

They waited until evening before carrying out their task. It was straightforward enough and unlikely to arouse suspicion. Deverell had been seen about Westminster, even if the true nature of his position was unknown. Marbeck was less familiar here, but both could rely on their appearance as men of some status. Having spent the day in discussion they were ready: two unlikely allies, in an unsanctioned operation to discover a cache of gunpowder – enough to blow up the Parliament Chamber.

'I mentioned the vault,' Deverell said as the two of them walked past Westminster Hall, hatted and cloaked. A pair of gentlemen on some late business, they attracted only passing looks from those who were about. 'It's the first place I'd search . . . It's at ground-floor level and runs the entire length of the building. A woman named Mistress Bright, as I recall, leased it from John Whynniard to store coals in. But she's gone, and someone else rents it now – I don't know who. Perhaps we could find out.'

They passed the Hall, in the lane between the two gates, with St Margaret's church on their right. But as they walked under the second one Marbeck slowed. 'Whynniard? But I heard that name, last night.'

'He's Keeper of the Old Palace,' Deverell explained – then, seeing Marbeck's expression, he stopped.

'He's also Thomas Percy's landlord here,' Marbeck said.

They stared at each other. From the river came the cries of watermen, still plying their trade in the dark. Between the river and where they stood was the Lords' Chamber. Without speaking they started off again, Deverell leading the way round the building to a pair of heavy doors. Finding these locked, they halted. 'This is the vault,' he said, his brow furrowing. 'And it isn't even guarded.'

Marbeck looked up at the tall windows: the Lords' Hall itself, on the first floor. Turning, he peered along the river front to the Parliament Stairs, where a torch burned. Almost directly opposite, as he'd reminded himself already, was Lambeth. He faced Deverell, who nodded.

'It would be easy enough to slip across, in a covered boat,' Deverell said quietly. 'Distract the sentries perhaps, while you unload your barrels at the stairs and roll them up to the doors. You'd need to make several trips, but if anyone asked, you could say they were kegs of wine or ale, and brandish a key . . .'

'Is there another way in?' Marbeck asked. Excitement stole over him: he was close to a discovery . . . He could feel it.

'From above,' Deverell said. 'The Great Chamber itself. And I think it's time we stopped padding about like tomcats, don't you?'

They walked around the building, through the Cotton Garden and thence through the Painted Chamber, deserted just now. But at the main entrance to the Lords', it was a different story. Guards stood about, some smoking their pipes. When the two official-looking gentlemen approached, a pair of sentries moved to block their way, crossing halberds.

'Who comes here?' a sergeant in a buff coat demanded, striding up. 'Pray, state your purpose.'

'William Catherwood, servant to the Lord Secretary,' Deverell answered haughtily. Marbeck followed suit, giving his John Sands alias.

'We wish to inspect the state chamber,' Deverell added. 'Ensure that all is in order for His Majesty's arrival on Tuesday. There may be a daily inspection, from now on.'

'Your orders, sir?' the sergeant enquired in a phlegmatic tone. 'You have written instructions, I assume?'

'You'll assume no such thing,' Deverell snapped. 'I can get one and return, of course, but I wouldn't want to disturb My Lord at this hour. He'd want to know who was the cause of it, if I did.'

'True enough, Master Catherwood,' Marbeck put in as the sergeant blinked. 'I could wait here while you go to Salisbury House, in case there's a change of guard.'

'One moment, sirs, if you please . . .' The sergeant looked at each of them in turn, but the battle was already won. Like most Crown intelligencers, Deverell too was a consummate actor when he chose. Without expression, he and Marbeck stood their ground as the man stepped aside and spoke to his fellows. Other guards were looking in their direction, but no difficulty seemed imminent. Finally, the sergeant faced them and said: 'You may look about the hall, sirs, but I'll accompany you – if that's to your liking.' And since his expression said clearly that he was coming along in any case, Deverell agreed. A few moments later a small door set within one of the larger doors was opened, and the three men stepped through.

The sergeant had a lantern, which he raised as they entered. The Lords' Chamber was spacious, its tall windows letting in a little moonlight. Here stood the King's throne on a dais, with benches around it on three sides and tables for officials. The place was still and silent, like a vast, empty church. Deverell and Marbeck, with the sergeant on their heels, walked its full length, making a show of looking around. As they expected there was nothing to see; their real destination lay beneath their feet, reached by a door at the far end. But when Deverell said he wished to inspect the vault, their guide became obstructive.

'That's private, sir . . . rented out to reputable citizens, for storage and such. No one can get down there without a key – which I don't have.'

'Indeed?' The spymaster looked him over until the man bristled. 'And why is that?'

'Because it's private, as I've said. You may try the door for yourself, if it please you.'

'I'm not accusing you of lying, sergeant,' Deverell said dryly, 'only of incompetence. We speak of the King's safety here: his, and that of the entire Council. If I were a Papist assassin who wished to conceal himself somewhere close by, the vault would be one place I'd choose – wouldn't you?'

'Perhaps I would, sir,' came the stiff reply. 'And no doubt it will be checked, closer to the opening . . . It's days off, yet.'

Impatient as ever, Deverell was about to make some retort, but feeling a tug on his sleeve he checked himself. Both he and the sergeant turned as Marbeck said: 'I have a solution to our difficulty, sergeant. If I can open the door, will you let me go down and take a peek? Master Catherwood can remain with you, as a guarantor of my good will. I'm no assassin . . . I'll even leave my sword here. It will take but a moment, then we can return to My Lord Secretary and speak of your willingness to aid us . . . your worthiness, as a protector of the King's person.'

Beside him, Deverell breathed out in quiet approval. The sergeant, however, didn't like it; nor, it seemed, was he susceptible to flattery. But when he began to ask the obvious question – how he intended to open a locked door – Marbeck was ready for him.

'It's a skill I learned in Queen Elizabeth's service, in Ireland,' he said. 'I helped storm a few strongholds, by the simple means of picking locks.' Reaching in his pocket, he drew out his bodkin and showed it. There was a moment . . . then at once the man's expression changed.

'You served in Ireland?'

'At Yellow Ford, Kinsale . . . and other places.' Marbeck put on a grim smile. 'Need I add more?'

'Nay, you needn't.' The man lowered his gaze and, after a moment, held out the lantern. 'Do as you wish, sir. I'll wait here as you say . . .' He glanced at Deverell. 'If you agree?'

'Of course.' Hiding his relief, Deverell nodded.

So, after unbuckling his sword and laying it aside, Marbeck left them both and went to the vault door, where he set down the light. Whereupon, for a fleeting moment, he saw himself at the gates of the Walden House in Crutched Friars . . .

He forced the thought aside and busied himself. It didn't take long; the lock was old, like the door itself, its hinges stained with rust. There was a final, muffled click; he turned the handle and the door squealed open. Catching up the lantern, he raised it to reveal a set of stone stairs. Without looking back, he descended; though he didn't know it, his persistence was about to be rewarded.

The vault was broad: a great, cobble-floored room with arches at either side. Down the centre ran a row of thick pillars, supporting the floor of the Lords' Chamber above. The place was dirty and littered with debris: bird-droppings, twigs, lumps of coal. A pile of empty sacks lay against one alcove, a few wooden planks by another. There were smells too: of old timber, damp mortar and coal dust, along with the ever-present reek of the river. Lifting the lantern high, Marbeck walked slowly down the middle of the room . . . and halted. Before him, spilling out of one alcove, was a great heap of brushwood tied in bundles, almost blocking his way. Beyond it, he realized, was the entrance where he and Deverell had stood.

And suddenly, his pulse was racing. He put down the lantern and took off his hat and cloak, placing them on the floor. Then he stepped forward, seized the nearest bundle of faggots and pulled it aside. Another followed, and another . . . He began to work faster, raising dust as he threw each one down; then he stopped and took an involuntary step back. Heart pounding, he caught up the lantern and lifted it . . . and realized he was almost shaking.

He had uncovered a great hoard of barrels: three dozen or so, packed tightly together. Moreover . . . He raised his eyes and let out a breath.

Where they stood, he guessed, was more or less directly beneath the King's throne.

SIXTEEN

In Marbeck's chamber at the Duck and Drake, somewhat shaken, the two intelligencers sat by the light of a single candle. They had turned the matter about, examined it from every side, yet the facts were unavoidable. Moreover, there was the dreadful knowledge that, apart from the movers of the terrible plot, it seemed likely they were the only ones who knew about it.

'I'll say it again: I commend your nerve,' Deverell murmured. 'None would have guessed what you'd found, when you told the sergeant all was safe and well.'

Marbeck barely heard him. In his mind's eye he still saw the truncated pyramid of barrels, disappearing as he replaced its covering of brushwood. At least, he thought, he'd kept enough presence of mind to conceal his discovery. Finally, he looked up. 'So . . . do we go to Monk, or over his head to the Lord Secretary?'

His companion made no immediate answer. The enormity of the discovery was still sinking in, along with the burden of responsibility both men now carried. Taking up the bottle of ale he'd brought from the inn, Marbeck drank and passed it to him.

'You do realize,' Deverell said, after taking a restorative drink, 'that were you and I of a different religion – and eager for a change of government – we need only go about our business and say nothing?'

'Except that the vault might be inspected soon. In which case, we're traitors for not reporting what we know.'

'But you already told the sergeant that all's clear – so we might appear traitors anyway. Though it's more likely no one will trouble themselves to search the place . . . They can't even be bothered to guard the vault doors.'

'True enough,' Marbeck allowed.

'Or even . . .' Deverell gave a snort. 'Were we wicked

enough, we could seek Catesby and his friends and throw in our lot with them – demand handsome fees for our silence.'

'We could,' Marbeck said dryly. 'Instead, we'll take the whole tale to our masters and relieve ourselves of this weight.' Then he frowned: Deverell looked as if he were trying not to laugh.

'We might be deemed heroes,' he muttered. 'We save the lives of the King and Queen, the Privy Council and half of England's nobility – we could find ourselves knighted.'

Marbeck met his gaze . . . and he too suppressed a laugh. 'At the least,' he said. 'In time, we might even take our seats in the very building we've saved from destruction . . . How does Lord Deverell sound?'

'By the Christ.' Suddenly, Deverell looked alarmed. 'I believe you're almost serious.'

'No more than you,' Marbeck replied, gazing levelly at him. 'Don't think I haven't been tempted to turn traitor. I was once offered a villa in Barbary, with servants and a harem.'

'Perhaps you should have accepted,' the other said, with a touch of sourness.

'I felt as if a madness had come over me in that vault,' Marbeck mused, after a short silence. 'It was like a vision; nothing I've seen before compares with it. And to think I reminded Monk of the time someone tried to blow up the Queen's bedchamber – even then, I didn't countenance something like it happening again.'

'In God's name, who would?' Deverell shook his head.

They sat in silence again, while from below the noise of the inn rose. For Marbeck, the England he knew teetered on the brink of disaster. There was little doubt that, were such a quantity of gunpowder set off by someone who knew how, the effect would be, in Monk's word, cataclysmic. King James would certainly be killed, and many of those near to him. In the fear and mayhem that followed, the rebels, as he now thought of them, would be able to mount the rising they'd no doubt planned; within days, the nation could be plunged into a civil war. He drew a breath and glanced up to see Deverell watching him.

'I know,' his fellow-intelligencer said. 'It's almost beyond my ken, too.'

'That servant of Percy's . . .' Marbeck frowned. 'Calls himself Johnson. He's an ex-soldier, and a bold one – and he resides within yards of the place. He could be the one charged with setting the explosion.'

'You're not thinking of confronting him?' Deverell said sharply. 'We'd need evidence.'

'I wasn't,' Marbeck assured him. 'We have a few days yet . . . We should do nothing to arouse suspicion until we've talked to Cecil – or Monk, in the first instance. He can hardly refuse to listen now, if we both make report. If he did, I'd drag him to the Lords' myself and show him the—'

'No – not Monk.' Deverell cut him short. 'I don't trust him, Marbeck . . . Indeed, I wonder now if I ever did.'

Marbeck eyed him. 'Do you care to elaborate?'

The other got up restlessly and took a few paces about the small chamber. 'Let's start with Prestall. Monk told you he would interrogate him, didn't he? Instead, the fellow turns up dead in the Thames. And more: why was Monk so ready to dismiss your report of Catesby's actions? I'll admit I was sceptical too, but . . .' He frowned. 'Now I piece it together, it could look as if the man's blocked both your investigations and mine. He told you to go off and watch Percy, while—'

'The men who were waiting to kill me,' Marbeck broke in. 'I wonder why they came there, even though I've realized how they knew where I lodged.' He drew a breath. 'I should have forced them to tell me who sent them. But after finding Curzon's body, I'd little thought for much else.'

'It's too late for regrets,' Deverell said impatiently. 'Think now – what do your instincts tell you?'

'Not a great deal, on the face of it,' Marbeck replied. 'If any man's loyal, I'd swear Monk is . . . or so I always thought. He almost worships Cecil . . . He'd lay down his life for the man.'

'As would we all,' Deverell replied. 'Especially since . . .' He hesitated. 'Especially since our Lord Secretary makes sure he has enough leverage to force each of us to do his bidding.' He turned about, standing by the window in the dim light.

Marbeck gazed at him, then nodded. 'You too?'

'Oh yes . . . An indiscretion, years ago, that could have cost me my reputation.' His companion managed a grim smile. 'Some say the Earl of Salisbury's more clockwork than flesh and blood; that every man – especially his agents – is a commodity to be evaluated and docketed. If it's any comfort, Marbeck, he's always kept you in the cubbyhole marked *highly valued.*'

They fell silent again; an unspoken understanding passing between intelligencers. Finally, Deverell sat down on the bed and let out a sigh. 'So: it's our cool-headed Lord Secretary we must go to. Tell him everything – including our suspicions about Monk. He'll listen – he's too clever not to. And when he inspects the vault for himself . . .' He shrugged. 'Then, it's out of our hands.'

Marbeck had been gazing at the floor. 'Something Monk said struck an odd note with me,' he admitted, looking up. 'After batting aside my suspicions, he said he hadn't noticed a stack of barrels anywhere about Westminster . . . and yet that's precisely what we've discovered.'

Deverell look uneasy. 'Is it possible?' he said, frowning again. 'Could he truly be a part of something so dreadful? It's hard to believe – the risks of failure are terrible . . .'

'As they've always been,' Marbeck put in. 'Think of the conspiracies of the last twenty years. Babbington, Essex . . . just two of those who paid with their lives. And those more recent . . . Raleigh languishes in the Tower still, half-mad with protesting his innocence.'

'I know . . .' Deverell sighed. 'Well then: shall we wait for dawn, then go to Salisbury House?'

'Can you delay until later in the morning?' Marbeck asked suddenly. And when the other showed surprise, he added: 'Of course we'll attend Cecil. But if you'll give me an hour or two, I've a mind to go elsewhere first.'

Deverell gave a start. 'You can't mean to talk to that whoreson priest again?' he demanded. 'What's the use? I'll admit he as good as told you he knew about this plot, given under the confessional. But what could he add now that we don't already know?'

'I'm not sure he can add anything,' Marbeck replied; then he frowned. 'And I doubt hard questioning would work, even if you had time to put him to it.'

'I wasn't going to suggest it,' the other muttered. 'His kind seem to think pain is their friend . . . that it brings them closer to paradise.'

'I still think it worth an attempt,' Marbeck persisted. 'If I learn nothing, we've lost nothing. You could wait here, and I'll return by eleven of the clock . . .'

'No.' Deverell shook his head firmly. 'I follow your reasoning, but I won't delay – the matter eats at me like a canker. I'll go to Cecil, make full report and tell him you'll attend him later to confirm what I've said.'

'Very well.' Marbeck let out a breath. 'I was about to add that we should try and get some rest, but . . .'

Deverell threw him a withering look.

So at last, after the most troubled night he could remember in years, Marbeck left the inn in the grey light of early morning and walked to the Ivy Stairs. Hailing the first boatman to appear, he ordered the man to take him across the river and down to St Mary Overies. From here it was a short walk to the Clink prison, where he presented himself to the gatekeeper. Without ceremony, he pressed a half-angel into the man's hand.

'I'm one of faith, who wishes to see Father Cornford,' he said, sounding as nervous as he could. 'I believe he'll hear my confession . . . as I believe you're a merciful man, master. There would be further garnish when I leave . . . An hour would serve me.'

The warder looked him up and down, even as he pocketed the coin. As hard-faced turnkeys went, this one was a cut above most. But it was well-known that, for a fee, anything was available at the Clink; bribes were customary, even demanded. 'Might I know your name, master?' he asked. 'If another takes my place he should know, so he may let you out.' A sly smile appeared. 'We wouldn't want you to be detained in error.'

'It's Tucker,' Marbeck said. 'Lawrence Tucker.'

A shout startled him. He looked round and saw the barred grating at street level, through which several dirty hands stretched towards him. At once a chorus of pleading arose, the wretched inmates begging for alms and food: anything that might bring fleeting relief to their misery. Steeling himself, he waited for the turnkey to unlock the outer door, then passed through . . . and soon gagged at the stench that assailed him.

For, like most of London's gaols, the Clink was a hell-hole. Marbeck hadn't had reason to visit the place in years, and even he was taken aback by the conditions. Having passed through another door, where a second warder eyed him expectantly before pocketing his own fee, he found himself in the main chamber, crowded with prisoners of both sexes. It was filthy, with rank straw underfoot. All the inmates were ragged and dirty, some half-naked for want of basic attire. At once he was surrounded, men shouting in his face; soon he had no choice but to draw his poniard and drive them away. Yet women still clung to him, pawing at his good clothes, offering him any favour he chose. Other prisoners were sitting or lying against the walls, many of them sick. Finally, overwhelmed by the sea of human wretchedness, he took one woman's arm and drew her aside.

'I seek Father Cornford,' he said, raising his voice above the din. 'Here's a penny for you . . .'

But no sooner had he produced the coin than the pathetic creature grabbed it and tore herself free, letting out a shout of laughter. Gritting his teeth, he looked about and settled on a barefoot man, as thin as a rake, who stood grinning at him.

'The priests . . . Where are they held?' Marbeck demanded. 'There's a penny if you tell me.'

'Priests?' The man's grin vanished. 'What have you brought – money, food?' At once he too was pawing at Marbeck's clothing, obliging him to seize the fellow and hold him at arm's length.

'The Jesuit priests,' he began . . . but there was a squeal of hinges behind him. Looking round, he saw a door open and yet another turnkey appear.

'Come through, sir,' the man said, assessing Marbeck's status at a glance. 'If you can pay the entrance fee, I'll convey you.' Then, his manner altered in a trice, he turned on the skinny inmate and dealt him a blow with his open hand, sending the fellow reeling away.

Somewhat breathless, Marbeck stepped through the door and heard it shut. He was in a vaulted passageway lit by tallow lamps, one of the oldest parts of the building. The stench was as bad, though the noise had diminished somewhat. He saw dark archways and more doors, then stiffened as the turnkey laid a heavy hand on his shoulder.

'Shall we say a shilling, sir?'

Having found the coin, Marbeck held it out. 'I seek Father Cornford,' he began, but the other was already nodding.

'I know why you've come, though I've not seen you before.' He surveyed the newcomer briefly, then: 'They lodge together . . . pass freely between each other's cells. Go and conduct your business, then ask for me – Plainstaff. I'll have another shilling to take you back.'

'How many are here?' Marbeck asked.

'Priests?' The man shrugged. 'I haven't counted . . . Are we done?'

So Marbeck paid him and was let through a third door, the din of the main prison lessening at last. Here the change was marked: there was a sense of calm and some attempt at cleanliness. And two further things struck him: one was a low murmur of voices, exclusively male; the other was the smell of incense. Left to his own devices, he walked down the passage to where several barred doors stood open and was confronted by a cassocked figure emerging from one of them, who stopped in surprise.

'Your pardon, sir . . .' The elderly man who faced him was no Jesuit but a Marian priest, one of a rare breed who were now being replenished by the secret infiltrators from the Continent. Eyeing Marbeck, he asked: 'You . . . Are you one of the true faith?'

'I'm looking for Father Cornford. Is he nearby?'

'Ah . . . I see.' The other nodded towards one of the open cell doors. 'I'm Father Ambrose – you've no message for me, then?'

'I regret not.'

The priest gave a thin smile and moved off. Subdued, Marbeck walked past one cell, where another priest knelt with bowed head, and approached the one Father Ambrose had indicated. As he did so he slowed, unsure what to expect. At the doorway he stopped abruptly as a black-robed figure appeared to block his way: he had forgotten how tall Father Cornford was.

'Why . . . Master Tucker, is it?' The man stared at him. 'Of all those I might have hoped to see, you must be the last.'

Marbeck looked and was relieved: Cornford had not been tortured as he'd feared. In fact, he appeared to be in remarkably good spirits. The tiny cell held only a stool and a narrow cot, but it was clean; to his surprise, on one wall hung a crucifix.

'It took me aback too, at first,' the priest said; he was even smiling. 'The degree of freedom I and my fellows are allowed, I mean. Yet others were here before, who have made great strides – and we have many good friends on the outside.' He stood back, motioning Marbeck to enter. 'Though I find it hard to believe you're one of them.'

'I admit that I'm not, father.' Marbeck stepped into the cell. 'Though I've come seeking your help, in one way.' He kept his eyes on the priest. 'Do you recall our last conversation, in a cellar at Great Willoughby . . .'

At that, Cornford's face clouded. 'How can I not? I pray hourly, yet . . .' He gave a start. 'Has something happened? Please tell me – we're late with receiving news in here.'

'It's not what you might think,' Marbeck replied. 'But there's danger yet.'

A moment passed, in which the priest seemed to be judging him. After a while he relaxed slightly, though there was a sadness upon him now. Finally, he said: 'If you've come to ask me to break the seal of confession, you've had a wasted visit. You know I cannot.'

'I do know – but it may not be necessary. Will you not help me to help others, and perhaps save lives?'

Cornford stared . . . then something surged up, altering the man's whole demeanour. Hope radiated from him, and involuntarily he lifted a hand, almost in benediction. 'Speak, then. Say what you've come here to say . . . I pray you!'

And within a short time the prisoner's hopes were indeed realized, in part at least, as the terrible burden he carried was lightened somewhat. A planned assassination of King James was about to be thwarted, he was told; even as the two of them spoke in this gloomy little cell, matters were being put in hand.

But what followed was unexpected, and by the end of that morning, Marbeck would have to reassess everything he knew.

SEVENTEEN

It was soon apparent that Father Cornford could tell him little, once Marbeck had revealed his discovery in the vault beneath the Lords' House – for it seemed that he hadn't known such details after all. He'd believed that there was a bold project in train to restore the Catholic faith in England, but he knew nothing of gunpowder. All he would admit was that he was acquainted with some brave young Catholic gentlemen, who were filled with anger at the king and resolved to carry out some long-planned scheme, with or without sanction. Which was why, in a place he wouldn't name, Cornford had reluctantly agreed to give the sacrament to several of them who'd taken a solemn oath, without asking questions. As for the man who'd told him more, under confession: Cornford prayed for him. Perhaps at least one of the circle had grown fearful of what lay ahead and wished to withdraw, he said. Yet none, he was certain, would betray their fellows: things had gone too far for that.

The two of them stood in silence for a while. For Cornford, who was at first shocked when Marbeck – after swearing him to secrecy – told him of the planned explosion at Westminster, relief was tempered with the knowledge that the movers of the plot were at large and could try again. And while he himself yearned for change, he insisted that what he'd told Deverell was true: his Society forbade acts of terror. Faith and persuasion, by deed and by example, were his only weapons.

'Then it's no use my mentioning names to you,' Marbeck said finally. 'Catesby, perhaps . . . or Thomas Percy?'

The other shook his head.

'Even though you know they'll be taken? For now the plan is uncovered, they'll certainly be brought in, sooner or later. My masters will seal the ports, watch the roads – the entire nation will be on alert. Meanwhile, they'll question those they hold already, by cruel means . . . which includes you, father.'

'You warned me of that already, in the cellar at Great Willoughby,' the priest said, somewhat tiredly. 'I repeat: my fate is in God's hands, as is the fate of those other men.'

'Will you at least tell me about one named John Johnson?' Marbeck asked, his patience thinning. 'A man from Yorkshire, tall and heavy-bearded?' His hopes rose as a different expression appeared on Cornford's face – only to vanish again.

'I've no need for silence there,' the priest replied. 'For I never heard that name, nor do I recognize the man you describe.'

'Very well.' Marbeck sighed; it was time to admit defeat. Deverell had been right, and the visit was pointless. With a final look at the captive, he was about to take his leave when the other half-raised a hand.

'There's something I can and will say,' he said. 'Since this business is now about to be exposed to the world, you claim . . . and I've no cause to disbelieve you, Master Tucker; even though I'm sure that's not your true name.'

He hesitated, then met Marbeck's eye. 'Have you not thought that others besides the ones I spoke of may know of it and are merely letting the plot ripen, for their own purposes?'

'In fact, the thought has occurred to some,' Marbeck said, concealing his unease; he was more troubled by that notion than he could admit. 'You needn't rack your own conscience any further – all will be sifted in time.'

'Will it?' Cornford wore a thin smile. 'Can you be certain?'

'I can,' Marbeck said stiffly. 'As shrewd as you are, father, there are men as clever, or even cleverer than you—'

'I don't doubt that,' the priest broke in. 'Yet you might ask yourself who has most to gain from letting this terrible drama play itself out until the last moment.' His smile faded. 'And what motive might lie beyond the mere foiling of yet another Catholic plot . . . Do you follow me now?'

Marbeck made no reply.

'I think you do,' Cornford said. He drew himself to his full height, the change in his manner striking: from one of stoicism to something like severity.

Marbeck felt the man's strength and knew that his talk of facing torture was no bluff: here was courage of a kind he had only seen in hardened soldiers. 'Will you not say more, even now?' he asked.

'Do I need to?' The other raised an eyebrow. 'When the answer's here, standing before you?'

'In what manner?' Restlessly, Marbeck moved to the door and turned to face him. 'I've no time for riddles, father.' As he spoke, he imagined Deverell at Salisbury House, making his report to the Lord Secretary. 'I feared you would tell me nothing – but it matters little in the end. I'll bid you farewell; you know we won't meet again.'

Father Cornford gazed at him in silence. Finally, he turned away and bowed his head.

So Marbeck left the cell and walked to the door by which he'd entered. He banged on it and called the name Plainstaff. After a moment the turnkey arrived, peered through the bars and gave a nod. Still thinking over what Cornford had said, Marbeck waited for the door to be unlocked, then passed through it. But when he started to walk towards the second door, he felt a sudden tug at his belt. Whirling round, he realized that the warder had snatched his poniard from its sheath.

'Where d'you think you're going?' he said softly.

Immediately, Marbeck tensed. 'Has the price of getting out gone up, then?' he asked harshly. 'How many shillings is it now?'

'I fear shillings won't cover it, my friend . . . nor even angels, for all that.'

Plainstaff was grinning at him . . . and even as realization swept over Marbeck, he saw the far door open. Another turnkey appeared – and this one held a sword.

'We must detain you, master,' he said.

Swiftly, Marbeck assessed his chances – but when his hand went to his scabbard, it was seized in a grip stronger than his own. Plainstaff held him, forcing his hand behind his back – and the next moment the other man's sword was at his throat.

'You're a Papist,' he hissed. 'You told the gatekeeper so yourself – and you've been consorting with a seditious Jesuit. You're not leaving here.'

'By whose orders?' Marbeck demanded. 'Tell me, or by heaven I'll—' He broke off as his own poniard was thrust against his side, hard enough to prick the skin. Taking a sharp breath, he locked eyes with the swordsman. 'You're making a mistake,' he snapped. 'When my masters find out who . . .'

He stopped himself as another feeling arose: one of terrible suspicion. His thoughts whirling, he found himself pushed violently through an archway. Then he was marched down a passage, his hands clamped together and a blade at his neck. Around a corner the three of them went, into a narrow way with a door at the end. Plainstaff took his sword from him, while the other man produced keys. This door, however, didn't merely squeak: it scraped the floor horribly, as if it were rarely opened. He glimpsed a pitch-dark cell beyond, then he was thrust inside . . . to fall headlong over something in his path. The door closed and a bolt slid into place, as Marbeck got up and turned – only to stop short when a voice came out of the darkness, from somewhere by his feet.

'Who's there? Keep back! I have a knife . . .' There was a rustle of straw as the man scrambled away. 'Stay there!' he shouted, from higher up; he was crouched by the door. 'Tell me your name!'

But only silence greeted him, until at last the new prisoner spoke in the dark. 'It's Marbeck.'

A gasp, then: 'Good God . . . are you in jest?'

'Do you think I'd give my name, if I hadn't recognized your voice?' Marbeck said, his spirits sinking. 'Shall we talk of bees, or do you require further proof – John Cutler?'

It turned out that there was a rushlight in the cell, in a tiny alcove. Marbeck discovered it when he lit a flame with his tinderbox, so at least they had a little light. Cutler, it transpired, had neither tinderbox nor the knife he'd claimed to possess. Haggard and pale, his hair a tangled mess, the one-time intelligencer looked like some Bedlamite who had been incarcerated here in error. But once they began to talk, sitting on the stone floor with only straw to cushion them, he appeared to be in a sharper frame of mind than Marbeck had feared.

'You were right, of course, in Croydon – about the gunpowder, I mean,' he mumbled. 'I knew it wasn't ale in those kegs—'

'You knew?' Marbeck broke in harshly. 'Then why in God's name didn't you say that?'

'I know – forgive me. I . . .' The other shook his head miserably. 'It seemed such a bind, Marbeck – reporting to Monk, who rarely believes what I say anyway. I've made a life down there, you know. I once wrote a letter, saying I wished to cease intelligence work, but he claimed he never received it. Still, they left me alone . . . I'm harmless, I suppose.' He looked up. 'Then you visited . . . and a few days later, they came for me.'

Marbeck frowned. 'Who came?'

'The usual sort . . . You know them. They arrived by night, said they had orders to take me to Monk, but it was a lie. I was brought here like a common villain . . . I've even lost track of the time.' A puzzled expression appeared. 'What day is it?'

'Saturday,' Marbeck murmured. He sagged, feeling close to despair. Three days remained until the opening of Parliament; his fervent hope was that Deverell's report had been believed. Surely, his own absence would then be noticed? He looked up to see Cutler peering at him.

'I've an idea what's behind it all, you know,' he said.

'Have you, indeed?' Marbeck searched his eyes for the wild look he had seen before and was relieved not to find it. 'Tell me, then. For we seem to have enough time for tales.'

'I will . . . but first, will you recount what's occurred since you left my home? For it seems to me that – assuming you returned to Monk and made your report – my arrest followed hard upon it.'

'So it would appear,' Marbeck said thoughtfully. 'Very well – I'll be brief.' So he told his own tale: the same account he'd given to Deverell, in the King's Head, as well as what had followed – for what did it matter now? They were both power-less: two intelligencers imprisoned for reasons yet unknown, while events marched on outside. But even as he ended the saga with his arrival in the cell, his own suspicions were gathering . . . until he stopped in some unease: Cutler was nodding eagerly.

'I'd swear it's because we knew about the gunpowder!' he

said fiercely. 'Someone had to silence us before we blabbed further – you especially, after what you found in the Lords' vault. Those men who came for me lied – they could have carried a forged warrant. So perhaps, as you fear, Monk has indeed turned traitor . . .'

Suddenly, the man was mournful. 'Who can be trusted, Marbeck?' he blurted. 'This is a wicked profession . . . Mayhap we deserve to be mewed up in a place like this. We've done – I've done – terrible things in the Crown's service, even to the taking of a life. That wasn't what I intended, back when I was the fencer you knew. I fought men for money and prestige . . . before I let myself be flattered into thinking I could serve my Queen – just as you did. Young cubs who knew it all and feared no one . . .' He shook his head. 'If nothing else, I've had time to think here in the dark. I can only pray I'm released, for heaven knows what will happen to my bees. Best keep out of everything else . . . Did I not say that to you once?'

Having no words of comfort, Marbeck was silent. Yet his mind was busy: Cutler's words had triggered something. A theory was gathering: a shape forming, from the jumble of events and from his suspicions. Deverell's mistrust of Monk . . . Cutler's arrest, as well as his own . . . and then there was Cornford's question: *Who has most to gain from letting the drama play itself out until the last moment?* And, more cryptically still: *The answer's here, standing before you.* What was standing before him just then, but a Jesuit priest?

Then he saw it – and the shock propelled him to his feet, startling Cutler. At the wall, he span round and gazed at his fellow prisoner, who peered up in alarm.

'In God's name, what's wrong?' he exclaimed.

Marbeck didn't answer.

'A rat, was it? They're here sometimes . . . I've heard them.'

'Not a rat . . .' Marbeck leaned against the rough stone wall, drawing long breaths. The stench of the cell was powerful, but he was almost accustomed to it already. Glancing round the cramped space, he eyed Cutler. 'Can we get something to drink in here? They've left me my purse, and my mouth's parched.'

'You have money?' At once Cutler brightened. 'Why didn't you say so? My purse is empty, but those varlets outside will bring anything for a price . . .' He hesitated. 'I doubt they'd let us go outside, though, as they do with some.'

'No . . .' Recalling the words of his turnkey – that even angels wouldn't cover the bribe – Marbeck was of similar mind. Slumping to a sitting position, eyes level with his fellow, he drew another breath and said: 'I'll call someone soon, say we can pay for food and drink . . . and blankets. Does that please you?'

'Why, you're a saviour,' Cutler breathed. 'You bring light, as well as sustenance . . .' A frown appeared. 'So what startled you?'

'Let's say I was in a fog,' Marbeck said. 'But I believe it's lifted. Shall I lay it forth?'

'If you wish . . .' Cutler looked uneasy. 'Is the gunpowder not the reason we're here then, you and I?' Suddenly, he shivered. 'I confess I've feared the worst, once or twice: the possibility that I'm considered a risk – even a traitor, if they choose to name me such. And you know what happens then.'

But Marbeck shook his head. 'I don't think you need fear that, Cutler . . . nor do I, for that matter. I think you're here as a mere precaution, while I'm here because I'm a nuisance: one who flouts orders and follows his nose, to the great annoyance of some.' Calmer now, he even managed a wry smile. 'But there's one man who long ago ceased to be annoyed by that trait . . . who even encourages it. Having seen it bring results at times, he lets me make my own paths – so long as, in the end, they all lead back to him.' He stopped, not needing to say more.

'You mean our Lord Secretary?' Cutler spoke low, as if afraid of being overheard. And when Marbeck remained silent, he shivered again. Quickly, he seized armfuls of straw and wrapped himself, hugging his body as if the cold had suddenly worsened. 'Set forth your deduction, then,' he said at last. 'But don't take too long – I need drink to warm me, as well as a blanket.'

'I will,' Marbeck said. 'But before striking a bargain with our gaolers, I'll count what's in my purse, so we may eke it out. For I fear that you and I will have to endure each other's company for some time yet.'

'How long?' Cutler's unease was back. 'And how can you know?'

'Three days at least, I expect,' Marbeck told him. 'Until the danger has passed – or rather, until that day a group of desperate Papists think is to be one of jubilation. Once they learn that their plans are as dust, they'll flee for their lives . . . Not that it'll help them. After that, I think we'll likely be let out of here, though what may follow afterwards, I don't know.'

And with that, he began to spell it out.

EIGHTEEN

Lord Robert Cecil, Earl of Salisbury, Secretary of State
and the most senior member of the King's Privy Council,
had been aware of the gunpowder plot for days, Marbeck
believed, or even longer. As the man had once told him, without
needing to boast: there was nothing he didn't know about –
and if there was, he made sure that he learned of it sooner or
later.

'It sits well enough,' he told Cutler. 'Cecil's had all the
reports of Papist activity over this past year – he must have
known something serious was in train. When I went to Monk
more than ten days ago, he was weighed down with business.
And he ranted about the number of Jesuit priests at large . . .'
He paused, shaking his head. 'Why didn't I begin to see it
then?'

'See what?' Cutler still didn't understand. 'Even if Cecil
knew of the plot, with the King away for the summer, he might
have simply been gathering evidence—'

'I'm certain he did that,' Marbeck broke in. 'But it wouldn't
be enough for him. He'd rather let the whole scheme ripen,
as Cornford put it, to the very last, before apprehending the
movers of it. After all, Catesby and his like are watched . . .
though they've been cleverer than we imagined, putting things
in place under the noses of people in Westminster. No doubt
many a bribe was paid . . . but no matter. For even then – when
Cecil's trap was sprung and the danger lifted – what would
be the outcome? Just another Catholic plot foiled, followed
by more arrests and executions. But once Cecil turned it about
. . .' He almost smiled. 'The Lord Secretary's never been one
to miss an opportunity . . . That's what Cornford was trying
to tell me.'

'You mean, he intends to blame it on the Jesuits?' Cutler
was shocked. 'Are you saying he would even risk the King's
life to do so . . . Use him as bait?'

'Of course not. Cecil never acts without weighing the risks.'

On his feet, Marbeck moved about the cramped cell to stretch his limbs. An hour had passed since the two of them had eaten and drunk of the simple fare brought by the turnkeys, after a price was agreed.

Wrapped in a blanket, warm and sated, Cutler was in better spirits than when Marbeck had first found him. But he was drowsy, struggling to take in the scale and boldness of the strategy. Lowering his gaze, he yawned. 'Well then, if all is as you say, it's the most dangerous game I ever heard of,' he said at last. 'Even for *Roberto il Diablo.*'

'I'd have to agree,' Marbeck said. 'But think on it. He has enough priests in custody – in this very place, as well as else-where – to put a strong case together. Under hard questioning some will break; they're but human. By the end they'll admit to anything, put their names to any document to make the suffering stop. Catesby and Percy are known Papists, whose arrest and execution would solve little – but the Jesuit missionaries are of a different stamp. They serve Rome directly and mean to bring the nation back to her – not by force, but by a war of attrition. That even scares Cecil, as it does Monk.'

'So, you believe Monk's a part of it?'

'He has to be.' Marbeck frowned, piecing it out yet further. 'He tried to put me off, told me to behave myself and watch Percy – because Cecil ordered him to. Sending me to seek you out in Croydon was perhaps a mistake . . . When I returned, his manner had changed.' He gave Cutler a wry smile. 'You may be harmless, as you say, but you put me on the scent. I was uneasy, hearing your tale . . . yet it was by sheer chance I listened to a talkative blacksmith and went to look for a gunpowder mill in Godstone.'

They were silent for a while, mulling the matter over. But for Marbeck, one thought grew: that he had been sidelined once again, and not entrusted with the business of intrigue and entrapment that had been going on in secret. How many of Cecil's other intelligencers might know of it, he couldn't guess. Perhaps Monk was the only one; he suspected Deverell had been as much in the dark as he had.

'Cecil's always hated the Jesuits, as his father did,' Cutler said, almost to himself. 'Ever since Robert Persons escaped capture and got to Rome, where he still holds office.'

'Precisely so,' Marbeck agreed. 'And with the schools flourishing, in France too now, he sees the threat grow ever stronger. Hence, what better opportunity could have arisen than this reckless scheme to blow up King and Council? How he learned of it doesn't matter – he may not even have known the details. But once he's poked around, produced enough evidence to show the Jesuits were behind it, he'll have all the help he needs to hunt them down and put them to trial. An attempt on the King's life is treason, so the worst kind of executions would follow: a deterrent to others, and a hard blow to their Society – they'd be discredited in the eyes of every monarch in Europe.' He let out a breath; despite his resentment, he couldn't help but be impressed at the clarity of Cecil's vision.

'And now the King has returned, you say?' Cutler put in.

'I heard he came back to London on Thursday – Halloween. And it wouldn't surprise me if a search is now being planned for the night of the fourth, the eve of the opening of Parliament. The gunpowder will be found, and the King and Queen will be safe, while pursuivants stand ready with a list of men to apprehend . . .' Marbeck paused as a thought rose. 'The one who minds Percy's house by the Lords' Chamber should be high on that list.'

Again, Cutler showed surprise. 'You mean, you believe the King was never in any real danger?'

'I'd swear to it,' Marbeck said. 'Even Cecil wouldn't dare use him as bait, as you put it.'

But even now the magnitude of the danger subdued him, as it had when he'd torn away the brushwood in the vault and seen the great heap of barrels – and again at the Duck and Drake, when he and Deverell had faced the matter. As so often before, he had to admire the needle-sharp mind of the Lord Secretary, not to mention the little hunchback's cool courage. Few men could have turned the matter to their advantage so skilfully . . . He paused, and a smile appeared unbidden.

'What amuses you now?' In the dim glow of the rushlight, Cutler was frowning at him. 'You said we're but pawns in all this – or nuisances, to be kept out of the way. I for one don't relish another three days in here, even with those comforts your purse may bring.'

'Nor do I,' Marbeck answered. 'Yet I can't help but imagine the outcome, when Cecil chooses the moment to take his evidence to the King. His position will be unassailable. Those who hate and despise him, his rivals on the Privy Council . . . they'll all be thwarted. James Stuart will never cease rewarding the man who saved his life and his monarchy.'

'Well . . . by heaven, I think I've heard enough just now.' Cutler sighed, shaking his head. 'Will you let a man sleep, so he can forget this witchery for a few hours?' He found a leather mug they'd been given and drained it.

'If they don't release us in three or four days, I'll try some other way to bribe the guards,' Marbeck said finally. 'My money will be gone, but there's my sword and poniard . . .' He frowned. 'Though it's likely they'll have sold them and deny they ever saw such.'

'Very likely,' Cutler murmured tiredly.

'Yet, there's my belt and doublet . . . Have you anything to offer?'

Again, Cutler shook his head. 'I came here in my workaday clothes, without even a cloak to keep out the chill. Now they're fit for naught but rags . . .' A frightened look appeared. 'My bees, Marbeck . . . who will mind them? No one even knows I'm here!'

Suddenly, the man was distraught, his fists clenched. He looked about helplessly, then finally lay down, pulled his thin blanket around him and turned his face away. Nor did he react when Marbeck moved closer to him and spoke low. 'Three days . . . four at the most. Then I'll try and find a way to get us out.'

There was no answer. Straightening up again, he stepped to the wall and leaned back, staring into space . . . whereupon the rush light sputtered and went out.

But there in the pitch dark he made his resolve – and this time he would not be swayed: his days as a Crown intelligencer were over. Let Monk, even Lord Cecil, threaten him as they liked: he had done with skulking in shadows and spinning tales, risking his life for purses begrudgingly given – and finding betrayal at every turn. His last thought, as he sat to take some rest, was of Meriel: once all was understood, would she be willing to listen? When she saw his resolve was genuine, would she allow him one more chance? He pictured her care-worn face, in the doorway of her father's house, before she was snatched away from him. With a heavy heart, he closed his eyes and waited for sleep.

Three terrible days followed.

To begin with, having no means of measuring time, both Marbeck and Cutler soon lost track of it. Though Marbeck was able to barter for more light, after a while the two of them agreed to go without it and use his dwindling purse to buy food and drink. Thereafter they passed the hours fitfully, swapping tales and, when they were used up, falling back on childhood stories. Meanwhile they grew dirtier by the hour, having only weak beer to drink and no water. From time to time Marbeck summoned the turnkeys by banging on the door, using all his wits to bargain for sustenance. He was forced to endure their mocking looks, knowing full well, as they did, that his money would soon be gone. After that, disaster loomed: a prisoner who was penniless was nothing more than an encumbrance and would likely be put in the Hole. His only hope then was to beg charity from passers-by through a grating: the one Marbeck had seen on first arrival, when he had come here to see Father Cornford. Already, it seemed like weeks ago.

On the first day, as he wrangled with Plainstaff or one of the other men, he asked the hour. When told it, he made a scratch in the wall with his bodkin. But after a while he believed the warders were playing games, giving false answers for their own amusement. Finally, certain that was the case, he gave up and tried to reckon the passage of time himself. But it was no use: after many hours in the windowless cell, he no longer knew whether it was day or night.

Then there was the problem of Cutler. For a day and a half, at least, his fellow intelligencer had remained calm enough, apart from moments when he fretted about his bees and his empty cottage. He even fretted about his market customers in Croydon, who would no longer be able to buy his honey.

Sometimes he lapsed into fantasy, and the wild manner
Marbeck had observed when they'd last met reappeared. He
began to harbour notions of feigning sickness, so that when
the guards opened the door he and Marbeck could overpower
them. When Marbeck pointed out the unlikelihood of such a
scheme succeeding, given the number of locked doors that
separated them from the main gate, Cutler grew angry and
accused him of cowardice. But Marbeck would merely turn
away and scratch the wall with his bodkin.

'What are you writing?' Cutler demanded one time, when
they had long since grown sick of each other's presence.
'Or are you drawing? Can you see in the dark now, like a
dunghill cat?'

'I can see you, Cutler,' Marbeck threw back, a warning note
in his voice: his own temper was almost spent, which troubled
him somewhat. 'Or smell you, at least . . . so don't try putting
any of your foolish notions into practice. I'll spike you if I
must.'

'I don't doubt it,' the other growled. 'Mayhap you should
do so while you may . . . for if I spend another hour in here,
I'll likely lose my senses. Who knows what might happen
then? I'll be the Tom o'Bedlam you took me for, when you
came to my door – a harbinger of doom!'

Marbeck didn't answer. He heard Cutler breathing in the
dark and steeled himself for any move: the man's desperation
was becoming a threat. When nothing happened he at last
began to relax, and a crippling tiredness swept over him. He
had slept only for short intervals since the first day; now it
was telling on him.

The thought alarmed him. Though he hadn't yet told Cutler,
his money was gone, and he was hungry. Soon, he would have
to admit it and call the turnkeys. Unless . . . A worse thought
shook him: would the two of them be let out, after all? Perhaps
the master of the Clink had orders to starve them, to leave
them until they were merely food for the rats . . . Heavily, he
lay down in the fetid straw and closed his eyes. There was a
rustling close by, but he no longer cared.

And then, only seconds later it seemed, he was shouting.

'I'm not done!' he cried: he was answering a turnkey, the

man he'd asked how many priests were held here. 'You should have counted – shall I loosen your tongue, you—'

'Marbeck!'

With a cry he sat up, lashing out. His fist connected with something; there was a yelp, then he was gripping the guard by the throat. 'Tell me how many!' he cried. 'Or I'll—'

'Marbeck! For God's sake . . . it's me!'

He froze, panting; he was awake, with Cutler trembling in his grasp, hands clamped desperately about his wrist. At once he released his fellow, jerking backwards in dismay.

Spluttering, Cutler spoke out of the dark. 'You whoreson wretch – you tried to kill me!'

'It was a dream . . . Forgive me.' Breathing hard, Marbeck forced himself on to his elbows. 'How long was I . . .? No, you don't know . . .'

'Listen, please!' There was a different note in Cutler's voice; Marbeck heard it, frowning in the gloom.

'What is it?'

'I said listen!' the other insisted. 'Come to the door. Put your ear to it and you'll hear . . .' He paused, then: 'At least, I pray to heaven you do, and I'm not dreaming too.'

They crawled through the stinking straw, until Marbeck felt the door's rough timbers. Placing his head against it, with Cutler kneeling beside him, he listened intently. He heard a distant hum and guessed it was merely the murmur of the prison, the wretched inmates of the main chamber. Then . . .

'Church bells?' He swallowed, his mouth as dry as dust.

'It's St Mary Overies.' His voice shaking, Cutler whispered close to his ear. 'They're tolling the bells – it's an alarm!'

Marbeck drew a sharp breath – and fear swept over him, reducing him to despair in a moment. Cutler was right: the bells were tolling, as violently as any sexton could work them. It was an alarm, as Cutler had said . . . which meant only one thing: the worst had happened, and his theories were as nothing.

He cursed his own folly. He'd convinced himself that all was well, when it wasn't: for some reason Deverell had failed to report to Cecil . . . nor had Cecil known of the gunpowder in the vault. The King was dead and probably Cecil too . . . Hell was unleashed: the plot had succeeded.

In dismay he sank down, his last shreds of hope draining away. Cutler was silent . . . whereupon, what had become the most unexpected noise of all sounded: almost a shriek, which shook them both. It was the scraping of the door, which now opened wide. There followed light that, though dim, was as a powerful sunbeam to the prisoners, stabbing their eyes. But even as Marbeck shied away from it, the voice of Plainstaff the turnkey sounded from behind.

'There's no need to soil your breeches, gents,' he said. 'I bring good news: you're leaving us. How's that for a sunny afternoon?'

NINETEEN

t was Tuesday, the fifth of November, and as the turnkey had said, it was a fine afternoon.

Blinking in the sunlight, hungry and dirty, Marbeck stepped out of the doors of the Clink. Behind him came the shambling figure of Cutler, staring about as if in a foreign land. Even the stink of the Thames was balm to them both; the cacophony of church bells – dozens of them ringing out at once, from St Mary Overies and over in the city – was sweet music. Dazed by the suddenness of their release, they stumbled down to Bankside and found it crowded. Then at last Marbeck's fears disappeared, for the news was on everyone's lips: the King was safe.

There had been no explosion, they learned; the opening of Parliament had been prorogued. News was still coming from Westminster, but the gist of it was clear: a wicked conspiracy had been foiled. The vault of the Lords' Chamber had been searched in the small hours of this morning by Sir Thomas Knyvett, Keeper of the Palace of Westminster, and a great quantity of gunpowder discovered.

Once he'd absorbed the facts, Marbeck sat down in the road before Winchester House, in no hurry to get up again.

Cutler slumped down beside him; the man was still wrapped in his dirty blanket from the prison cell. 'Thanks be to God,' he said weakly.

Marbeck said nothing.

'They had orders, at the Clink . . . That's why they were so eager to get rid of us.' Cutler's voice shook: he was shivering. 'You were right – they were charged with keeping us until told otherwise. It means Cecil has matters under control . . . It must do.' With growing excitement, he gripped Marbeck's arm. 'Don't you understand? We're free – I can go back to my bees!'

Feeling drained, Marbeck turned to him. 'I thought it strange that they returned my sword to me,' he murmured. 'My poniard's gone, but no matter.'

Cutler stared. 'Did you not hear me? You're free – you can thumb your nose at the whole pack of them, go where you please!'

'Yes . . . you're right, of course.' Marbeck managed a smile. 'I'd surely welcome some soap and hot water, and fresh clothes. I've a chamber at the Duck and Drake—'

'You told me already,' Cutler broke in. 'You'd best go there at once . . . You look like you've escaped from Bedlam.'

'As do you,' Marbeck said. It was true: Cutler's hair and beard were wilder than ever, his clothes like rags. There was a light in his eye that might have alarmed some, but Marbeck knew him too well by now. 'You'd better come with me,' he added. 'I've some spare attire you can put on. If my credit holds, you can eat and drink while I go out and gather news.' His face clouded. 'I must find Deverell . . .'

'Oh no – I can't possibly delay.' Quickly, Cutler got to his feet. Though pinched and emaciated, there was a determination within him that brooked no argument. He looked along the street, out at the river with its myriad boats, then pointed at London Bridge, looming to their right. 'There's my road: Long Southwark. The walk will do wonders for me . . . I want to see fields and woods.'

'You intend to walk?' Marbeck exclaimed. 'It's ten miles to Croydon . . . You'll keel over before you reach Newington.'

'I think not,' Cutler replied briskly. 'If I look like a beggar, then I can become one. I'll walk, cadge a ride – crawl if I have to. I must get to my cottage and my bees. Neighbours will aid me . . . and come next market day, I'll be doing business again.'

Marbeck drew a breath, but knew resolve when he saw it. Slowly, he got up and, having nothing else to give, offered his hand.

The other took it and, without another word, walked away. He turned by St Mary's Dock, making for Long Southwark and his journey homewards.

Marbeck watched until he was lost to sight, then looked towards the Bridge. Since he hadn't even a penny to summon a boat he faced a different walk, through the city to the Strand; then he remembered something else: his winnings from the primero game.

The cache of gold and silver coins, in his old chamber at Skinner's: of course, he should go there first . . . Had he really forgotten about it? But then, with Curzon's murder . . .

He started walking, past the great church with its bell still tolling . . . then he slowed. *The place will burn down, destroying everything,* Monk had said; *It'll probably be a blessing . . .*

Forcing the grim notion aside he walked on towards the Great Stone Gate, picking up scraps of conversation as he went. Through the morning and the early afternoon, it seemed, while Marbeck and Cutler had languished in their cell, the momentous news had been spreading. People stood talking, or hurried to the stairs to hail boats. In the city, bells were still clanging . . . and now columns of smoke began to appear. Halting before the gate, where there was an excited throng, he stopped a passer-by.

'Is there a fire?' he asked, pointing across the river.

'You clown – those are bonfires!' The passer-by, a rough-looking fellow in a brewer's apron, jeered at him. 'All of London's rejoicing at the King's escape – see for yourself!' Whereupon, noting Marbeck's appearance, he wrinkled his nose. 'If they'll let you across,' he muttered, and stalked off.

A moment later Marbeck realized what the man meant. His own words came back: *They'll seal the ports, watch roads . . .* Only too aware of how he looked, he approached two guards who stood at the bridge entrance. For once, he hadn't the energy to bluff.

'I need to go through,' he said.

The men, armed with swords and halberds, looked him over. 'Who are you?' one of them demanded. 'State your business.'

'I'm John Sands, servant to the—' He broke off in time, before someone truly took him for a madman. While the guards stared he backed off, turned and left the roadway.

On Bankside again, he began to gather his wits. Of course

Cecil and the Council would have moved to secure both cities: London, and especially Westminster. Much as he'd tried to forget it of late, he was still Marbeck the Crown Intelligencer; now, Marbeck-like thoughts crowded in. Had Robert Catesby, Percy and others been apprehended? Had Percy's servant Johnson been taken? Was the King now at Whitehall? What of the kidnap threat to the royal children – were they safe?

He walked along the river, reasoning as he went. Men passed, looking askance at his clothes: good quality, yet badly soiled. As for his rapier, they would think it stolen . . . He stopped. The sword: it had been back in his possession for less than an hour; now he must part with it again, for it was his only asset.

A short while later, unarmed but with money in his purse, he was at the Falcon Stairs, trying to act like the gentleman he was. After all, he was not the first to pawn such a valuable possession . . . whereupon he thought suddenly of Curzon. Somehow he had managed to keep the memory away, until now . . .

'You, fellow – get out of the way!'

He swung round to see a well-dressed gallant, buckled hat and all, gesturing impatiently at him. 'That's my boat,' the man added, his nose in the air. 'Be off!'

Marbeck looked and saw others jostling behind him. Meanwhile a skiff was pulling in, the boatman gripping the jetty post . . . whereupon one thought overrode all others. His anger surging, he shoved the gallant backwards into the crowd of waiting passengers, knocking the fellow's hat flying and provoking a chorus of shouts and curses. Two seconds later he was in the boat, tugging at his purse. When he drew out a silver coin, the waterman blinked.

'Take me to Paul's Stairs,' Marbeck snapped. 'I'm on royal business. There's a shilling for you – refuse, and I'll have you arrested. Come, what say you?' He held the man's eye, until he flinched.

'Good Christ . . . I believe you.' The fellow gulped and shoved his oar against the jetty. In a moment, to the fury of those left behind, the boat was turning with the current.

'Now, row like the devil,' Marbeck added, sitting down heavily. 'I meant what I said – so bend your back!'

Less than a half hour later, however, he stood in St Martins, gazing at the blackened ruin of Skinner's bowling-house. And from the bottom of his heart, he cursed Levinus Monk. The spymaster's words were as his actions, it was said; just now, Marbeck wished heartily that they'd been empty words.

But they hadn't. The fire had been out for days, he saw: perhaps since the very day he'd stood in the room by the Jewel Tower and told Monk of the sword fight that had taken place within. Rain had since turned the burnt timber, thatch, and everything else into one great, soggy mass. Not surprisingly, the buildings on either side had been damaged too: this was London, where people lived cheek by jowl. Fortunately, it looked as though those fires had been put out quickly, leaving the oak frames still standing. With a sigh, Marbeck surveyed the devastation and accepted defeat. Somewhere underneath lay his hoard, won off Thomas Percy with a knave-high *fluxus*. But there was no denying what would be found now, were he inclined to sift through the wreckage long enough: molten coins, congealed into a shapeless lump of metal.

A thought sprang up, which almost made him laugh. 'I bluffed to get it,' he said aloud. 'So there's my reward.'

He turned about and walked the crowded streets, through something close to mayhem. Here in the city, the news of an attempt to murder the King seemed to have struck a more urgent note than on shiftless Bankside. Bells still rang, and bonfires were being lit in many places, people emerging from their doors with fuel. Soldiers passed in two and threes, while the taverns were bursting. Men and women stood about on corners, eager for news. It appeared there had been mutterings of a Spanish conspiracy. A mob had assembled outside the ambassador's house and only dispersed when the frightened man threw money down to them. Some reminded their fellows of the omen: the eclipses of the previous months . . . Was there yet more danger to come? Meanwhile a watch was on all the gates, and a company of the King's horsemen had been seen galloping out of the city, heading westwards. Moreover, it appeared that parliament was not prorogued after all, but sitting in emergency session. But yes, the King was safe; England was safe . . . for now.

Through it all Marbeck walked as if in a daze, picking up rumours as he went and discarding most of them. The French were behind it, or even the Irish – they could never be trusted; it was a hoax – there was no gunpowder, only barrels of earth; the barrels had been found a week ago, but no one had acted . . . Gradually, however, a consensus seemed to be forming: that this was yet another plot by desperate Papists, foiled by the Lord Secretary, a man hated by many but grudgingly admired. If there were anyone cleverer in all England than Lord Robert Cecil, Marbeck thought, he had yet to hear of him.

He skirted Paul's and walked through Ludgate, which was also guarded, out into Fleet Street. People were on the road, on horse and foot, but he ignored them. After he'd passed through Temple Bar, however, where sentries regarded him darkly, he slowed pace and finally stopped before the gates of Essex House. It was closed up, with no sign of habitation. He thought briefly of the gaiety he had found within the mansion, the night he'd gone there with Curzon and played primero in the Blue Room. Where was Thomas Percy now?

But he relaxed then, letting out a long breath; it was no longer his concern. Let Monk say what he liked . . . if, indeed, Marbeck ever saw him again. He was finished as an intelligencer: his resolve, made in the darkness of his foul prison cell, was unshakeable.

At a brisker pace, he walked the short distance to the Duck and Drake and entered by the side door. As expected the inn was noisy and crowded, but in the din nobody paid him much attention. He reached the stairway in the passage, where he found one of the drawers having a surreptitious smoke.

'Jesu, Master Tucker . . .' The man snatched the pipe from his mouth. 'What's become of you?'

'Long story,' Marbeck said. 'Will you have some hot water sent up – and a ball of soap, if you can find such?'

'I will . . .' The drawer stared at him. 'Have you heard the coil? Some devils tried to blow up Parliament!'

'I heard,' Marbeck said, one foot on the stairs. Seeing that his credit appeared to be intact, he added: 'I'll have supper and a cup of Rhenish too . . . No, make it a jug.'

In his chamber at last, he went to the window and looked out. Evening was falling, and he could see lights at Somerset House. Beyond was the Savoy, and further off Salisbury House: a stone's throw away, yet for Marbeck it might have been an ocean's width. Even if the Lord Secretary had returned home, and was even now in the private chamber in his great house, he was as unreachable as he was indomitable.

Moving about the room, he peeled off his filthy clothing, piling it in a heap. The itching that had troubled him in the prison had continued since his release: now he found the lice, in his clothes and on his body. Finally, stark naked, he wrapped himself in a sheet and waited for the means to get himself clean. Once he was restored, when he had eaten and rested, he would go out and conduct business. There were men he might borrow money off while he made his plans. He would seek out Deverell first, then Monk, and tell them of his decision. Afterwards he would take Cobb from the stables and ride, far away from London. But before that he would try to see Meriel . . .

He sat on the bed, feeling as though a weight had been lifted from him. He'd vowed before that he would quit the Crown's service, more often than he could recall. Now the decision was made, he felt only relief.

He was still sitting, gazing at the rushes on the floor, when a servant girl arrived with a cheerful grin and a brimming pail. Supper was delayed, she informed him, because the hostess was so busy. But if he cared to wait, being a regular gentleman, he would receive satisfaction. Marbeck nodded and favoured her with the first real smile he had worn in many days.

Two hours later, clean and with a full stomach, he slept like a dead man. He slept all night and through the early morning, through the rattle of wheels on the Strand, the cries of carters going into the city and the cracking of their whips. He slept as the inn stirred into life, the wenches clumping on the stairs and the drawers coughing. Finally, he awoke with the morning well advanced, to a day of cloud . . . and sat up with a start. Deverell was sitting by the window, as calm as could be.

'I didn't like to rouse you,' he said. 'I'm pleased you're safe and well . . . Would you care to hear my tidings?'

TWENTY

Despite his new resolutions, Marbeck couldn't help his innate curiosity. Having dressed, he shared a late breakfast in his chamber with Deverell and listened to the man's tale. And quite soon, even the limited news Deverell could impart held him in silence.

'It seems there were many in this circle of plotters,' his fellow intelligencer told him. 'Robert Catesby, as you surmised. Ambrose Rookwood, Francis Tresham, Robert Keyes and others . . . Papist villains all. Even Lord Digby's part of it, I heard—'

'And Thomas Percy?' Marbeck broke in.

'Him also.' Deverell nodded. 'Indeed, he looks like one of the prime movers; he was back at Essex House only the day before the explosion was set, dining as bold as you like with his cousin, the earl. The earl too has a lot of explaining to do, though I doubt the man knew much about it. The story's emerging piecemeal, with much still to be uncovered. As for Percy – he's now fled to the Midlands, I gather, where some of the others have gone. They won't remain free for long: horsemen are scouring the shires already.'

He fell silent, letting Marbeck absorb the intelligence. As when they had last sat here together, the enormity of the plot – and the implications, had it succeeded – took his breath away. Finally, he frowned and said: 'The servant. The man I encountered at Percy's house . . .'

'Calm yourself, for he's taken,' Deverell answered, with grim satisfaction. 'Caught red-handed, would you believe – hiding in the vault with a slow match ready to set the charge, and booted and spurred ready for flight. He's been conveyed to the Tower. Hard as iron, I hear: he told them nothing, almost spat in their faces. But I'll wager he won't stay silent for long.'

Marbeck lowered his gaze, picturing the tall man in the house at Westminster, smiling as he described the place as being like a rabbit-hutch. 'I'll wager another thing,' he said. 'That his name's not Johnson.' Suddenly, he looked up. 'Aren't you curious to know where I've been these past days?' he asked sharply.

'I am,' Deverell replied. 'For after we parted, I was detained at the Lord Secretary's pleasure . . .' He paused, meeting Marbeck's eye. 'I hope you're not suspecting me of anything untoward?'

'Not at present,' Marbeck said. 'But I'm eager to hear.'

The other gave a shrug. 'Well, there's little to tell. I went to Salisbury House as I said, demanded to see the Lord Secretary . . . but can you guess who I saw instead?'

'Monk?' Marbeck frowned again. 'I've thought about him a good deal, of late. But please, finish your tale.'

'Very well . . .' Deverell too was frowning, at the memory. 'There was Levinus Monk, in a chamber of his own, as comfortable as you like. The Lord Secretary was too busy to see me, he said. He also said that the old room by the Jewel Tower was no longer safe, though I couldn't see why. Then he heard me out: your discovery in the vault, the whole story, including your going to question the priest—'

'And?' Marbeck broke in impatiently.

'And then, he arrested me.'

Marbeck let out a breath. 'Did he, now.'

'He did. I had a room to myself in the house, food and drink, even books to read. I wasn't allowed tobacco, since the Lord Secretary won't permit it. I could venture as far as the garden, where I was greeted by my protectors, as they called themselves. They were my gaolers, of course, who had orders not to let me leave until further notice. Until last night, when it seemed they finally got that notice. I went first to my wife, who was frantic with worry, then this morning I came here. And that, Marbeck, is the whole of it.'

'You didn't see Monk, after he detained you?'

'Not until last night, very late. A short conversation, telling me what I've since told you. You're to speak to no one else, I should add, until you've seen him.'

'Of course . . .' Slowly, Marbeck nodded. 'No doubt he assumes that I'm still obedient and ready to be sent on my next errand. That I should accept temporary imprisonment without complaint – and emerge unchanged, even grateful for my release.' He drew a breath and stood up. 'But that's not how it will be, Deverell . . .' He looked away briefly, then turned. 'Would you care to hear my own account now – even though it's a good deal less pleasant?'

Morning turned into afternoon, and afternoon too was advanced by the time the two men had finished their discourse. By then both were weary and somewhat angry: Deverell as much as Marbeck, for the way he too had been edged aside.

'We've always known Monk would serve Cecil to the very end,' Deverell said finally. 'Though he himself may trust us, whatever orders our Lord Secretary hands out, he'll obey them to the letter.' He eyed Marbeck. 'Mayhap this time he'll regret it, if you're truly resolved to withdraw from the service.'

'I am,' Marbeck said shortly. He was restless, eager to be outdoors.

His fellow, too shrewd not to judge his mood, stood up and stretched his own limbs. 'I'll leave you, then. I should have mentioned that, as far as Monk knows, I came to order you to attend him and nothing more. When you do see him, I'd be obliged if whatever he tells you comes as news . . .' He hesitated. 'You do intend to see him?'

'Indeed. I'd prefer to tell him of my decision face-to-face.'

'Then I'll say farewell. We're unlikely to meet, after this.'

Marbeck nodded, but said nothing.

'I almost forgot . . .' At the door Deverell turned, fumbling at his belt. Having produced a small purse, he held it up. 'I have to give you this, for immediate disbursements.'

He threw it, unhurriedly so that Marbeck could catch it . . . and as he did so a notion occurred to the latter. 'It came from Monk, I assume?'

'Naturally – who else?'

And he was gone, pulling the door behind him before Marbeck could say that he knew he was lying.

But that same evening, when Marbeck finally made his way to Salisbury House, he was denied entry.

He was at first taken aback, then annoyed. The two men who confronted him, soldiers rather than servants, wouldn't let him beyond the gate. Even when he gave several different cover names, and spoke of urgent news for Levinus Monk, they remained adamant. They had orders to admit no one who wasn't on their list, they said, and Marbeck – alias John Sands, alias Giles Blunt, alias Lawrence Tucker – wasn't on it. When he asked politely to see the list, he was refused. Finally, feeling not only angry but somehow empty, he turned and walked off.

He went to the stables then, to see that Cobb wanted for nothing, and paid a small sum on account to the phlegmatic Oliver. Then he walked, to clear his head. Though still bitter about the treatment handed to him, he had continued to piece things together. For in the aftermath of the Gunpowder Treason, it was certain that not only was the Lord Secretary working himself to the bone, but also his most trusted lieutenant, Monk.

After all, he told himself, a hue and cry was in progress. Reports would be coming in from Crown officials and those charged with rounding up known Papists, as well as pursuing the fugitive plotters. There would be investigations and interrogations, messages flying back and forth by the hour. No doubt King James would be holding council, demanding the presence of his Secretary of State. Marbeck knew well enough that he himself was of small importance, until assigned to a mission. But in that matter, he thought grimly, Monk was about to be disillusioned. Whereas the Lord Secretary, he guessed – were Marbeck ever allowed into his presence again – would fix him with his cold eye and mention his obligations to the Crown. If still unsatisfied, he might threaten action for past misdemeanours . . . but if it came to that, Marbeck was resolved now to call his bluff. Cecil, he believed, would let him go in the end. The man may be like a well-oiled clock, and devoid of sentiment, but even he would have no relish for seeing one of his best intelligencers executed.

Finally, weary even of his own company, he returned to the Duck and Drake and drank enough to make himself sleep.

Thursday dawned dry but cold, with a taste of the coming winter. Restored in body, but with a restless energy, Marbeck roused himself at the inn and went out. Within a short time he had crossed to Bankside, retrieved his sword from pawn and bought a serviceable poniard from the same dealer. Re-crossing the river, he returned to his chamber and set about selecting the few clothes he needed. These he made into a pack, ready for travelling. The rest he gave to one of the wenches to sell as she pleased, or even to burn. By midday his tasks were done, so he took a light dinner at the inn before venturing out into the Strand. Soon he was at the Ivy Stairs, where having nothing better to do just then, he sat down to watch the river traffic.

It was over, he realized: he had yet to see Monk, but his old life was drifting away from him already. Plots and stratagems, even the wiles of Charlotte and her Spanish master, need concern him no further. He guessed that the woman was making haste to quit England, if she had not done so already . . . By rights he should make a full report of her actions to Monk. He thought then of MacNeish, who had played him along too – he'd never thought the Scotsman capable of such guile. But then, who in the end could fathom another man's mind?

After an hour, he was cold and cramped. Boats came and went, the watermen's voices sharp in the cold air. He rose finally and started to make his way back to the Strand, when a blur of movement caught his eye: just ahead of him, someone had seemingly darted round the corner. With sudden suspicion Marbeck quickened his pace, emerging into the busy Strand. He halted abruptly, peering about – then at once, he was running. He was in pursuit: of a slim figure in a blue coat – and now he recalled MacNeish's admission and knew his instincts about being followed had been correct all along.

Towards Ludgate his quarry ran, dodging horsemen, carts and passers-by – but Marbeck, running with renewed vigour, was gaining on him. For a moment he lost sight of his man, then caught a glimpse of him ducking into a side-alley. In a moment he had turned in after him . . . only to slow down in grim satisfaction: it was a dead end.

Caught like a rat, the fugitive cowered at the far end of the ginnel, looking desperately to left and right. But there was no escape, and he knew it. Steadily, Marbeck approached him, regaining his breath while he reached for his sword . . . then as he drew near, he spoke.

'Blue Donal.' His anger rising, he closed in on the wretched man, who was quivering with fear. Indeed, before Marbeck could even speak, he was babbling.

'Mercy, master . . .' He almost choked on his words. 'I'm a poor man, with a parcel of bairns to feed . . . For the love of God, will ye no' spare me?'

'Spare you, Donal? Why – should I have some grievance against you?' He halted within a yard of his victim and let him quake for a while. This Scotsman was no red-bearded highlander of MacNeish's stamp, but a raw-boned townsman from the Edinburgh streets, dark-haired and weasel-faced.

Wetting his mouth, Donal swallowed and said: 'I . . . I fear ye might have, master. If ye've been talking with the man MacNeish, I mean . . . then, I wouldn't believe everything the big fellow tells ye. I just run errands, as it were . . . keep mysel' out of trouble, as best I can.'

'Indeed?' Keeping his hand on his sword-hilt, Marbeck fixed him with a stern look. 'Does dogging my every move count as keeping out of trouble, then? For it brought a good deal of inconvenience to me, I can tell you.'

The other shivered and gulped, struggling for words. He cut such a sorry figure, in fact, that Marbeck felt something akin to pity. He was a poor man, when all was said and done . . . like the men who had waylaid him at Skinner's. At that thought, he stiffened. 'By the Christ,' he muttered. 'Was it you who told a pair of men-at-arms where to find me? For if so, you'd have helped me to my death.'

'No, master, I pray you . . .' Quickly, Blue Donal found his voice. 'I know naught of such . . . I was hired to follow you about for a while, I admit such, and God forgive me for it. I had to watch your lodging – the bowling alley, that is – and report when you came and went.'

'And you're still doing so, it seems,' Marbeck said dryly. 'Perhaps you're unaware of recent events . . . that the lady who paid you and MacNeish to do her bidding is exposed as the agent of a Spaniard?'

At that, Donal jerked as if he'd been struck. 'You toy with me, master,' he said quickly. 'I—' He broke off, eyes darting everywhere.

But Marbeck drew a long breath, for all was clear to him. He pictured Charlotte, sitting rigid in her nightgown, telling him of her master Juan Roble. *His reach is long* . . .

'I speak true,' he said, with a shake of his head. 'I'd guess you've not seen the lady of late, in which case you wouldn't know. But as we're both gamblers, I'll wager you she's long since left the house where she stayed – maybe left England. There'll be no more payment, and you've been serving an enemy of the state . . . Somewhat unwise, just now, I'd say. So . . .' He paused, to let the import of his words sink in. 'Would you take that wager?'

Then, as the wretched man stared at him in mingled dismay and terror, he gripped his sword-hilt and summoned his most menacing tone. 'I thought not. So instead, would you care to tell me the whole of your tale – here and now?'

Blue Donal gave another gulp and managed a nod.

TWENTY-ONE

In the light of what he now knew, Marbeck decided to wait until the following day before leaving London.

It was Friday, the eighth of November, and apart from the inn-folk at the Duck and Drake he had seen no one since his talk with Blue Donal. This morning he busied himself making purchases, weighing carefully what remained in the purse Deverell had given him. He went to the stable, saw that Cobb was well-fed and spoke to Oliver; he would leave in the afternoon, Marbeck said, and asked the stableman to make up a feedbag for the horse. After taking dinner at an ordinary he walked by the river again, then returned to the inn. But in the Strand, someone appeared suddenly to block his way.

'Master Tucker?'

'Not I, my friend,' Marbeck said, with a shake of his head. 'You mistake me for another.'

The one who confronted him, however, gave no sign of moving. Whereupon with a frown, Marbeck recognized him as one of the armed men who had refused him entry to Salisbury House, two days ago. 'Master Tucker . . . or Master Sands, if you will,' the guard went on. 'I have orders to invite you to a room where someone you know waits.'

'Invite me?' Marbeck echoed. 'Most kind – on another occasion I'd be delighted. As it is I'm occupied and will choose my own time to pay my respects.'

The other grinned. 'He said you'd likely reply in such a manner. So I was told to offer this on account . . . More will follow when you attend him.' He reached in his pocket and produced a gold sovereign, allowing Marbeck a moment to reflect.

'I'll admit your timing is good,' he said finally. 'Yesterday, I'd have rammed that coin down your gullet and made you swallow it. As it is, I'll accompany you, provided you tell me I'm going to see Levinus Monk and no one else.'

'It's Monk,' the other admitted, his grin disappearing; he'd sensed that only a straight answer would serve. He held out the coin and Marbeck took it. This was no time for wounded pride: he needed money – and more, he needed to look his spymaster in the eye and tell him he would no longer do his bidding.

So with a curt nod, he allowed the soldier to lead the way. And some twenty minutes later, having walked the length of the Strand and passed by Charing Cross into Whitehall, he was admitted to a small, ground-floor chamber close to the Privy Gallery. There at last, after the most momentous week he could remember, he confronted Levinus Monk again; but as so often in the past, the man confounded him by going immediately on the offensive.

'By heaven, Marbeck, why couldn't you take the hint?' he thundered. 'Why couldn't you have left things alone, just for once, and done as ordered? You think I enjoyed having you clapped up? You and Deverell – even that fool Cutler?'

He was on his feet, beside another table cluttered with papers and writing materials. In fact, the place was such a close replica of his former chamber by the Jewel Tower, for a moment Marbeck was almost disoriented. But there was a window here, even if its view was only that of a stone wall. Gathering his thoughts, he remained silent and let Monk have his say.

'I knew how your mind moved,' the spymaster went on. 'As I understood only too well what you'd uncovered. You think after all this time, I don't know your strengths? Perhaps I should have foreseen you'd turn something up, before the time was ripe. As it was . . .' He hesitated. 'My hands were tied. I won't say more: I think you understand.'

'Just now, I'm not sure what I understand,' Marbeck said. His thoughts were on the prison cell, where he and Cutler had pieced together their theory: that the Lord Secretary himself had allowed the Gunpowder Plot to come to fruition. Was he about to get some answers at last?

For a while Monk said nothing. The man was more than tired, Marbeck saw: he was near to exhaustion. He took a stool near his table and sat, motioning Marbeck to do the same. 'And don't tell me you'd prefer to remain standing,' he said

in an acid tone. 'What I'm about to say will take some time
. . . and even you will find it better to listen in some comfort.'

So Marbeck took the only other stool and sat down facing
him. Whereupon Monk picked up what looked like a hastily
scrawled report and scanned it briefly.

'It may interest you to know that I didn't order you to watch
Thomas Percy merely to keep you out of my way,' he said,
looking up finally. 'He was of real interest to us . . . But in
any case, that's history now. The man died this morning, killed
in a fight at Holbeach House in Staffordshire, where he and
his friends had been cornered. Robert Catesby died with him.
They stood back to back, I gather, and were shot by the same
bullet . . . Most economical.'

Marbeck took in the news in silence. Briefly, he saw Percy,
eyeing him over the card table at Essex House, telling him
they would play again; that, too, was now another closed
chapter.

'Others were also slain,' Monk went on, in a matter-of fact
tone. 'One Rookwood was wounded, and the survivors were
captured, to be conveyed to the Tower. For such treason, their
deaths will be terrible: the worst the Crown can devise—'

'Johnson,' Marbeck broke in suddenly. 'Percy's servant,
who kept the house by the Lords' . . .'

'Ah yes . . . Him.' Monk set the paper aside and eyed him
grimly. 'He's an ex-soldier, fought in the Low Countries for
the Spanish. He's been a busy man, these past years – even
went to Spain, seeking support for a rising. He was sent
packing, I gather . . . Philip wanted no part of it. The fellow's
from York – born a Protestant, would you believe? But it's
often the converted ones who turn out to be the most fanatical,
isn't it?'

'Do you know his real name?'

'We do now. It's Fawkes: christened Guy, but calling himself
by the Spanish name, Guido.' The spymaster paused, shaking
his head. 'It took them two days to get even that out of him.
I never heard of any man who could withstand the tortures he
has endured.'

Marbeck lowered his eyes, remembering the tall man
who faced him at Percy's house and the strength that

seemed to flow from him. Then, suddenly, he looked up. 'Father Cornford . . .'

Monk stiffened. 'What of him?'

'He tried to warn me. He was in torment, because of what he'd been told in the confessional—' He broke off as a hard look came over Monk's features.

'He'll pay the price for his silence!' he snapped. 'Can you imagine the consequences, had this vile plan succeeded? The King dead, likely most of the Council too . . . an heir to the throne held hostage, or spirited away to be raised as a Papist? England would be drawn into a fearful conflict – or worse, towards the rule of Rome!'

'And yet . . .' Marbeck ventured, causing the spymaster to frown. 'The matter is – that was never going to happen, was it?' And when the other merely blinked, he added: 'Call it speculation . . . one of my theories, whether you scorn it or not. But the truth is . . .' He paused, choosing his words. 'The fact is, Monk, I'm tired of keeping so many secrets. Indeed, I wonder you don't feel the same, at times.'

The spymaster's frown deepened, but no answer came.

'Then, whether you do or not, it's all chaff now,' Marbeck went on. 'I've done a deal of thinking these past weeks – especially in that cell at the Clink, stewing in my own filth. And putting together a picture, too . . . Even poor Cutler saw it, after we'd talked it over.' He paused, meeting Monk's fierce glare. 'We were there because we were an irritant: two hapless intelligencers, working in the dark. He stumbled upon gunpowder being taken through Croydon, I followed it to Lambeth, and . . .' He shrugged. 'You know the rest, just as I know why you had to keep me out of the way, until things had been allowed to come to fruition.' He managed a wan smile. 'I confess, I never thought even My Lord Secretary would take such a risk: letting matters play out until the last moment. Then, no other man would have the nerve. Unless . . .' A suspicion rose suddenly. 'Unless the whole plot was false from the start—'

'Enough!' Monk was on his feet now, looking fiercely at him. 'You go too far, Marbeck – not for the first time! That's sheer nonsense. The plot was as real as it was wicked – even

Cecil didn't know of it until recently. A letter was sent a week before the opening of Parliament, warning a certain nobleman to stay away . . . but that too is history now. In truth, you know as well as I that whatever My Lord does is for the safety of the realm. His whole life is dedicated to England's good – as was his father's. Do you truly think he would play with the lives of the King and his entire government?'

'No . . .' Marbeck drew a breath. 'He plays with the lives of expendable folk – men like me. Yet there was still a grave risk, was there not? I saw the barrels myself—'

'The powder was decayed!'

Marbeck froze, staring at his spymaster. For it was clear that, for once, Monk had overstepped himself. Flushed with anger, the man sat down and put a hand to his head.

The silence grew, until Marbeck was tired of it. Finally, having thrown caution aside, he spoke his mind. 'Well, that would make sense,' he said. 'After long journeys, being manhandled and left for long periods, gunpowder may separate into its parts. In which case, it wouldn't have exploded. For all his pains, Fawkes's match would have done little but make a fire, perhaps – and that would have been discovered.' He exhaled deeply. 'The King was never truly at risk – but no one must know of it. Am I correct?'

'In God's name, Marbeck, what do you think?' As always, Monk was recovering quickly. Finding a cup, half-concealed by papers, he took it up and drank. 'Even My Lord needs public opinion, at times,' he said, wiping his mouth. 'The nation's enraged at what might have happened. We can use it to move against the Papists, strengthen laws . . . You know as well as I do of the danger within our own borders. We spoke once of the Jesuits at large – imagine another forty Cornfords, winning over converts even as we speak. Would you have them left to their own devices?'

Marbeck gave him no answer. The matter was clear at last, and it left him feeling almost numb. Cecil had indeed played a dangerous game, but the danger had been assessed and deemed acceptable. Now the Lord Secretary had triumphed: it was perhaps his finest hour. And henceforth, as Marbeck himself had said, he would be unassailable.

'Needless to say, you'll repeat not a word of what I've said in this room,' Monk said to him. 'Otherwise, regrettably or not, I'll have you killed immediately.'

Marbeck looked up, met the man's eye and knew it was no bluff. But then, he expected nothing else . . . and now, at last, he felt it was time.

'You need have no fear of that,' he said. 'Yet, regrettably or not, I came to you for two reasons. One was to take whatever payment is owed me. The other was to tell you that I'm quitting your service. But first . . .' and as the other stiffened, he raised a hand. 'First, I've a little codicil to add to the lengthy report My Lord Secretary's no doubt penning. Call it a parting gift, if you like: a mark of my goodwill.'

Monk stared at him, then with an effort sat down. Whereupon, without preamble, Marbeck laid forth the frightened testimony of Blue Donal, given to him in a freezing alley by Ludgate the previous day. It had sobered him, but after sifting the matter in the light of what had happened since he'd set foot in Essex House, it was all as plain as daylight. In a measured tone he told Levinus Monk of Charlotte de Baume and her attempt to end his life. Then he spoke of her master: Juan Roble, the renegade *espionar* who had quit the King of Spain's service and worked for his own ends. Finally, to join the final link in the chain, he reminded Monk of his own words.

'King Philip wanted no part of the planned rising, you said, and refused the importuning of Guido Fawkes. But other Spaniards, it seems, were less scrupulous . . . in return for riches, when all was over. In a Catholic England they could live well – even sue for a pardon from their own king, perhaps, when he saw what had been done. Likely, the Pope would reward them, too. So whether he likes it or not, My Lord Secretary will have to concede that there was Spanish involvement of one kind. It puts a somewhat different light on his scheme, does it not?'

He stopped then, knowing Monk would piece out the tale for himself. Marbeck would hardly have made it up; he saw that the spymaster had not taken eyes off him for a moment.

Finally, after taking a fortifying sip from his cup, Monk spoke. 'So this Frenchwoman . . . this Madame de Baume, who claimed to be kinswoman to the French ambassador, was here as Juan Roble's envoy? She could have carried words of support to the plotters. Money too, perhaps . . .'

'Likely so,' Marbeck put in. 'And part of her mission was to snuff my life out into the bargain . . . Kill two birds with one very attractive stone.'

He was silent then, recalling the breakfast in Charlotte's bedchamber and the sweetened wine with which he'd almost been poisoned. He would never forget it, nor his last sight of her, sitting like a statue.

'Well . . .' Monk let out a long sigh. 'Is there more you wish to tell me, or . . .?'

'I don't believe so,' Marbeck replied. 'Except to say that my unwilling informant Blue Donal is now clapped up in the Counter. I thought you might wish to question him yourself, so I had him charged with trying to lift my purse. Since he'd been ordered to betray my whereabouts to others, by which I almost lost my life, I thought he got off lightly. Let's call him my parting gift to you, shall we?' He paused, then: 'As for Madame de Baume, I fear you may be too late. Having been detained for some days, I was unable to tell you of her. But that, I fear, is no longer my concern.'

Monk looked as if he would speak, but held his tongue; the man was stunned at last, which gave Marbeck some satisfaction. 'You heard me aright,' he added. 'I'll repeat it: I'm leaving your service. And if you've a mind to threaten me, I should add that I've weighed up the attendant risks and, like My Lord Secretary, decided to run with them.'

There followed a silence. Seeing that Marbeck wasn't in a mood to listen to argument, Monk merely drained his cup to the dregs. Finally, summoning a brusque manner, he shoved a pile of papers aside and opened the familiar chest.

'Your payment,' he said, and threw the purse.

'My thanks,' Marbeck said as he caught it.

'As to the matter of your decision . . .' The spymaster gave a sigh. 'I can but convey your words to the Lord Secretary, at the next opportunity.'

'Naturally.' With a brief nod, Marbeck rose to take his leave. He caught a look in Monk's eye, one of sly calculation, before it vanished. 'Although . . . there's one final matter that may interest you,' the spymaster said.

With a wry look, Marbeck waited.

'With all the excitement of late, such everyday matters tend to get overlooked,' the other went on, giving him a bland stare. 'Yet for most of the populace life goes on, does it not? Affairs of state move apace, but others require more mundane attention. I speak of a forthcoming marriage, at St Olave's Church in Hart Street. It's the parish church for the people of Crutched Friars, among others. The groom is a well-known lawyer, Richard Verney. The banns have been read, I understand, and all is arranged.'

Controlling himself, Marbeck stood very still. Finally, seeing he had no choice but to enquire further, he said: 'Since you're so well-informed, might I ask when the date is set for this wedding?'

'Tomorrow, at noon,' Monk replied. 'Or so I'm told.'

Without a word Marbeck turned on his heel and moved to the door. With pulse rising he opened it, but before he could step over the threshold the spymaster spoke up.

'The matter is, with all that's going on,' he said, 'it's unlikely I'll have that opportunity for quite some time: to pass on your decision to my master, I mean. And it's likely even you don't feature in his thoughts just now, Marbeck. Should your name arise, however, I could mention some small investigation I've sent you on. Meanwhile, you may take some time to think—'

'I don't need it,' Marbeck broke in, containing his feelings with an effort. 'I've said what I came to say, and there's an end to it.'

'I understand,' Monk said quickly. 'But who knows how you may feel in a month or two? We all need a holiday at times, Marbeck – even I. I've a notion to see my home town again . . . That's Ghent, as you know. It's mighty cold there in winter. But then, I imagine wherever you plan to go to will be the same just now . . .'

He had raised his voice during the last sentence, but to no effect. Without looking back Marbeck left him, making a point of banging the door. The latch rattled, and then there was only the sound of his footsteps receding along a stone passage.

Outside he walked briskly, his hand gripping his sword-hilt until the knuckles ached. Out through the Court Gate he went, looking straight ahead. Charing Cross loomed before him, with The Strand opening on his right. Without slowing his pace, he strode to the Duck and Drake and entered. A short time later, with the reckoning settled and carrying his belongings, he was making his way to the stables. Finding Oliver absent he readied Cobb, left money for his keep and tied his bags to the saddle. Then he was mounted, feeling the horse's eagerness match his own: a desire to ride out of London into the fields, and thence through open country until it grew too dark to see.

But it was no use. They got as far as Highgate before he reined in, the breath of both horse and rider clouding in the cold air. Turning Cobb about, he peered downhill towards the sprawl of London, hazy in the smoke from thousands of chimneys. After picking out the tower of St Paul's his eyes roved eastwards: the distant spires of Bow Church, the Guildhall, St Anthony's, and finally St Helen's. The small church of St Olave was not to be seen, but it was only a short distance further.

He drew a deep breath, shook the reins and began riding slowly, back towards the city.

TWENTY-TWO

Under a cloudy sky, several wedding guests had assembled by St Olave's to greet the bridal party when they walked down from Crutched Friars. In view of the season, vows would be exchanged inside the church instead of at the doors; the parson was already within, warming himself. Outside, a number of parishioners had gathered from mere curiosity, while the group of invited guests stood apart, their status obvious from the quality of their clothes. No one paid much attention to a man clad in plain black, who appeared a little before noon and stood on the edge of the crowd.

For Marbeck it had been a near-sleepless night, in his old chamber at the Duck and Drake. More than once he had cursed himself for his desire: the need not only to see Meriel, but in the end to punish himself too, by watching her marry another man. It was partly sheer curiosity, he knew: to see whether she would go through with it, given what she'd told him the last time he saw her. But he remembered the desperation in her gaze as he recalled her weariness when she spoke of putting an end to the conflict with her father. Perhaps it was, as she had told him, the only life she could make for herself. Outwardly calm but with a turmoil of thoughts, he stood with the other bystanders and waited.

Mercifully, the wait was short. A murmur of voices arose, and all eyes turned towards the end of Hart Street, where it bent away into Crutched Friars. Soon the party appeared, splendidly dressed, bride and groom at its head . . . and Marbeck's heart thudded: for the bride looked happy.

Along with others he watched the approaching group, managing to keep out of their sight. The bridegroom was neither more nor less than he'd expected: a middle-aged lawyer in a fine gown, round-faced and beaming, his grey-speckled beard neatly trimmed. Close behind him stepped a company of gentlemen and ladies, richly attired, bejewelled and smiling. He scanned the group warily for Meriel's father, but failed to see him. He did see an elderly woman who could be the servant Goody Joan, recalling with a pang of regret that she would have been Meriel's midwife. Friends and relatives followed, in cheerful conversation. All was well, it seemed . . . but why should it not be? It was an occasion for rejoicing, with feasting and merrymaking to follow, and at once Marbeck knew he had no place here.

Could he really have thought otherwise? He'd seen enough already; now, he had no desire to witness the ceremony. With an emptiness inside him, he was on the point of edging away, yet he lingered. Perhaps it was unwise, but he wanted to take a last look at Meriel before she entered the little church. The couple were at the doors now, people craning their necks for a glimpse of the bride in her fine gown of lilac and silver, her head covered with white lace. At the last moment she lifted her head – and seemed to look directly at Marbeck. Then without another glance she turned and, hand-in-hand with her husband-to-be, entered the church.

The others followed, crowding the entrance, joined by those who'd waited in the street. Soon only the backs of the last few guests could be seen, while the onlookers began drifting away. But Marbeck remained where he stood, motionless and without expression: for that look from the bride had stunned him.

The woman wasn't Meriel.

For a moment he thought his mind was playing tricks, that his wishes had overridden his senses. From a distance, as the group approached, he had assumed that the fair young woman in the bridal gown was she. He'd seen her smile and allowed his gaze to shift to the others. Only at the church door, when he met her eye, had it struck him. Then, in his mind's eye, he saw Monk's sardonic gaze. *The groom is a well-known lawyer, Richard Verney*, the spymaster had said; he'd made no mention of the bride.

His thoughts racing, he turned from the church and walked to the corner, where the street joined Mart Lane. Several bystanders stood about, talking of the wedding party. He picked out two likely informants, managed a smile and approached them.

'Your pardon, mistress . . .' Bending his head, he fixed on the older of the two women. 'I came to see the wedding – or rather, to see Master Verney and wish him well. But I've yet to learn the name of his bride – do you know her?'

'I do, sir,' the woman answered. 'She's Mistress Wallbank, a cousin of his. They've known each other since they were children.'

'Of course . . .' He nodded. 'Yet, now I think on it, I heard he was betrothed to another – a daughter of Thomas Walden?' He raised his eyebrows and waited, but he had to work hard to appear only mildly interested at what followed.

'Oh, sir . . .' The woman's eyes widened. 'Plainly, you haven't heard. Mistress Walden ran away – left her father's house, more than a week ago. But even before that, the wedding had been called off, so I heard. She . . . Well . . .' His informant hesitated, whereupon her friend, a pinched-looking woman with a hard eye, spoke up instead.

'She was a wanton,' she said sharply. 'A sore trial to her father, who is a fine gentleman. If you care to know what I think, Master Verney is well rid of her. Nor did he take it to heart, being the strong man he is, but settled matters at once with the Wallbank family. It was meant to be – even if there was an uncommon speed about it all, banns read quickly and all. But no matter – he's made a good match, and so has she.'

There was a pause. The pinched woman, having said her piece, drew her cloak about her and eyed her friend, who was blushing.

'Oh, my dear,' the friend said with a sigh. 'You've a tongue like a viper's – but that's the nub of it, sir, and no lies told.'

She looked at Marbeck, who merely nodded and moved off.

The afternoon waned, and he was in the Pegasus in Cheapside. He had been there for hours and had lost count of how many, but unlike on the last occasion he'd sat here, he wasn't drunk. The same mug of watered sack stood before him, as it had done since his arrival, still half-full. The only reason he'd not been troubled by the drawers was that one of them remembered him, as the man who'd emptied his purse and told him to take the money for his daughters.

'Whatever you desire, sir, call upon me,' the portly fellow had said as he served him. 'You look to me like a man who needs to reflect. None shall disturb you – that's my promise.'

Marbeck had indeed needed to think, but his ruminations had achieved little. Over and again he ran conversations with Meriel through his mind – especially the last one, when he'd stood at her father's door and demanded that she go with him. That night, when he'd sought refuge in Charlotte's bed, he hadn't expected to see Meriel again. Now it seemed as if everything had changed, but he was unsure what it meant. If she had indeed fled her father's house – and he had no reason to disbelieve the women in the street – where would she go? Not to her sister's, for she would be found. Her other friends would surely be known to Thomas Walden, who would lose no time in searching for her. Nor, Marbeck was certain, would she seek out their mutual friend and his fellow intelligencer, Joseph Gifford. Gifford would shelter her, of course – but he was away now, on some mission for Monk. Which left one question: why had she not tried to find Marbeck?

That, he decided, troubled him most of all. Meriel was shrewd; moreover, she knew him well, as she knew the kind of places he frequented. Surely, she could have traced him to the Duck and Drake? He'd been in prison for some days, but even so . . .

He forced himself to face it: the possibility that she didn't want to see him. What kept his hopes alive was the belief that her feelings for him remained strong, whatever else had passed. Perhaps even now, he told himself, she was searching London for him, though the notion was daunting. To scour this city of two hundred thousand souls – an ants' nest, a mass of nooks and crannies – was beyond one person's powers. And by the same token, how could he possibly find her? Perhaps she'd left London – did she know people elsewhere who might offer a refuge, if only a temporary one?

But at that, he almost laughed. Here he sat, one of the Crown's best intelligencers, who'd tracked men here and abroad, in towns and cities, to houses and hovels. He had found a priest hidden in a wall, yet he had no idea where to look for the woman who had been his lover.

He got up at last, drained his mug and left a coin on the table. The inn was filling up, evening already drawing in. Out in Cheapside, he walked to Goldsmith's Row and turned into Friday Street, intending to make for Ludgate by the south side of Paul's. He had nowhere to go but back to his lodging, where he would pass one more night. Beyond that . . . He had few thoughts beyond that. He was a man with no home and no purpose.

His mind drifting, he was almost at Watling Street when they seized him.

He had been followed, of course; he cursed himself for his carelessness, even as he struggled. But this time he was outmatched: he knew it as soon as two pairs of strong arms pinned him, while a third man closed in quickly. He was drawn into a side-alley, dark and deserted, little more than a passageway. Breathless, straining against the weight of two heavy men, he was dragged backwards, his heels bumping on cobbles. Nobody spoke – nor would they, he knew: they were hard fellows, the kind he had even commanded himself. Their gloved hands dug into his arms as they forced him halfway along the ginnel, midway between Friday Street and the Old Exchange. There at last they stopped and slammed him against a wall, so hard that his breath was driven from his body.

With his back to the brickwork, arms outstretched and as immobile as a scarecrow, he could only face his chief attacker. Only then did he see that the man was masked . . . and thought of his assailants at Skinners', black scarves covering their faces. But this was no hired ex-soldier, desperate for payment: he was a seasoned professional, who now lifted a pistol and aimed it directly between Marbeck's eyes.

'Am I allowed to ask a question, before you rub me out?' he asked, struggling for breath.

No answer came; but none was necessary. He saw it clearly and realized he should have entertained this possibility sooner . . . perhaps since he'd closed the door to Levinus Monk's chamber in Whitehall. *Regrettably or not, I'll have you killed* . . . The spymaster's words rang in his head. But that, of course, was before Marbeck had told him he was quitting his service, after which everything the man had said meant little. Who else knew that he would be at St Olave's church – as he knew that Marbeck would be unable to stop himself going there? He had been watched since then, by men who knew how to remain invisible. He had been watched as he talked to the women on the corner, and then followed back to Cheapside. He'd been watched as he came out of the tavern, followed until a suitable spot presented itself to his assassins. For he was no longer merely an unruly and undisciplined intelligencer, a trial at times, yet tolerated because he brought results. He was now a risk, and a serious one at that. Perhaps he should be flattered, he told himself, for being considered so important . . .

He blinked: all these thoughts had rippled through his mind in seconds. Before him all was unchanged: two burly men on either side, holding him fast, just outside his field of vision. Before him loomed their leader, gloved and masked, his pistol levelled. Marbeck gazed down the dark cavern of its muzzle . . . as he had stared down the one held by Thomas Walden, what seemed like a long time ago. At that moment, he recalled, he'd thought his troubles could be solved by merely allowing that angry man to pull the trigger; now, he had no choice.

He drew breath and waited. There was a faint rasp and a click as the hammer was drawn back – then a great bang that deafened him, and a lurid flash that blinded him. In a daze, he sagged, feeling his arms let loose . . . then he hit the ground, all his strength gone.

Whereupon he looked up and realized he hadn't been shot.

But someone else had: one of the two men who'd held him. A heavy-set figure, he now lay on the ground to Marbeck's left, blood welling from a gaping wound in his temple. His companion, no less heavy-set, was slumped on Marbeck's right, apparently dazed by a blow. And even as he stared, the third figure – the man who would have killed him – bent over the pursuivant and produced a dagger. He dealt two sharp thrusts into his victim's chest, then stepped back as blood gushed forth. In a very short time two men lay dead in the ginnel, which was becoming awash with their gore.

A moment passed, but Marbeck didn't try to get up. Instead, he peered up at his rescuer, who had been poised to end his life, but was now wiping the blade of his poniard on the breeches of the last victim. Words failed him; he had been about to die, and now he wasn't.

'Good Christ, Marbeck, won't you rise?' the man demanded, straightening up. 'The shot will raise an alarm, and you're about to get your breeches blooded. Do I have to lift you?'

It was Deverell.

Somehow, Marbeck found his strength. It seemed to come back piecemeal, to one part of his body at a time. He got up, his ears still ringing, found he wasn't too dizzy and put a hand out to steady himself. Leaning against the wall, he could barely see the face of his saviour in the gloom.

Finally, he spoke. 'Monk's orders, I take it?'

'Of course.' Deverell pulled his mask down, looked swiftly to one end of the alley and then the other. 'Come,' he snapped. 'We must cut through to Old Fish Street, to a house where you'll be safe.' He nodded towards Friday Street, where a figure had appeared in silhouette; soon there would be others.

'Well then, I'm in your hands,' Marbeck said. And he began to walk, stepping over the trickle of blood that flowed into the runnel. Gaining the far end of the alley, he followed Deverell out into the Old Exchange, which was quiet. Thereafter, walking side by side, the two of them headed downhill.

They crossed Watling Street, paying no heed to passers-by, who in any case saw only two gentlemen making their way to the junction of Knightrider Street and Old Fish Street. Here Deverell turned to his left, leading the way towards the opening of Distaff Lane. But before it, he stopped at a door and knocked. Almost at once it was opened and Marbeck was being ushered into a dark hallway. He was aware of muffled voices, before finally entering a dimly-lit room, where Deverell at once went to the window. He peered out, then, apparently satisfied, pulled a curtain across and turned to Marbeck.

'All's well,' he said. 'I'm sure we weren't followed . . . Even Monk wouldn't have thought it necessary, this time. You're safe, though I don't advise you staying here longer than a night.' He drew a breath. 'Well – are you content?'

'I believe so,' Marbeck answered weakly. Seeing a stool, he gestured towards it. 'May I?'

'I think you should, before you fall over,' Deverell said. 'Then I think I'll take a cup of something strong . . . Do you care to partake with me?'

TWENTY-THREE

I t was not a 'safe house', in the sense of one used by the Crown's intelligencers: just now such a place would not have been safe at all. It belonged to a friend of Deverell's: an invalid who lived in a back chamber, cared for by his daughter – a spindle-thin girl who looked often at Marbeck, but was too shy to speak. After night had fallen, with a bellman calling the hour outside, he sat and heard his rescuer out in silence.

'The facts are not propitious,' Deverell said. 'You're a dead man . . . I have to inform Monk of that. I took his instruction last night, without comment or complaint. He knows I loathe him, but he also knows I'll do as ordered . . . Why should I not? There was little affection between you and I in the past, and in any case, you were a threat that had to be removed. Indeed, you are still, dead or not . . . You must see it yourself.'

After a while, Marbeck nodded. 'How will you explain the deaths of those two in the alley?'

'I'll say you fought like a demon, of course. You're not an easy man to kill – Monk knows that. You stabbed one of them and knocked my hand aside as I fired the pistol, so the other poor fellow was hit instead. After that, I ran you through with my sword . . .' Deverell gave a shrug. 'He'll believe me in the end. I'd hardly return to his service if I'd betrayed him, would I?'

'Is that what you intend to do – remain in his service?'

'What other life am I suited for?' the other replied. Then with a frown, he added: 'For that matter, what other life will you have? You can't stay in London – you know that.'

'I do . . .' Marbeck looked away. Only hours ago, his mind filled with thoughts of Meriel, he'd had little care for his own future. Now, it looked as if he might have none at all.

'Nor can you go back to the Duck and Drake,' Deverell was saying. 'If you wish, I'll go there and gather your belongings. I'd better fetch your horse too—'

'There's no need,' Marbeck broke in. 'Besides, Cobb won't let another man lead him nowadays. I'd be grateful for my pack; it's not been opened, since I was supposed to be gone yesterday. Tomorrow, at first light, I'll go for the horse. I doubt the stables are watched . . . As you said, I'm a dead man, am I not?'

A weariness swept over him. Despite everything, he believed he would sleep this night; tomorrow, he didn't care to think upon. It struck him that vague notions of going back to his family in the North were as chaff: nowhere in England was safe. So – had it come to this: that for all his loyal service, he had little choice now but to flee the land of his birth and offer his skills to another power, as men had tried to persuade him to do? Was he, in the end, no better than Charlotte de Baume after all: a spy – even a killer – for hire?

'There is, of course, one other possibility, albeit slight.'

He looked up to see Deverell watching him.

Taking a drink of the weak wine they'd shared, his rescuer thought for a moment, then said: 'It's a very long shot. But were we to go to Monk together and spin a different tale . . . Were you to throw yourself on his mercy, claim you never intended to leave the service, but were angling for better payment—'

'No.' Marbeck met his eye, letting the other see his resolve. 'I won't do that. Even if it were possible, I could never trust him again; nor would he trust me. As for our Lord Secretary . . .' He shrugged. 'Once he got wind of it, he'd order my death just to be safe, after he'd weighed the risks, as he always does. We're expendable, Deverell . . . even the best of us. Which includes you.'

They both fell silent. The hour was late, the owners of the house already abed. Finally, Deverell rose and said he would go home to his wife. 'You should have married, Marbeck,' he said quietly. 'When all's said and done, a man needs a little comfort . . . even you.' And he went, saying he would return in the early morning.

After he'd gone Marbeck sat in the dark, until the midnight chime of Paul's sounded. Then he lay on the rush-strewn floor, on a bed of his own clothes, and let sleep overcome him.

At dawn, cloaked and hatted, he left the house in Old Fish Street. He had his pack and had bidden Deverell a hurried farewell. When they'd parted, there was nothing left to say; a brief handshake had to serve.

Hurriedly, he made his way through back streets, to the stable in St Martins. The place was in gloom, with no light showing. Finding the entrance barred, he knocked gently. After a while there was a stir within; a door creaked open, and Oliver appeared in shirt sleeves.

'Master Tucker?' The ostler blinked in the dim light. 'What's the coil? It's unlike you to come at such an hour . . .'

'It's the last time,' Marbeck said, and pushed his way in.

In the semi-darkness, with the warm smell of hay and the muffled stamping of hooves on straw, he relaxed slightly. Cobb was in the farthest stall as usual and lifted his head at his master's approach. For a while horse and rider stood, Marbeck stroking the animal's mane. Behind him, Oliver was making a spark to light a lantern.

'It's just you and me now,' Marbeck said softly, rubbing Cobb's forehead. 'Let's shake London dust from our feet, shall we?' Then he turned, saying: 'Can you make up a bag of feed for him, with oats? A bigger one than before.'

'I can.' Having hung up the lantern, Oliver faced him, digging his pipe out for his first smoke of the day. 'But see now,' he muttered, 'when you said it was the last time, do you mean you're taking Cobb away for keeps?'

'I do,' Marbeck answered. 'You've no need to fret – I've payment here and a shilling for yourself to toast my departure. Would you have a dried apple or two you could spare?'

'I might . . .' Oliver stuck his ancient pipe in his mouth and summoned a faint smile, which was a surprise; as a rule he was the most morose of men. Marbeck watched him go off towards the tack-room, which often served as the man's bedchamber.

Moving to the harness rack, he found Cobb's saddle and

bridle. He was about to ready the animal, when a sound made him turn. Oliver was standing by the open door to his lair, still wearing the grin which, to Marbeck's eye, looked somewhat forced.

'Will you step in here, sir?' he called. 'There's a reckoning made up for the time Cobb's lodged here – only, I don't read too well. If you'd care to run your eye over it, make sure all's fair and good, we'll settle up. 'Tis not for myself . . . My master's a stickler for such frippery.'

Marbeck hesitated, but only briefly; everything should appear as normal. Putting down the saddle, he walked across the straw-covered floor. 'I always thought you were the owner of this stable, Oliver,' he said as he reached the door. 'Or part-owner, at least . . . I never knew you had a master.'

Oliver was already in the dusty little room, rustling papers. Marbeck squeezed inside, between piles of old harness and assorted jumble. Seeing the man bent over a shelf with his back to him, he stepped forward . . . and came up with a jolt as something solid was jammed against his spine.

'Did you not?' a harsh voice cried. 'Well, that shows you don't know everything, Tucker!'

Marbeck stood rigid. He felt hot breath on the back of his neck and smelled the odour of strong drink. In front of him, Oliver was backing into a corner, out of reach. His grin was gone . . . and once again, Marbeck knew the bitter taste of betrayal; as he knew who it was, pressing a pistol to his back.

'Turn round slowly – and no tricks!' Skinner ordered, his voice hoarse as a rusty lock. 'My hand's somewhat shaky of late . . . I wouldn't want to shoot you before I'm ready.'

So Marbeck turned about carefully, his hands away from his sides, and faced his old landlord. He blinked, for the man was a sorry sight: haggard and unkempt, with a mark on one cheek that could have been a burn. He wore the same clothes Marbeck had last seen on him – when he'd sat on the floor of the bowling alley, his arm dripping blood. That arm was bandaged, but it didn't prevent the man from holding, with both hands, what turned out to be a caliver: an old army gun, cocked and primed.

'Well-a-day . . .' Marbeck allowed himself a sigh. 'How long have you been bedding down here, Skinner?'

'How long?' the other echoed. 'Ever since my house got burned down – for I'd nowhere else to go! But now my luck's turned, has it not? I want to see you cack your breeches, Tucker – for you've precious little time left on this earth!'

There was a stir from behind. 'Not in here,' Oliver said harshly. 'Take him outside, as you swore you would, else the horses will take fright and bolt.' The man was nervous; Marbeck heard him shifting from one foot to another. It was he, of course, who had told Skinner he would be arriving today to collect Cobb.

Now, without taking his eyes off his captive, Skinner let fly an oath at Oliver. 'Don't wet yourself, you whey-faced javel!' he sneered. 'You think I want to start a fire?' A savage glare appeared. 'I don't know how, but I'd swear you're the cause of the last one, Tucker! Everything I owned was in that house – all of it, gone up in flames! As for me – I'm lucky to be alive!'

'I'm very glad to see it,' Marbeck said lightly. His reward was a jab in the ribs with the gun-barrel that made him wince.

'Drop that fancy sword!' Skinner yelled, shoving his unwashed face close. 'Your poniard too – move!'

Unhurriedly, Marbeck loosed his belt and let it fall to the floor.

'Now get outside – Oliver, open the whoreson door!'

It was done in some haste. With obvious relief Oliver brushed past them, stumbling through the stable to the yard door. He unbolted it and swung it outwards, letting in milky daylight. Marbeck, the caliver's barrel pressed hard against his ribs, allowed himself to be driven out to the yard. As he went he threw a last glance at Cobb. The horse gazed at him from his stall, then was gone.

'Over there, by the wall!'

Skinner had taken a step back and was motioning to Marbeck. Weighing his options swiftly, and deciding that on this occasion they were somewhat scarce, Marbeck complied. The yard was small, surrounded by high walls lined with bales and sacks. A dung-heap, covered against the rain, filled one corner. Backing away from his captor, hands loose, he moved to a wall and stood still.

'Do you mark this?' Skinner cried, his face contorted with rage. He meant his injured arm, which Marbeck now saw was so stiff that he could barely move it. 'Barber-surgeon says it'll never heal properly! That's your doing, Master Give-You-Goodnight! You and your smart swordplay . . . You've ruined me! I wish to God I'd never set eyes on you – you were a trial, right from the start. A bad penny . . . Nay, a bad omen. You arrived hard upon the sun's eclipse – my beloved said so, the one you scorned to greet when she sat at my table! And here you are, hale and hearty, set to ride out without a care in the world. So what do you say now, before I splatter your guts across that whoreson wall?'

But for answer, Marbeck said nothing.

'I said: what do you say, before I end your stinking life?' Shaking with anger, Skinner moved towards him, levelling the caliver. Even then Marbeck didn't speak; there was a vestige of defiance within him yet, which would have its way. And then, to Skinner's further rage, a calmness came over him.

Three times within a fortnight, he reflected, he had stared down a gun-barrel. Twice he had been fortunate . . . Suddenly, he recalled the words of his boyhood mentor, Ballard: *Once may be deemed a near-miracle, my boy*, the old player had said; *twice may be coincidence – but three times? No man will credit that . . .*

He glanced up then: at the grey November sky and the rooftops, with wisps of early-morning smoke drifting across. The people of London were lighting fires, cooking breakfast . . . There was a sound of hooves, from somewhere beyond Aldersgate. In the Tower, men who had failed to blow up the King waited to be tried and hung for treason, the one thing certain to follow upon the other. In Whitehall Palace, King James lay in his curtained bed, while his children slept safely in theirs. At Salisbury House, the Secretary of State would already be at his desk, his crookback frame propped up on cushions. While somewhere, perhaps a long way from London, Meriel might be waking . . . Whereupon Charlotte de Baume's words came starkly to his mind: *What would it matter, if you are slain by a lord or a lackey . . .?* He let out a breath: was this pitiful rogue, then, to be his executioner?

Suddenly, a laugh welled up. Of all the dangers he'd faced – at the hands of trained assassins, expert swordsmen and marksmen – the notion that his life could be snuffed out by a low-life wretch like Skinner seemed the most supreme irony of all. He faced the man then and allowed his laughter to spill forth.

'By the Christ, you think I won't do it?' Skinner cried. He was beside himself with fury. Shaking yet resolved, he aimed his caliver at Marbeck's heart. Beyond, just inside the doorway, Oliver stood grim-faced but resigned, fiddling with his pipe.

Marbeck faced his nemesis . . . but even at the very last, a flicker of hope remained. After all, he'd been in similar predicaments before and survived them somehow; was there yet time for a Ballard trick?

He swallowed, his smile gone . . . then he stiffened in dramatic fashion, throwing a look of alarm over Skinner's right shoulder – whereupon Oliver chose that precise moment to drop his pipe. It fell with a clatter on to the cobbles and broke in two.

Skinner gave a start and whirled round – whereupon Marbeck whipped his bodkin from his pocket and leaped . . .